ONCE UPON A TIME

ONCE UPON A TIME

Edited by: C.L. McCollum & August Clearwing
Associate Editors: Elaine Titus & Gerald Sallier
Cover Design by: Emma Michaels
Arrangement by: August Clearwing

ISBN-13: 978-1514326497 (Herding Cats Press)
ISBN-10: 1514326493

HERDING
CATS
PRESS

www.herdcatspress.com

Proceeds to benefit RAINN—Rape, Abuse and Incest National Network.

Fairy tales are more than true: not because they tell us that dragons exist, but because they tell us that dragons can be beaten.
~ Neil Gaiman, *Coraline*

Contents

To anyone currently on a journey towards their own happy ending,
this is for you.

Introduction

From August Clearwing
Author, Editor & Project Manager

The first fairytale stories didn't have happy endings. And, while I cannot promise that all of ours do either, I *can* promise that by enjoying this anthology, you are contributing to the happy endings of nearly 300,000 survivors of abuse each year.

Because few people read long-winded introductions, I will keep this one brief. Never did we expect such astounding talent would be willing to offer up their services for our cause. After the amount of fun we had putting together the *Dark & Stormy* anthology, we decided to up the ante and invite additional authors and artists to contribute to RAINN: the Rape, Abuse, and Incest National Network. Our invitation was met with an overwhelming response from our fellow authors and artists in our online communities, many of whom already personally support the RAINN foundation all by their lonesome.

As survivors of abuse, or family of survivors of abuse ourselves, we want to let anyone who is currently experiencing, has experienced, or will experience abuse to know that it *does* get better. While it is sometimes impossible to believe: **you are not alone**.

Talk to someone. Get help. Contact RAINN at 1.800.656.HOPE and tell your story.

C.L. and I have never been more proud to be a part of, much less direct, any project in our lives than we are this one. We are humbled beyond words that fellow creatives, both friends and strangers, gave us their trust and time and gifts to organize all of this.

Much like with our previous anthology, the only rule we supplied our authors was that the story must begin with *'Once upon a time'*. From there, the sky—and in some cases *space*—was the limit.

We hope you enjoy the epic worlds we've crafted for you. Thank you for all your support.

August Clearwing ~ June 2015

Ravens for Johannes

- Emma Michaels & Michael Cross -
Illustrated by Rebecca D. George

Once upon a time, the only loyalty Johannes had ever known, despite all of his years, was the faithfulness and devotion of his master, the king of the land, for his people.

The king had taken Johannes in from a world cruel to homeless children. Where once he would have died in the night on a frozen street, now he had a palace over his head. The kingdom was rich and everywhere Johannes turned he saw gold. But nothing shone so brilliantly as the king. To Johannes, his master was more precious than any riches.

The day came when the king fell deathly ill. For the first time since coming to the palace Johannes knew despair. Faithfully, he tended to his king. But no force on earth would halt time or the pull of death.

"My faithful servant and friend," the king whispered, "I am dying. Do not cry for me. I have lived a good life with a dear friend and servant at my side. I know I can trust you to keep my son safe."

Johannes bowed his head. "My king, I will do whatever you wish. Only please do not die."

"Oh Johannes. If only I could live forever. I'd love to see my child grow up. Do it for me. Stay beside him. Watch him skin his knees and wipe his tears away. Guide him when his heart is broken and teach him

1

to love again. Don't ever desert him in his time of need. And beware the king from across the sea. Keep my son away from that portrait."

"I swear. I will always serve him. Until the day I die, I so swear."

The king smiled. "Thank you, my friend."

He let out his last breath, and the birds outside fell silent. Not a whisper was heard. The king's loyal cat, Sebastian, who was never far from the king's side, bowed his head. The cat, like Johannes, had been taken in as a stray, and since had been the king's constant companion, warming his lap and soothing away his troubles with gentle purring. Johannes reached out a hand and closed the eyes of a man who was not only his king and savior, but friend.

"Always," Johannes whispered, and the cat next to him meowed his agreement.

———————◆———————

"Higher, your majesty," Johannes called out. "It's just a bit higher and to your left."

Mathew, now King Mathew, reached where he was told and grabbed tightly onto the branch. "Aha!" he cried. "Look, Johannes. I have done it!"

Johannes smiled and gave a small nod. "Yes, your majesty. You've done it."

The king's cat, Sebastian, gazed up at the young boy. "Johannes, how can you let him climb a tree? He could fall to his death."

Johannes' smile grew. "He's a child. Let him be fearless for a bit longer."

Sebastian sighed. "Just remember he doesn't have nine lives."

Johannes chuckled and waved to the young king. He caught the laughing royal in his arms as Mathew jumped down.

"I was so high up, Johannes."

"I know, your majesty. I bet you could see the whole world from up there."

King Mathew grinned. "I could. I really could!" His young face fell. "I wish I could have seen Father."

Johannes fell silent. He reached out a hand and rested it on Mathew's head. "You might not have seen him. But I promise you, little king, he could see you. He was smiling down at you."

King Mathew's face brightened. "Did you hear that, Sebastian? My father could see me. I'm going to climb a tree every day so that he can always see me."

Sebastian rolled his eyes. "Well done, Johannes. I'm going to start losing my own lives just from worrying."

King Mathew laughed and scooped up the cat. He hugged Sebastian to him tightly and ran.

Johannes watched Sebastian's worried face. But he knew better. Sebastian, for all of his worrying and pondering, loved the young king as much as he did. If not even more. Mathew came to a sudden stop and put Sebastian down. He stared intently at a door off to his side. Sebastian glanced back at Johannes. Both knew what door the young king had stopped at.

King Mathew's eyes never left the door. "Johannes?"

"Yes, your majesty?"

"Why do you never let me go in this door?"

Johannes kept his gaze on Mathew. "It's just an old section of the gallery."

"But what's in there?"

"Nothing of consequence."

Sebastian tore his gaze away from the door. "What is it?"

"Something you should never look at, young king."

"I want to know."

Johannes took his hand. "If you see it, it will change your life forever. It will bring a great source of sadness into your heart that will never leave."

King Mathew's eyes widened. "As sad as my father passing away?"

Johannes' squeezed the little hand. "It would be even more painful."

Mathew nodded and let Johannes lead him away. But his eyes turned once more to the locked door. A small spark lit in his heart. One that would not be easily put out.

Sebastian watched them walk down the hallway. He meowed. "You won't be able to keep him away from there forever, tall one. One day the pull will be too strong. What will you do then?"

3

Johannes closed his eyes and took a deep breath. "That is another day. For now let him be a child. Let him be innocent and full of life and laughter."

Sebastian watched Mathew and servant walk away. "You're playing a dangerous game, old friend. You should listen to this wise old cat. Before it's too late."

———————◆•———————

The years passed and the young king grew steadily from a child into a young man. He had grown fearless, something which tried both Johannes' and Sebastian's patience.

"Johannes, I command you to show me that room."

Sebastian hissed in annoyance. "Young king, he has told you many times the room is forbidden. Just forget about it."

"Listen to me, you great big ball of fur," King Mathew said. "I want to see in that room. I want to know."

Johannes frowned at the young man. "What good would knowing do, your majesty? I have told you before it will bring great sadness into your heart."

"I don't believe that. Now, servant, do as your king commands and open that door."

Sebastian's eyes widened. King Mathew had never referred to Johannes as *servant*, even during moments when he was cross with him. Johannes gazed evenly at the young man.

"As my king decrees," he said. Sebastian's ears wilted at his words. Both knew what the opening of that door would mean for the whole kingdom.

Johannes reached into his pocket and withdrew the only key in the whole castle that would open the door. He unlocked it and threw it open. The heavy wood opened silently and without protest despite the many years it had been since it was last moved.

King Mathew took a hesitant step forward into the darkness. His eyes slowly adjusted until he could see a single ray of light shining down on a portrait on the wall adjacent to the door. His breath caught, and his heart raced when he could make it out. His feet moved of their own accord toward the far wall until at last he stood beneath it.

It was a young girl. Fair haired and arms outstretched as she held a tiny bird in her hands. Her gaze was on the bird, but it was like she was staring only at the young king.

She was the most stunning girl he had ever seen.

"Johannes?" he said when he finally found his voice.

Johannes, dreading what he knew was next, stepped inside the room. "Yes, my king?"

"Who is she? She is so beautiful."

Johannes sighed heavily. "She is known as the 'Princess of the Golden Roof,' or of the great gardens far to the east. She is Sophia, the daughter of the ruler of the lands across the sea, who is the sworn enemy of your majesty."

King Mathew didn't take his eyes off of the portrait. "You mean he was my father's enemy."

Johannes looked grave. "You inherited your father's kingdom and with it his enemies."

"But surely after all of these years that king would hold me no ill will. My father is dead and the past with him."

Sebastian could no longer hold his tongue. "Great king, I am but a humble cat, but I have a long memory. Know that it is as Johannes has said. He will always view the ruler of this kingdom as his enemy."

"I love her," Mathew whispered.

Sebastian snorted. "How could you love someone you have never met?"

"Ask her to come to me, Johannes."

"Are you daft?" Sebastian said. "What if the old fool did as you asked? Even if by some miracle this girl who doesn't know you would agree to leave the only home she has ever known, what do you think her father would do when he finds out?" Sebastian slapped his paw down. "War. Everyone in this land would face an army."

King Mathew rested his hand over his heart. "I'll win her over. You'll see, Sebastian. She'll be mine. I will wed her, and her father will agree to it."

Sebastian made a sound reminiscent of coughing up a hairball. "Humans!"

"Your majesty?" Johannes pleaded. "Please forget her and any idea of winning her heart. I promised your father I would watch over you. To keep you safe."

But it was far worse than Johannes could have imagined. For the young king had no intention of letting sadness break his heart. No, he had something else in mind.

He had a plan.

———————◆•———————

"This is madness!" Sebastian meowed. "Are you really going to let him do this?"

Johannes gazed out to sea. Dread filled his heart. He knew he should try harder to stop Mathew. Even if he had to sink the ship to do it. But what difference would it make? He knew King Mathew's disposition. The young royal wouldn't give up even if he had to row all the way.

"Will you come?" Johannes asked.

Sebastian shook his head. "We cats do not like open sea."

Johannes' face fell.

Sebastian pattered up to him and placed a paw on Johannes' hand. "Fret not, my foolish friend. I'm an old cat, but I have a few tricks up my sleeve. You will not be alone."

Johannes nodded and stood up. He took a deep breath and boarded the gangplank.

"Johannes!"

Johannes turned back to Sebastian who watched him from the shore. "Remember," Sebastian said, "you're only human. But you have a loyal heart. The king believed in you. Have faith and don't give up."

Johannes nodded and waved to his friend. "Be safe, my small friend."

"And you as well, tall one."

———————◆•———————

Johannes descended into the cabin. For three months, Mathew had written and entreated the princess to give him her hand though she had never written back. But King Mathew had expected this. While he waited, he had Johannes bring him everything they had in the royal library about the land across the sea. He learned a great deal. The land to the east was filled with nature lovers. They were great sculptors and artisans who dedicated much of their talents in honor of the animals there.

That was where King Mathew got his idea. "Johannes? Bring me our kingdom's greatest sculptors. I want you to have them fashion as many statues of animals as our fastest ship can carry. Have them do it in gold. Tell them to polish the statues until they shine like the sun."

Johannes gazed evenly at the young king. It was a mad idea. But he recognized the creative genius. "As you wish, your majesty."

Now the nation's fastest ship was filled with a precious cargo worth more than mere gold. It bore the hopes of the young king, and the greatest worries of Johannes who feared he was bringing his ruler to his death. If his enemies learned of this voyage, they would never make the eastern shores.

"We shall disguise ourselves as merchants," Johannes said.

King Mathew frowned. "Merchants? How will I be able to approach Princess Sophia if she thinks I am just a mere merchant?"

Johannes raised his eyebrows. "Do you think you stand a chance of meeting her if you were to declare who you really are?"

At this Mathew fell silent. He knew Johannes was correct. "Do as you think is best, Johannes. I will follow your wisdom."

Johannes smiled wearily. "I wish you had felt that way while in our kingdom, my king." He turned and paced the deck. His thoughts were of the approaching land. The voyage was long, but they would arrive far too soon for Johannes' liking. He had to come up with a plan to keep his charge safe.

"You!"

Johannes turned at the sound of the shrill voice. He saw a black raven flying alongside the ship.

"Are you Johannes?" it cried out.

Ravens were devious creatures. They had long memories and never forgot a face. Johannes chose his words cautiously. "Yes, I am Johannes, servant of the king."

The raven nodded and landed next to him. "Sebastian sends his regards. I am here to serve you."

Johannes knelt down and held out his hand to the dark bird, who climbed tentatively onto his outstretched palm. "Sebastian sent you?"

The raven nodded. "He spared my life when my brothers and I were but chicklets. We owe him a great debt. He thought I could help you."

Johannes nodded excitedly. He didn't know what the bird could do to help him, but it was comforting to know that he would not be alone.

"Do you know how I might get the Princess of the Golden Roof to see my king?"

The raven thought for a moment. "I can carry a message for you to her if you want? All animals are welcome in her kingdom."

Johannes gave a slight nod. If his plan worked, Mathew would have his chance to win over the princess. "Go to her and tell her that a merchant from across the sea has brought her riches from the land of her dreams. Tell her that she has only to meet me at the docks, and I will show her wonders beyond compare."

The raven nodded and took flight. Johannes watched him disappear from view. *Am I a fool for helping him, your majesty?* he thought. *Will my actions get your beloved son, my king, killed?*

———————◆———————

"We're here at last," King Mathew said. "Quick Johannes, bring me to the princess!"

Johannes placed a hand on the king's shoulder. "Have patience, your majesty. Please trust me."

King Mathew grew quiet and gazed into the older man's eyes. "I trust you, Johannes. You've always been faithful despite how I've treated you. But please don't make me wait too long. My heart aches to set eyes on her. My ears long to finally hear her voice."

Johannes nodded. "It won't be long." He stepped out of the cabin and went ashore. He found the raven waiting for him.

"Johannes!" it cried. "I did as you asked. The princess received your message, although I do not know if she will come."

"Thank you, dear friend," Johannes said. "Give my thanks to Sebastian and safe journeys home."

The raven flapped its wings. "Good luck, faithful Johannes."

Now Johannes waited. *I don't know if my plan will work,* he thought. *But I won't give up. I will keep the king safe and help him.*

Soon a great golden carriage arrived, and a beautiful young woman stepped out. Johannes recognized her from the portrait. She was even more breathtaking at the height of womanhood.

"Your highness," he said. "I have come from across the seas with gifts from another realm."

She gazed at him suspiciously. "We have many wonders here, merchant. Many like you have come with promises but rarely deliver. Show me what you speak of."

He bowed and withdrew a small golden box. He opened it and a tiny golden bird rose out of the box. Johannes wound the box and the bird began to sing.

The princess' face lit up at the song. "I know this song well." she said. "My mother used to sing it to me as a child."

He handed the box to her.

"Take it," he said. "It is a gift. I have many more wonders for you on my ship. Will you come see them?"

She gazed at the box and then up at the ship warily. But her eagerness won over her caution. "Yes, merchant. I will come see you. But I warn you that I will not tolerate disappointment."

The princess allowed herself to be led onto the ship and down into the hold. She clapped and cried out excitedly at the many wonders that Mathew had made for her. "It is all so beautiful!"

Turning to the captain, Johannes smiled. "Make sail for our homeland in all haste."

The ship's captain looked uncomfortable. "Beggin' your pardon, but are you sure this is wise? I won't be party to kidnapping a girl. Especially a royal no less."

"It will all be alright," Johannes said. "Tell the king to wait for us on deck."

The captain sighed and gave the order to set sail, and before long, they were far from land. It didn't take long for the princess to realize the ship was rocking. She ran to the deck and gazed out in dismay.

Johannes held up his hands. "Wait, your majesty. Please hear me out. I assure you that you are safe."

"Liar!" she cried out. She pulled out a small knife from her gown and brandished it before her. "Turn this ship around now or face my father's wrath.

"Hurry, my foolish king." Johannes whispered to Mathew as he walked up. "Speak to her now or we will never see another dawn."

"Princess Sophia," King Mathew said. He took a small step forward. "Please wait. I am royal, and your equal. I beg you to hear out my plea. I suffer from a painful malady that only you could cure."

She grew silent. "What ails you? I will not have any creature, even one so full of treachery as you, suffer on my account."

King Mathew took another step forward until the point of her blade rested on his chest. "Fairest princess, no—you are more than a mere princess. You make the great beauty of the sun pale in comparison. I saw a portrait of you not long ago. You were a child. Now I see you before me, and my heart soars like a shooting star." He placed his hand over her knife-wielding one. "My malady is this: I love you. My faithful servant warned me that the moment I laid eyes on you it would mean great suffering. Now I understand why. Because if I don't have you by my side, if I cannot love you every day forth from here on, then I beg you to end my suffering and my life by your own hand. If you would save me, then spare my life, accept my love, and become my wife."

Princess Sophia gazed at him with wide eyes. She looked down at her blade before she glanced back up.

"You're insane!" She pushed him over the side of the ship into the waters below.

———◆———

Johannes gazed at the miserable young man who shivered under the blanket. "It was a valiant attempt, your majesty."

King Mathew scowled at his faithful servant with chattering teeth. "Don't say it, Johannes."

"Say what, your majesty?"

"The 'I told you so' speech."

"I would never tell you I told you so, your majesty."

"You just did." King Mathew looked glum, his lower lip protruding in a petulant manner. "Now what do I do, Johannes? She has rejected me..."

Johannes thought for a moment. "Allow me to speak to her."

He bowed to the young king before he climbed to the deck to where the princess, who had not left in all that time, stood gazing back toward her homeland.

"Your highness," he said as he bowed. "May I bring you a blanket for warmth?"

Princess Sophia shook her head. "No. I want nothing from you or that lunatic."

Johannes smiled patiently. "He can be a bit crazy," he said. "I do admit that. But it is only because his heart is so filled with fearless longing."

The princess glanced at Johannes. "Fearless longing?"

Johannes nodded. "He wasn't lying. I feared showing him the portrait that my king had found on a ship that was bound for your kingdom. It was meant for your father, the king of the East. He never forgot that my lord took it and has held a grudge ever since."

Princess Sophia gave a small nod. "The portrait was the last thing my mother ever painted before she passed away. It was very important to my father."

"The young king treasures it, too. You are as important to him as the portrait is to your father."

At this Sophia's face softened. "Do I really mean so much to him?"

"And more," Johannes replied. "I have known King Mathew since I held him in my arms as a babe. He now lives and breathes only in the hopes you might smile at him. To requite his love."

The princess glanced back out toward the sea. "He doesn't even know me. How can he love a girl he doesn't know?"

"Your highness," Johannes said, "what you must ask yourself is not that. But rather if he loves you this much now, how might his love grow for you once he does know you, and has even greater cause to love you?"

She bit her lip. "The animals of my father's kingdom have long told me stories of great loves. I had thought they were just stories."

"If you have faith, you can make the story real, your highness. But only if you willingly give him a chance."

She turned back to him. "You sound so sure of yourself. Do you really have so much faith in him? You are just a servant. What has he done to warrant such admiration and love?"

Johannes smiled. "Do you want to find out?"

She nodded. "I do."

———◆———

"King Mathew, I will give you a chance but only one," she warned him. "If I find your heart isn't true, my father's wrath will be terrible and without mercy."

The young king knelt down and took her hand in his, pressed his lips to it and smiled adoringly at her. "Then I pray that you and my faithful servant Johannes will stay by my side and always keep me true until I breathe my last breath."

For the first time, the princess smiled at him. "I think your servant's faith is well founded."

Johannes smiled at the warm scene, but his heart was troubled. Not long after the princess had gone to Mathew and accepted his proposal, another raven visited him.

It was smaller than the first and flew very quickly. "Are you Johannes?" it called out. "I bring word from Sebastian. The king is in danger!"

"I am Johannes."

"Beware, Johannes!" it cried out. "Beware!"

"What is it, my feathered friend?" Johannes called.

"I bring word from Sebastian. The king of the east has learned of King Mathew's treachery. He has sent word to a horse loyal to him that shall throw the king from his saddle when he mounts. Whatever you do, do not let King Mathew ride him."

Johannes grew silent. He had feared war, but an assassination attempt? He found it difficult to believe the king of the eastern lands would stoop so low.

"Thank you for the warning, friend raven," Johannes called out. "Tell Sebastian we will arrive soon."

Now, with the shores of their homeland approaching, a challenge waited. He had to stop King Mathew from riding a horse that would be the death of him. The raven's warning was strong.

I will have to act fast, Johannes thought. He knew King Mathew would foolishly want to show off his horsemanship to the princess.

Before long, the ship docked. Protocol decreed the king be the first off the ship, but Johannes stepped out ahead of him and strode quickly down the gangplank.

Gasps of disbelief rose from the ship and shore. "What is that servant doing?" the onlookers called out.

King Mathew frowned, but squeezed the princess' hand. She watched Johannes silently as he hurried over to where a large white stallion with a gold bridle and saddle awaited the king. Johannes grasped the reins.

"I know where your loyalties lie," he hissed to the horse. "I will not let you hurt *my* king."

The stallion blinked at Johannes. "How do—No, I will not fail the eastern king. Be gone! You are but a servant."

"No!" Johannes cried and shoved the horse back, who reared on his hind legs. He swatted the stallion's rump and sent it running.

"Johannes!" Mathew barked. "What are you doing? I wanted to ride that horse to the castle."

Johannes thought fast. "Forgive me, your majesty. I foolishly thought you would wish to ride in a carriage with your bride to be."

"Oh," King Mathew said. He gazed thoughtfully and gave a small nod. "Yes, you are right, Johannes. I should ride with her. Thank you."

Johannes bowed and called for a carriage. He rode next to the driver as they set forth for the castle with Mathew and princess safely within.

Soon after they set off, a small dark shape flew toward the carriage. Johannes strained his eyes until the shape revealed itself to be a large, dark raven.

"Johannes!" it cried out. "Beware! The king of the eastern realm has set a trap for the King Mathew. If he wears the clothes that have been sent as gifts, he will surely perish."

Johannes' fists tightened. To refuse a gift from a royal was a crime. The king knew this. If King Mathew willingly rejected the gift, the king in the east would have his war, regardless of his daughter's wishes.

"Thank you for the warning, dear friend," Johannes called out. "Tell Sebastian I thank him too and shall see him tonight!"

"I will," the raven cried. "Protect our king, human."

"Always," Johannes whispered as he watched the raven fly away.

Soon enough the castle loomed ahead. In the courtyard were several boxes of gifts that messenger birds from the East had brought. When the carriage came to a halt, the young king looked out and saw the boxes.

"Look, beloved," he said. "Your father sends his greetings and his acknowledgement of our love."

Princess Sophia gazed at the boxes and nodded slowly, but her heart was troubled. She knew her father. All too well. She turned her gaze to Johannes who nodded, confirming her suspicions. She pleaded with him with her eyes to do something.

Johannes leapt off of the carriage and ran to the boxes. He ripped the clothes from them and threw them into a muddy puddle within the courtyard.

King Matthew's face reddened with anger. "Johannes," he said through gritted teeth, "what is the meaning of this? You would do this to a gift from the father of my future bride?"

"Your majesty," Johannes said. "I beg you to please believe me when I say that what I did was for you. I mean you no disrespect."

Mathew's eyes narrowed. Finally he took a deep breath. "Very well, Johannes. But enough foolishness for today. Do not presume to act for me again unless I tell you."

Johannes bowed deeply. He could hear whispers from members of the court behind him and voices calling for him to be punished. He sighed inwardly. He followed behind his king and princess until his eyes fell on a familiar face.

"Sebastian," he called out happily. "I received your warnings."

Sebastian nodded. "I got your thanks. Ravens never tasted so good." At Johannes' horrified look the cat chuckled. "I'm kidding, tall one. They are safe and sound. But our tribulation is not done yet. Another of the young brothers has brought word of a third and final plot."

Johannes faced fell. "If I act up again, I fear what the prince will do."

Sebastian nodded. "Be faithful and vigilant, Johannes." The cat glanced toward Mathew. "The great king of the east has decided that if he cannot have his daughter, he would rather no one will."

Johannes' face turned grave. "Surely he would not sacrifice his own daughter!"

The cat's ears pulled back. "He is torn with grief. He has lost the last memento of his wife and now his daughter. He isn't acting rationally, Johannes."

"What does he plan?"

Sebastian turned back to Johannes. "When the princess eats her meal tonight, it will be poisoned. She will die most horribly."

"I must stop her from eating it."

Sebastian nodded. "We will both go to the king. He will understand."

That night at the banquet hosted in the princess' honor, a great feast was placed on the table, filled with all kinds of food from all over the kingdom. A plate filled with delicious looking treats was placed before the famished princess.

"Your majesty," Johannes pleaded. "Do not let her eat anything."

King Mathew frowned. "What are you saying? She has hardly eaten a thing since we set out. Would you rather she starve?"

"Listen to him, young Mathew." Sebastian pleaded. "I beg you to listen."

"I tell you she must not eat from this table," Johannes insisted.

The king slapped his hand down onto the table. "Johannes, you go too far! First you presume and set my horse running and then destroy a peace offering from Sophia's father. Now you would force her to go without food?"

Johannes turned a pleading look to the princess. But she was hungry and did not see his concern. She reached for her plate. Bowing his head, Johannes faced his king.

"Always." he said.

He turned back to the princess and struck her hand away. She cried out in surprise. He grabbed her plate and ran, eating as he went. He might have simply thrown the plate down, but he could not risk even a lowly serf eating the poisoned food.

"No, Johannes!" Sebastian cried out.

"Johannes!" King Mathew shouted. He ran after him, grabbed him and threw him with the plate to the floor. "How dare you!" He grabbed the older man's head and bashed it against the floor. "You are false as a friend and servant."

"Stop, King Mathew!" Sebastian said. "You do not understand." He swiped at the young man with a paw, but he knocked the cat backward tail over ears.

"My king," Johannes gasped, "I have always and shall forever be your faithful servant."

"You have insulted my future wife!" King Mathew bellowed. "Do you think that you will get away with it? Well? Do you?"

But Johannes didn't answer.

"Answer me, servant!" the king roared.

Johannes' healthy pallor faded into purple. His breathing ceased.

"Johannes?" King Mathew said. His eyes widened as his servant turned blue. "Johannes!"

There came no response, and the young man felt the life drain from Johannes as he held him in his arms.

Eyes that had once been filled with joy and love faded to emptiness. Hands, once strong, fell limp to his side. It was only then that Mathew realized the truth. Sophia's meal had been poisoned. Unable to make the king see reason, Johannes had done the only thing he could. He ate the meal.

Sebastian limped over to him.

"What have I done?" King Mathew sobbed. "Oh Sebastian, whatever have I done…"

Sebastian bowed his head. "Faithful Johannes. You kept your promise. The king's beloved son is safe."

Johannes' body was placed in a magnificent stone chamber where fresh flowers were laid every day. Sebastian would be seen walking by regularly. The servants would whisper the cat would often speak to the air, as though to an invisible person that only he could see. The years passed, and the young king and princess were married. They had children and life was quiet. But Sebastian was troubled. A raven had brought word to him of a visitor from across the sea. And this time he wasn't sure if they could avert what might happen.

Yet he remained faithful—just like Johannes would have. And he came up with a plan. He whispered it in the night to the king.

Together they plotted and hoped with secret hearts.

———— ◆ ————

Finally the night came when the visitor arrived. The king and queen met their guest in the throne room.

King Mathew bowed before his father-in-law. "Welcome to my kingdom."

"I have come for what is mine!" the king bellowed. "I shall have justice or your head, princeling. Choose and meet your fate."

King Mathew straightened his posture and glanced at Sebastian. A raven stood next to the cat. It was now or never. "Before you exact your justice on me, great king, I ask that you hear me out. I have a deal for you. One that I think will be worth your time."

The great king's face turned pensive. "You seek to barter for your life? What deal could you possibly make me? You have taken everything away that matters."

"I know," King Mathew said. "You have given me so much. A reason to breathe, to love, and to fight for those I care for."

He dropped to his knees and held out his hands. "But now I come before you, great king, and I selfishly ask you for something more."

"And what would you dare to ask me for now, stupid prince?"

"A trade."

The king laughed. "I will not trade anything with you. No, I shall destroy you and all you hold dear."

"Father!" Sophia exclaimed. "Would you destroy me too?"

At this the king grew quiet. "No, daughter. My actions were thoughtless and cowardly. But no. I shall trade with this thief."

King Mathew grew quiet. *What would Johannes do?* he thought. He gave a small nod. Johannes had risked everything for him and in the end had given his life. King Mathew could do no less.

"Then if you will not trade with me," he asked, "will you make a wager?"

The king eyed him suspiciously. "What wager?"

King Mathew turned to Sophia. "Will you trust me, my love?"

She gazed into his eyes and nodded. "Johannes had faith in you. I will bet everything I hold dear on you."

He smiled at her, his face filled with love. "Thank you, Sophia." He turned back to the king. "My wager is this: I will gamble everything I hold dear. The love of my life, Sophia, my children, and even my crown."

Sophia gazed at him with wide eyes. But she kept silent.

Her father began to smile eagerly. "Oh? What is the wager?"

"That if I cannot offer you something that you want just as badly as what I have offered, you can take what I have wagered with you and return across the sea. I will give you my crown and go forth from the castle as a beggar. Nothing more. Nothing less."

The king stared at him in astonishment. He laughed and shook his head. "I thought you were a devious thief, little princeling. Now I saw you're just a fool."

King Mathew nodded. "Yes, I am a fool. Because I didn't trust the word of a man who has been more than a mere servant and friend. One who indeed has been a beloved father to me my whole life."

The king nodded slowly. "Very well. What do you want from me? Gold? Lands?"

Mathew held out his hand to Sebastian. "My loyal cat has told me that within your gardens is a bird whose feathers can return life to someone dead once a generation. Is this true?"

The king's shoulders stiffened. "How did you learn of this?"

Sebastian groomed a paw. "I have heard the story from your loyal subjects. When your wife passed away, you became obsessed with finding a way to bring back your dead wife. Only you couldn't, because her body had been lost at sea."

The king gave a weary sigh. "You are right. I have such a bird in my gardens who can do what you say." He glanced up sharply. "But why should I give its feather to you? What worthy reason could you give me that would equal such a prize?"

19

"A most worthy one," King Mathew said. "To restore the life of the man who sacrificed everything for me."

"For a servant? I said 'worthy.'"

"Father," Sophia pressed, "He was a worthy man. He served my husband all of his life. He kept him safe... He gave his life for mine."

"Very well. I accept your wager." He smiled coldly. "Now then, win your wager and offer me something that I could want more than you want that feather, your kingdom, my daughter, or grandchildren."

King Mathew gave a small nod and snapped his fingers. Two servants brought in a large object covered by a sheet. "I believe my father took this from you. It has brought me so much." He bowed his head. "And I thank you for that, great king."

The sheet was removed. The king gasped and clutched his heart. "It can't be," he whispered. "I never thought I would see it again." He wept tears and fell to his knees sobbing.

Mathew watched the king's face. "What have my father and I done?" he whispered.

The king and Sophia turned to him. Mathew shook his head. "Great king, I knew you coveted the painting. I thought to use it to win this wager... but I didn't know. I can see it in your eyes. The same love I felt when I saw it."

He stood and turned to Sophia. "Forgive me, my love. I must lose this wager. Even if I lose everything, even you, I cannot make your father bear the same pain that Johannes saved me from by bringing you to me."

Sophia's eyes were wet with tears. "I don't want to leave you, husband."

"And I don't want to leave you, wife."

The king watched them. "Your servant saved you from the pain that you would now spare me from. Even knowing you will lose everything you would still do this?"

King Mathew removed the crown from his head. "Johannes would do the same, your majesty."

The king was silent for a long time. He stared at the crown in Mathew's hands. Slowly a warm smile filled his face.

"If such a man has inspired a heart to become worthy of my daughter's love, I think I would like to meet him." He stood and offered a hand out to King Mathew. "Come, I accept you have won this wager. I shall take the painting to have something of my daughter and wife. I shall send for the feather. Your faithfulness will be rewarded."

Mathew bowed his head. "Thank you, great king."

He turned to Sophia who threw her arms around her father's neck.

"Thank you, father," she whispered.

Sophia's father was true to his word. By morning, a great bird of pure white arrived with a magnificent feather in its beak. The king presented the feather to the King Mathew who placed it on Johannes' body, which had been preserved in his memory. Breathlessly, they waited. Soon color returned to Johannes' cheeks. Warmth and life moved throughout his body. He sat up and smiled at his king.

"Your majesty."

"Faithful Johannes!" Mathew cried. "Welcome home! And well done, my dear friend and beloved servant."

Sebastian watched from afar and purred. "Well done, Johannes. The reward for your loyalty is the one thing you never had. A family that will love you and never desert you. Faithful until the very end."

Bridgette

and the Gruffz

- Steven Wilcox -
Illustrated by Bobbie Berendson W.

My first autograph!

Once upon a time, there was an enchanted forest. And in this forest, there lived a family of satyrs, The Three Brothers Gruffz. The eldest was Biggs, broad of shoulder and swift of hoof. Second was Midean, sharp of tongue and quick of wit. The youngest was Smalz, who loved poetry, yoga, rock gardening, and interpretive dance.

Each year, when winter released the woods from its icy grip, The Three Brothers Gruffz would go out into the forest and seek their fortunes, such as fortune was measured in their family.

Biggs was loved best by the ladies of the wood. He could lift a nymph in each hand over his head, and did so frequently. He could best a bear in a wrestling match, and rattle a tall tree's branches with a kick. His feats of strength and prowess were many, and he loved adding to the list almost as much as he loved recounting them.

Just as no foe would lock horns with Biggs, no fool would trade jibes with Midean. He could charm the leaves off an oak with a compliment, or set it ablaze with an insult. The ladies that preferred a quick wit to a strong arm flocked to him, and Midean never wanted for the attention of the dryads and sprites and other forest girls.

But, while they thought Smalz kind, and his gardens pretty, and his songs sweet, the ladies of the forest were quick to leave him as soon as one of his brothers passed by. Most evenings found the youngest Gruffz alone, while his brothers caroused, and cavorted, and made merry late into the night.

One day, as spring was warming into summer, Smalz found himself at the forest's edge. A brook babbled by, and over it was a bridge. Though the brook itself had lost much of its thawing swell, its bed was deep, and the bridge was raised by mound and stone so that even Biggs could have walked beneath it without stooping his head.

The bridge's timbers were fresh-hewn, the stones newly set, and Smalz looked around, searching for other signs that might explain its construction, like a village or a woodcutter's hut. He walked down the path, and commenced across the bridge, still looking into the distance. His hooves made a clacking noise on the boards as he made his way across.

"Who's that, trip-tropping across my bridge?" a voice asked.

Smalz looked down. A pair of bright yellow eyes peered up at him through the timber slats of the bridge.

"'Tis I, the smallest brother Gruffz. My friends call me Smalz. Forgive me if I've intruded..."

"Oh, nothing of the sort. Bridges are made to be walked over. I was just curious."

A tall, feminine silhouette unfolded from the shadows beneath the bridge. She stooped slightly to keep from bumping her head on its underside and stepped out into the sunlight. She smiled at him from the creek bed as she straightened up, and putting a hand on the railing, swung up on to it easily.

Smalz was taken aback, quite literally; she might have caught him in the chin with her leg had he not stepped away in surprise.

"Oh, sorry!" she apologized. "I didn't think you were so close. My name's Bridgette."

She was, head-to-toe, a sort of bluish green in color. Her hair was a deep, almost iridescent green, and a pair of short, uneven horns poked up from the top of her head. Strangest of all was her clothing, in that she was wearing any at all. She wore a simple, short dress made of animal skins that left her arms and most of her legs bare. Smalz knew it was a dress, from stories he'd been told, but he never imagined he'd actually see one. He was trying to compose a proper and flattering compliment for it when she started talking again.

"So, do you live nearby?" she asked, crossing her long, sturdy legs and fixing those curious yellow eyes and their still-more curious irises on him.

"I do, just in the forest, there."

"Oh, you are forest-folk, then?"

"I suppose I am, yes."

"Are you really so short, or are you bewitched?"

Smalz felt the heat of red creeping up his cheeks. His height was a source of considerable entertainment for his brothers, and she was probably half-a-head taller than Biggs. There was no cruel mirth in her voice, though, and her smile was guileless. He tried to think of a clever response, and failed.

"I heard that witches sometimes live in forests, is all," she continued, seeming to take no notice of his silence. "Are you going somewhere?"

"Oh, not really," he answered lamely. "I... I saw the bridge and thought it was new, and came to have a look."

"Do you like it?" she asked, clearly proud. "It's my first one... well, I mean, it's the first one that's *all* mine. My parents have one, obviously."

"Well, I don't have a lot of experience with bridges, but it seems... um... sturdy?"

"Well, that's what a bridge should be, above all else." She beamed, a purplish blush working its way through her verdant cheeks. He couldn't help but smile, and she smiled back, and he laughed, and she laughed. A proper satyr would have continued in this vein, and flattered her construction, or composed an ode on the spot to her prowess at hewing stone, but Smalz could never do those sorts of things off the top of his horns.

If she thought his lack of decorum reproachful, though, she made no sign. She seemed perfectly content to regale him with the engineering principles at work in this joist or that riser, and to seek his opinion on what manner of lichen she should cultivate upon the stones. She invited him underneath the bridge and, rather than expecting him to recite sonnets regarding the greenness of her hair, discussed with him the placement of the river stones in the stream bed beneath and near.

All concern over propriety faded at this. All the streams in the forest were occupied by naiads and nymphs, so he'd never had the chance to work water into his designs. A burst of creative giddiness took him, and he rambled on like a fool for the better part of an hour, pointing at this stone and that, and even getting into the stream to move one about when she expressed doubt the efficacy of the suggested arrangement. There was nothing Smalz liked more than rock gardening, except, perhaps, for yoga, but he knew better than to bring *that* up. No one cared about yoga.

Bridgette was likewise taken with the enterprise, and Smalz was able to, for a while, forget about wooing and cavorting. Though, as they sat in the cool shade of the bridge and lunched on pepper sandwiches, the thought of, perhaps, canoodling a bit occurred to him.

The opportunity never arose, though. As soon as the conversation lagged on one subject, she would ask him about something else, and, generally, it was something he had thought about a great deal, and he would get distracted from his proper satyr manners and talk to her about it. He did manage to ask her questions about herself, but they were inane and pointless ones, like where she came from and what it was like there, and not at all about what she thought of his biceps.

Bridgette hailed from the mountains that sat on the horizon, so distant as to appear purple in the setting sun. Her parents were the upwardly mobile sort. No sooner would they have a bridge put together to their satisfaction than they would start on another one—taller or bigger or longer or further up the mountain—and move under it. She had an elder brother who had moved out a few years ago after a spat with her father regarding the family business. He had always preferred caves to bridges, and had fallen in with rough sorts, and now their mother had worried endlessly about her daughter getting out on her own.

"She wanted me to study with my uncle," she explained. "He lives beneath a big, arched bridge in the south, and consults on their construction all over."

They were back on top of the bridge, watching the sun set. It was just wide enough for Bridgette to sit across it, her bare toes dangling off one edge while she leaned back against the opposite railing.

"But that wasn't the point. Just moving out? The point was to get out on my own. Really try to make it, you know?'

Smalz nodded. He was sitting next to her, chewing on a bit of long grass he had snagged from the bank.

"Yeah, to do it your way."

She sat forward at his response and looked at him. "Exactly! It's like, just because I want to build bridges on streams instead of mountain passes doesn't make me an anarchist, Dad!"

Smalz smiled, "It's still a bridge."

Bridgette scooched her legs up and turned towards him, "I know, right? Do you have family?"

He sighed. No conversation with a woman had ever gone as he preferred once his brothers were drawn into it.

"Yes, I have two brothers."

"Aw," Bridgette replied, scrunching up her brow sympathetically. "You don't get along with them?"

"No, we get along fine, they just… every time I'm trying to…" He glanced at her and looked down. "Anyway, they always ruin things. I know they don't mean to, they're just being themselves."

"Sounds like they're being jerks."

"Yeah," he smiled. "Just being themselves."

Bridgette laughed, and not a twittering giggle behind an embarrassed hand. It came from her gut, and rolled out, becoming a cackle as she pitched forward. She drew closer, and put her hand on his thigh as she laughed, and he was satyr enough to take it.

"Can I kiss you?" he asked. It was the right thing to do, even if it was the wrong way to ask.

She raised an eyebrow, and then narrowed her eyes as if to appraise him. Then she smiled.

"I'm not sure if you can, but I'd like you to try."

He was about to close his eyes and lean over to do just that when she laid a long, outstretched finger against his lips.

"Just not tonight. Come back tomorrow, and we'll see how it goes."

"Okay." He smiled, too befluttered to feel any disappointment at all.

Smalz and Bridgette said their goodbyes, and he promised he would return tomorrow to try and get that kiss.

On the way home, it was all he could think about. Perhaps he'd start with a song. She hadn't heard him sing. Most of the songs he knew were raucous and bawdy. What if she didn't like those kinds of songs? He didn't know what sort of songs they sung in the mountains, but perhaps he could get her to sing one. He'd always been a quick study with music, and he was pretty sure he could fake it and join in. If it was a romantic song, or even a funny one, he could lean in at some opportune moment and make the attempt.

It was nearly dark when he made it back to the glade where he and his brothers lived. The evening was already in full swing: Biggs had a fallen tree across his shoulders, and a pair of plump boggarts were dangling from either end. He was spinning this way and that, and the poor little fellows looked ready to come flying off at any moment. A group of four nymphs was giggling and twittering at the display.

Midean was nearby, a pair of dryads at his feet and another on one knee while he rushed through a ribald ballad, squeezing the ample rump of the one in his lap to make her squeal at the right times to punctuate the song.

He hoped he wouldn't be noticed. Normally, the way the girls ignored him made him feel almost a satire of a satyr. Tonight, though, he'd just as soon be left alone. He needed to compose a song, in case Bridgette couldn't think of one. It needed to be neither boring nor bawdy, and that was a difficult balance to strike.

He must have had too glad a gait, though, or been whistling, or otherwise appeared a bit happier than normal, for he had not made it halfway-round the clearing when Midean called out to him. "Hey there, little brother! You don't seem the least bit down in the mouth at all this fine night. Are you okay?"

Smalz tried to come up with something clever to say in response. He didn't need to match Midean's silver tongue. He just needed to hold the conversation long enough for the girls to get bored, and his brother would be drawn away, and he would be free to get to working on his song for tomorrow.

"I... that is, it's just that the night is fine, and the day was finer. Perhaps I got too much sun."

The girls giggled at the exchange, but Midean's canny brow raised.

"And what's made the day so fine? Hey, Biggs! I do believe the youngest Gruffz has been out, meeting secretly with someone that put a smile on his lips, and springs in his legs."

"Only one thing does that to a satyr," Biggs laughed, and spun on his hoof hard enough to pry one of the boggarts loose. The tiny sprite sailed through the air and landed outside the glade's edge with a pronounced *oof*. The nymphs applauded the feat.

"Aye, aye, one thing indeed," Midean echoed. "Dare we guess what plain and homely fae-girl saw fit to while away a day with Smalz?"

Smalz's cheeks burned. The nymphs giggled, and the dryads talked quietly behind raised hands. The one in Midean's lap nuzzled his cheek.

"Well, don't stand there, Smalz! Fetch her here! Let's meet the poor thing."

"She's not homely—" Smalz protested, and then nearly whacked himself betwixt the horns for his stupidity.

"Oh, so you *have* been with a woman all day," Midean jeered gleefully.

"A shy one, no doubt," Biggs cajoled. "Else we would have met her by now."

"Surely," Midean agreed, the dryad nuzzling his neck not distracting him in the least.

"No, she's new." Smalz tried to explain. "Come down from the mountains."

"From the mountains?" Biggs echoed. "What manner of fairy lives in the mountains?"

"I don't think she's a fairy."

"Smalz Oleander Ignatius Gruffz!" Midean cried out in mock horror. "Have you been cavorting with a *mortal*?"

The gathered forest girls burst out laughing.

"No!" he complained, feeling his blush deepen. "Well, at least, I don't think so. She has horns, and green skin. Humans don't have horns."

"Fairies don't have horns either," Midean pointed out. "Just us. And Fauns. And minotaur and centaur."

"Centaur don't have horns," Biggs said, dropping the log behind him. The remaining boggarts were obliged to scramble clear lest they be crushed by it.

"Sure they do," Midean insisted. "If they're part deer or elk instead of part horse. Have you been cavorting with a she-centaur, Smalz?"

"There are she-centaur?" Biggs asked, not bothering to let Smalz reply.

"Oh sure. How do you think they get more centaur?"

"She's not a centaur!" Smalz shouted.

Nymphs are notoriously skittish, and at his outburst, the whole lot gathered around Biggs 'eeked!' and turned into trees. The dryads glared at Smalz for frightening their sisters, and slipped away haughtily. Biggs gave chase, calling for them to come back. Midean glowered at Smalz and followed after. Smalz didn't really care, though. Tomorrow couldn't come soon enough.

The night was interminable, but it ended, as all nights must. Smalz had hardly slept a wink, but he made himself wait until after breakfast before he started down the forest path to Bridgette's crossing.

It was bright and warm, as a proper late spring day should be, and he was already considering what he and Bridgette might do after he'd kissed her properly. She had a peculiar knack for balancing stones on one another, and though he couldn't hope to match it, he had a few ideas of how to put it to use in the water-rock garden beneath the bridge.

His heart sank at first, when he cleared the forest and failed to catch sight of her, but felt silly the instant she stepped out of the shadows beneath her bridge and waved. Honestly, where did he think she'd gone?

He waved back. He tried to keep from sprinting the last hundred feet to the bridge, but failed.

"Hello again," Bridgette said, smirking beneath heavy-lidded eyes. Her dark skin glistened slightly in the sun. It looked soft and very warm, and Smalz suddenly wanted desperately to feel it against his.

"Hi," Smalz replied, knowing he was grinning like an idiot but powerless to do anything about it. "I had some arrangements I thought of last night that I thought we might try—"

"I thought you were going to try to kiss me."

Smalz blushed, "Well, yes, but afterward—"

Bridgette put her hands on her hips and smiled broadly, "Oh, sweetness, I don't know how much you'll be up for afterward."

Satyrly wiles abandoned Smalz completely at such a bold declaration, and he stood for a moment with his mouth agape, then managed to stammer. "Yes, well, I thought it best to be prepared."

She seemed ready, and more than willing, so Smalz leaned forward, and stood up on the tips of his hooves so she wouldn't need to lean down so far.

"Not here," she said. "Let's do it right."

Kissing in the cool shade of her bridge next to the stream babbling over their rock garden seemed ideal to Smalz, but he wasn't going to complain. Bridgette took his hand in hers and led him up the bank and on to the apex of her bridge's gentle arch.

"Here," she said. "Ready?"

Smalz nodded and moved closer. She was tall and lovely and broad in all the right places, soft and warm and endlessly appealing. He yearned to feel those pleasant curves pressed against him, to feel those arms around his shoulders and, most of all, those moist, dark green lips against his. Silently, he vowed that he would get this one right, and if he didn't at first, he would try again and again and again until he did.

And then she picked him up over her head and threw him into the creek.

The first slap of the water and the solid *thunk* of the streambed thereafter were surprises in their own right, but paled in comparison to the shock of being bodily tossed into them. His cry of surprise lasted a few moments too long, and he downed a considerable drought of the stream's cool water. He pushed up, knee deep and sputtering in shock.

Bridgette looked crushed.

"Well, you're going to have to try harder than *that*!" she scolded.

"Why—what?"

"I told you I didn't know if you could do it," she leaned over the railing, "but you said you wanted to try."

"And so you *threw me*?"

"I didn't hurt you, did I?"

"Well... no," Smalz admitted. In fact, as he looked, he noticed that the entirety of their work on the rocks the day before had been carefully and exactly moved up stream some forty feet, on the far side of the bridge. All of the other very large rocks had been cleared as well, leaving the stream deeper, and the bed little more than soft, muddy sand.

"Do you want to try again?" she asked, her tone worried.

"Try to what, exactly?" he asked.

"Kiss me."

"Well, yes, I should like to."

"Oh good," she said, sounding very much relieved. "Well, come up here and let's try again."

Smalz was dubious, but slogged his way out of the creek and up onto the grass, and then made his way back up on to the bridge.

And she promptly picked him up and threw him over the railing again.

This time he landed on his back. The smack of the water was prodigious, and he came up sputtering once more.

"Smalz!" Bridgette shouted down at him, disappointment and apprehension mingling in her voice.

"What!?"

"You have to try harder!"

"To kiss you?" he demanded. "I'm trying *very* hard, but you keep throwing me off the bridge!"

Bridgette flushed, her lovely yellow eyes widened with shock. Her full lips moved once, then twice, and no sound came out. Smalz watched her eyes narrow. Moments passed, and, when she spoke, she did so slowly, her sultry alto marred by a serrated edge.

"What. Kind. Of girl. *Do you think I am!*" she growled, her voice gaining volume and speed until she was practically roaring.

"Wha—" he started, but she wasn't waiting for him to reply.

"Mother warned me! *She warned me*! But did I listen?"

"Warned you about what?"

"*About you*!" She screamed. "About boys like you! Boys that would try to kiss me without throwing me off my bridge!"

"Why would I—"

"Because I thought you liked me!"

And now she was crying. Smalz swallowed against the lump forming in his throat.

"But I do! I like you very much!"

"Just not enough to throw me off my bridge!"

"I—I... what?"

"Stones and Mortar! I'm such an *idiot*! Go away!"

Left with little other alternative, he did. He climbed on the bank and ran into the forest as fast as his hooves would carry him, Bridgette's sobs torturing his ears long after their sounds had faded behind him. He felt wretched enough to be sick, and disappointment and confusion threatened to reduce him to tears as well.

A firm hand grabbed him by the left horn, and steered him in a circle.

"Smalz!" Midean spun him around once and brought him to a stop with a hand on his chest.

Smallz looked up and blinked in surprise.

"Pan's Pipes, brother!" Midean exclaimed. "I've been running after you for a mile at least!"

Smalz did a quick calculation, and realized with some relief that the bridge was much further away, and Midean would have been nowhere near it.

"Where are you going?" Midean asked.

"Um, I was—"

"Have a falling out with your centaur?"

"She's not—"

"Look, Smalz, it's not a big deal! So she got mad, no worries! That just means she likes you!"

Smalz looked at the ground and kicked a molehill. "Maybe she did."

"No. No. No. It doesn't work that way. Take half a breath, pick some flowers, go back, tell her you're sorry, and it'll be fine."

"Sorry for what?"

"Doesn't matter. What matters is that you came back, gave her a gift, and said so."

"I don't think—"

"That's right. Don't think. Just do it. You'll thank me later. Promise."

With that, Midean trotted away, leaving Smalz to consider. Ultimately, he was left with nothing but to follow his brother's advice. Picking flowers in the forest, though, was no trivial matter. Almost all of them belonged to this sylph or that dryad, and it took the better part of the afternoon and no small number of favors to get together enough to form a proper bouquet. He tried to arrange them in a way that she might like, and he thought it was very becoming, but his heart was still in his throat when he braved the edge of the forest again.

The sun was a few fingers above the mountains. She was there, sitting on her bridge, looking at the horizon, the light making her green tresses glow slightly.

She looked over her shoulder as he approached. Her eyes went to the flowers, and her face scrunched, fit to tear up again.

"I'm sorry," he blurted, all the well-formed flattery and wooing words evaporating from his mind.

She shook her head and wiped her eyes, and looked away. A few minutes passed, him standing there awkwardly, and her staring at the mountains. The sun had nearly touched them when he dared speak again.

"So, where *you're* from… you have to throw a girl off her bridge to kiss her?"

"Yup."

"What… what if you really like a girl, but she's much bigger and stronger than you?"

"Then you have to find a way. It isn't like you have to be able to do it every time. Or even most of the time. My mother can toss Father three times out of five. That probably seems really old fashioned to you."

She looked aside to him sharply, yellow eyes narrowed and flashing and daring him to agree. He dared not.

"No, nothing like that. I just… when a girl wants to be kissed here, you just… kiss her?"

"Well, I'm sorry to disappoint you. Stones! Father would have just eaten you by now."

"What?"

"And ground your bones to make his bread."

"That's a thing?"

"No, but that doesn't mean I'm some cheap fairy strumpet for you have your way with."

"I—I never… I wouldn't—"

"Fine."

Smalz winced, looking at the stream, but he'd promised he'd make this work, and make it happen, and he meant to make good on that promise.

"Look. Bridgette…"

"What, Smalz?"

"I… I really want to kiss you, and if I have to throw you off your bridge to do it, then I will."

"But you're tiny, and not very strong at all."

"Hey!"

"What? You aren't! You were so confident, though, so I thought, 'Hey! Maybe this little goat man has some trick you haven't seen yet'. But now I know you just thought I was easy—"

"I never said you were easy!"

"Were you planning on throwing me off my bridge?"

"No, but—"

"Then you thought I was easy!"

"That's not—I mean it! I'll throw you off this bridge. I'll do it right now!"

"Really?"

"Well, yeah, if you still want me to."

"You mean it?"

Smalz set his shoulders back, resolute. "Yes. I mean it."

Bridgette looked happy enough to hug him, but she threw him off the bridge instead.

"Hey! I wasn't ready!"

"Stones, Smalz! That's the whole point! Try to catch me off balance!"

And so he did, and so he failed, time after time, after time, until long after the sun had set. He'd never been much for roughhousing, even with his brothers, and he sorely regretted not putting in the time now. She was impossibly strong, and deft, and quick, and seemed to know what he was going to try before he did.

Night had properly set in, and he pulled himself once more out of the water and up on to the bank, breaths coming in great, tired gasps.

"Smalz…"

He closed his eyes and lay back. The grass had grown cold in the night, and felt positively frigid against his skin.

"Smalz!"

He looked up to see Bridgette standing over him, looking at him with concern.

"Maybe we should call it a night," she offered.

"Hey," he said, gulping air between words. "There's an idea: how about I come back tonight and push you off the bridge while you're asleep."

"Smalz, why do you think I sleep *under* the bridge? A girl can't let herself get rolled off by just anyone."

He groaned a little and sat up. "Of course not. Okay. Let's try again tomorrow."

She helped him up, and the two of them started walking towards the forest.

"What does it take to hold hands?" he asked.

"Hmm?"

"Say I wanted to hold your hand. Can I just do that, or do I need to, like, hit you in the head with a rock?"

She laughed, and grabbed his hand. She walked with him up the little path that led from her bridge, and, as they parted, he was so bold as to take her other hand, as well.

"Good night. See you tomorrow, Bridgette."

He was mostly dry when he made it back to the clearing. The usual din of laughter, singing and shouting was muzzy. Half-heard questions about where he'd been went unanswered.

He walked directly across, laid down in the soft grass, and fell asleep.

The next day passed more pleasantly, if without any more success on his part. He walked to her bridge, and was thrown off it a number of times. Then they took lunch, then whiled away a few hours arranging rocks upstream. Bridgette was always careful to toss him off the downstream side, into the place she'd prepared for him, but one couldn't be certain that would always be the case, and they would not see the rock-and-water garden damaged.

After that, it was back to the throwing and the splashing, and a few pointers on hoof position and proper lifting form, and then more throwing, but mostly, being thrown. They dined on pepper sandwiches and watched the sunset, followed by a comfortable walk, holding hands and a promise to try again tomorrow.

When he returned to the clearing that night, Midean greeted him with a brotherly arm about the shoulder.

"So, how'd it go?"

"Oh, pretty well."

"Good. Good. Why are you... wet?"

"Oh, I've been in the brook quite a bit today."

"That's great! Her name's Brook? That's a strange name for a centaur."

"She... oh. No. That's not it. Her name is Bridgette. She threw me in the brook."

"Whatever you want to call it, little brother, I'm just glad to see you stagger in and fall asleep after a hard day's work."

Smalz was too tired to straighten any of that out, and Midean was quickly distracted with other matters. Back to the soft grass he went, and fell asleep.

The next morning, due to the exhaustion or the long hours or both, he slept late. It was nearly noon when his eyelids fluttered open. In a trice, he was up and shaking the cobwebs from his head, and then he was off and running down the forest path to Bridgette's place.

He was nearly to the forest's edge when he spied Midean, crouched behind a mulberry bush and peering out towards the crossing.

"Midean, what are you—"

"Shh!" his brother shushed, and beckoned him closer. He crouched back down, and pointed towards the bridge. Bridgette was standing in the stream, bent over at the waist, with her head in the water. She had taken off her dress and wore just a tiny loincloth, which looked all the smaller for her height. Smalz was dumbstruck.

Midean nudged him in the ribs with his elbow, and smiled appreciatively as Bridgette stood up, her long hair sending water every which way. She ran her fingers through it, displaying her profile to great advantage.

"What do you think she is?" Midean asked, not looking away.

"That's Bridgette," Smalz explained.

"What's a brijet?" he asked, not looking away from the copious amounts of water pouring in rivulets down and through her ample curves.

"No, that's her name."

"Name? With a body like that, she doesn't need a name. What I mean is, what is she? She's too tall to be a fairy."

"I think she's a she-troll."

"Trollup."

Smalz's head snapped to look at his brother, and he had to fight to keep his voice down. "Hey!"

"What? That's what you call a she-troll. A trollup."

"Don't let her hear you say that. I know her—"

"You wish."

Midean made to stand up, but Smalz grabbed his arm with both hands and pulled him back down.

"No, I mean, I know her. She's who I've been going to see the last few days. Her name is Bridgette, and I really like her, so don't going making a Nick-Bottom of yourself."

"Oh. Oooh. *ooooOOOOoooh*. Oh. Wait, she's not a centaur—"

"Ugh! No, she's not, like I told you."

"Wait, how did you get…" Midean trailed off. Smallz followed his gaze and saw that Bridgette was scooping handfuls of water from the stream and washing her upper body with it. The brothers watched with respectfully stilled tongues until her task was complete.

Smallz started, "Yeah. That's the thing, I haven't—"

Midean punched Smalz in the shoulder. "Why not? What is *wrong* with you?"

"Ow! Nothing! Look, she won't let…"

Bridgette had started washing her thighs, and the two satyrs were obligated to watch again in silence until she had finished. Still unaware of her audience, she sloshed her way back upstream and disappeared beneath the bridge, presumably to dress. A few moments passed while the brothers tried to recall what they were talking about.

"She won't let me," Smalz said, remembering finally.

"Ha. Yeah, I can believe that. Here. Watch and learn."

"No, wait." Smalz tightened his grip on Midean' arm. "There are like, these rules."

"Heh. Rules."

"You can't do anything with her until you throw her off the bridge."

"Oh, I'll throw her off *something,* all right. "

"Seriously," Smalz insisted, and his tone seemed to penetrate his brother's satyrly haze.

His brother looked at him with some confusion. "Wait, really? Like, literally?"

"Yes!"

"Oh." Midean seemed to consider for a moment, then shrugged.

"Okay, so I'll go push her off the bridge or whatever."

Smalz raised an eyebrow. "I'd like to see you try."

"Then let go and let me."

"Did you *see* her?"

Midean whistled low, and smiled. "Oh yeah, I saw."

"I meant, did you see how big she is? She's taller than me by a head and a half."

"Pssh. So am I."

"No, you're not."

"Close enough."

To punctuate his assertion, Midean put a rough hand between Smalz' horns and shoved, sending him rolling backwards out of the bush. By the time he'd gotten to his feet, Midean was already half way down the path. Helplessly, Smalz crouched down to watch.

"Who's that, trip-tropping across my bridge?" he heard Bridgette call out.

"'Tis I, the second brother Gruffz," Midean replied in a loud voice. Smalz felt his stomach hollow out as she emerged and the two of them began speaking in tones too quiet for him to make out over the distance. For a brief moment, it seemed like he would lose Bridgette to the charms of his older brother. Midean took her by the hand and stood a bit taller to get his lips closer to hers. Her long, strong fingers wrapped around Midean's horns.

The twist of her hips was as sudden as it was artful, and she used the purchase of the satyr's horns to hurl him sidelong, over the railing. Midean hit the water with a splash and came up sputtering.

"Let me guess," she called down to him, smiling broadly, "you weren't expecting that."

Midean flushed and splashed his way out of the creek. He stormed up the path to the forest's edge, and did so much as spare a sidelong glance to his younger brother. Smalz waited until he was long gone before emerging from the thicket and making his way down to her. Bridgette beamed at him as he clopped up the planks to her.

"I hope Midean didn't upset you. I tried to tell him."

"After that mess with you, I was ready for it," she replied sunnily, then bit her lip. "Do you want to take another shot?"

"Very much so. But first, how did you do that to Midean?"

"Oh, that's a hip throw."

"You never threw me like that."

"That's because I like you. And I didn't need to."

"Can you show me how to do it?"

And so she did. She led him to a grassy spot to one side of the path and showed him how to stand, where to put his feet, how to grab her, and how to twist his hips and pick her up with his legs. The motion was unfamiliar, and they had to practice many times very slowly before he started to get the hang of it.

Once he did, they went up on to the bridge and tried for real. Unfortunately, he found he could scarcely get a hand on her, let alone get the hold right or move his feet correctly. Sometimes she'd move her arms inside his, and throw him instead. Sometimes she'd block his hip with her knee. Sometimes she'd just step to the side and let him pitch forward on to his face.

"You can't just try the same thing over and over again, Smalz," she chided. "Remember? Try to catch me by surprise."

Twice more he tried, and twice more he failed. The last time saw him back in the water, and the shocking cold was almost a relief. He was sweating profusely, and his knees and elbows were skinned and bruised from falling on the hard wooden planks. Once he'd had a chance to catch his breath, she welcomed him into the shade beneath the bridge and offered him a consolatory pepper sandwich.

After lunch, they gardened a bit, and then took a walk together along the edge of the forest. He picked a quick collection of hostas, elephant's ears, and fern fronds and tied them together and presented it to her. He showed her how to set it in her hair over one ear.

She thanked him, but it wasn't until he showed her reflection in the stream's placid waters that she understood.

"It's beautiful, Smalz!" she exclaimed, beaming down on him happily, then turning back to her reflection. He smiled at her wistfully. She bent down and turned her head to admire it more fully. Her profile was striking, and every satyrly bone in his body ached to make another attempt while she was distracted. But he refrained, knowing well she'd pound him senseless for even trying.

The sun was well-set when he finally made it home to the clearing. The sylphs, dryads and nymphs were absent, leaving only Biggs and Midean to greet him. Biggs was stroking his chin, and Midean leaned against a tree, chewing on a bit of long grass. Smalz felt the eyes of Biggs immediately. Midean seemed to be deliberately avoiding his gaze.

"Midean has told me a tale," Biggs began.

"Has he?" Smalz glared at the middle brother. Midean didn't meet the look.

"Indeed. I understand you've been wasting time with this centaur, talking to her and playing in the river instead of wooing and cavorting."

"She's not a centaur," Midean corrected, still staring pointedly into the night.

"I'm trying to woo her, Biggs!" Smalz exclaimed.

"Yes. Apparently you have to best her to have her."

"Well, to kiss her, yes."

"Ah. Then I shall best her and put an end to this," Biggs' normally cheery tone was fierce with intent.

"No need for that," Midean interjected. "She keeps letting him try. He's bound to get the best of her eventually."

"And all the while, she goes unkissed, unwooed, uncanoodled. In our forest!" Biggs countered.

"She built a bridge over the brook," Smalz could feel his own voice rising. "She doesn't even live in the forest."

"Close enough!" Biggs roared. "Our family's honor and reputation are tarnished, and I won't stand for it."

Biggs rose and stamped a hoof in emphasis.

"You're standing," Midean pointed out.

Smalz implored. "Biggs, I'm doing my best! You have to let me—"

Biggs raised a hand. "And I'm sure you conducted yourself well, but the time for half measures has passed. We are the Brothers Gruffz, and, between us, no woman shall resist. If she won't submit until she's been tossed from her bridge, then I shall do just that, worry you not!"

Smalz took a breath to continue arguing, but Biggs cut him off.

"Enough! My mind is made up, and that's that. Get some sleep, brothers. Tomorrow, I'll make her mine."

Biggs stalked from the glade with purpose, and Smalz sat, dejected. Bridgette was lost to him either way. Either Biggs would best her, or she would win, and prove once and for all that she was simply beyond him. After all, if she could beat Biggs, what chance did he have? He sighed heavily, and put his head on his knees in defeat. He wondered if she *had* to kiss him if he managed to toss her, or if that was just a necessary step, given that she wanted to be kissed.

"You really do like this one, don't you?" Midean still hadn't moved from the tree. His gaze was still directed outward, his voice calm and contemplative, devoid of its familiar, sardonic edge.

"Very much so," Smalz confessed, before he could think better of it.

But Midean didn't mock him for it. He simply nodded, then added, "Then, let's just see what can be done."

———— ◆ ————

When Biggs roused Smalz and Midean from their slumber, it was already warm, despite being so early. Their eldest brother stalked excitedly around them as they woke, clearly eager to be on his way. Smalz had barely rubbed the sleep from his eyes when he was hoisted up and set on the trail.

"Ho now, show me the way!"

Obediently, Smalz lead his brothers down the now-familiar path. Resolute, he didn't dally, but led straight and sure to the forest's edge, where he caught sight of Bridgette, sitting in the shade of her bridge and soaking her feet in the water's cool.

Biggs pushed his way forward, and moved down the trail in a confident swagger, with Smalz and Midean falling into step behind him. Bridgette looked up, but said nothing until the first hoof touched the wooden plank of her bridge.

"Who's that, trip-tropping across my bridge?" she asked.

"'Tis I," Biggs replied boldly. "The biggest Brother Gruffz. You've had merry sport of my brothers, but I'm here now, and I *will* have you."

Bridgette swung easily up over the railing, landing in a crouch then

uncoiling slowly. Smalz noted with some satisfaction that even Biggs had to crane his neck to look into those beautiful yellow eyes.

"I'm not had for the wanting," she said, looking down at Biggs with a challenging smirk.

Biggs lunged forward, and Bridgette caught him as she had caught Midean, and made to throw him to one side. But Biggs bulled forward, his hooves clicking over the plank as he lowered himself and drove her back. Smalz's heart leapt into his throat as Biggs wrapped his broad arms around her waist and hoisted her off her feet.

Bridgette was crafty, though, and wrapped her arms beneath and pushed their bodies apart, dropping a leg back and forcing herself back to equal footing. Biggs released his hold and made for her hair, but she hissed and grabbed him by the horns and twisted.

Back and forth they raged. Bridgette was tall and fast, while Biggs was stout and broad. Bridgette's command of subtle holds and throws was matched by Biggs' stamina and dogged determination. The struggle was titanic, ranging from one end of the bridge to the other, and Biggs' hooves were gouging broad cuts in the planks as he sought traction.

Biggs lowered his shoulders and drove Bridgette against the railing, then grasped her around the thighs and made to heft her off her feet.

Midean put a hand on Smalz's shoulder and squeezed, and Smalz closed his eyes in dismay.

He nearly missed it. Bridgette locked her hands around Biggs' back and drove her hips down. With herculean effort, she lifted the biggest brother Gruffz off his feet and dropped him on his head. Dazed, Biggs couldn't resist as she grabbed him by the arm and one ankle and flung him sidelong over the railing. He hit the water with a crash, and Bridgette leaned over the railing to regard him, exhausted, but triumphant.

Midean released Smalz' shoulder and clapped him on the back and whispered, "Now."

"Ha! Not today, not *ever*," Bridgette called down to Biggs. "I'd sooner kiss Rumpelstiltskin's wrinkly ass as let you topple meEEK!"

Smalz struck her in the rump with his horns, head down and charging with all his might. The impact crossed his vision with stars, but he pushed through, and it was enough. He blinked his eyes clear in time to see Bridgette splash down next to Biggs. He waited for her to surface, his face screwed up in worry and apology.

Smalz struck her in the rump with his horns, head down and charging with all his might. The impact crossed his vision with stars, but he pushed through, and it was enough. He blinked his eyes clear in time to see Bridgette splash down next to Biggs. He waited for her to surface, his face screwed up in worry and apology.

Bridgette didn't look up at him as she made her way out of the creek. She hauled Biggs to the bank where he lay, face down and gasping like a hooked carp. Midean offered her a hand up, which she accepted and clambered out herself. She made her way to the top of the bridge, and to Smalz.

"Sorry," he said.

"I'm not."

And she wrapped her arms around his shoulders, leaned down, and kissed him. She *hmmed* pleasantly into his mouth, pressing herself against him. When she pulled away, Smalz felt woozy, but the smile on her face told him he had fulfilled his vow.

And so, they lived happily ever after, at least until she took him to meet her parents, but that is another story entirely.

In Scales, In Skin

- Erin Honour -
Illustrated by Rebecca Flaum

Once upon a time, in a cold metal jungle, a poor green snake lost her way. Human strangers had captured and carried her far, far away from her home, to a strange forest made of brick and steel. While they fed her and kept her warm, she ached to return home. However, the man who kept her had other ideas. He packed his bags and brought her aboard a bizarre floating box, lined with gears and with steam pouring out the top. She didn't like it at all; the wind dried out her scales, and she felt a slight, uncomfortable amount of pressure on either side of her head. Days passed, and the green snake decided that enough was enough.

And so one day, when she awoke from her slumber to find that the latch was open, she decided to make her escape. She slithered out the front, pausing to look over at the bed. The man was fast asleep, his arm dangled over the side of the bed as he snored loudly. *Good*, the snake thought slyly. She knew that once he was in this state, he would not be up for hours. She moved to the edge of the desk where her cage sat, and though it was quite a distance, she summoned her courage to slither down one of the desk's wooden legs.

Her stomach touched the hard polished wood floor; it felt pleasant compared to the chipped desk. Once more she glanced over, worried that she had somehow awoken the man, but he snored on. She knew she had to move quickly, and slithered out the door onto the main deck without a second thought.

There was that terrible wind again. That cold, cold wind, pushing against her as the ship soared through the sky. Tall ones walked by her, and one nearly stepped on her, all of them lost in their own world. She moved carefully between the large boots and pointed heels, her body getting colder with each passing second. If she stayed out here much longer, she would die, so she pressed on. She passed by an exposed wall and stopped, the sudden flush of warm steam rejuvenated her. Her eyes closed in fatigue and bliss from the warmth. She didn't know how long she'd been out there, but she needed a rest. When the warmth faded, she slid up between the gears, desperate for just a little more before she continued on. It was almost food time, and she was so tired that for a moment she considered going back to her cage. But she had come so far: the room she escaped from was far behind her, and the bridge of the ship came into view. Just a little nap, and then she would move forward. With dreams of delicious mice dancing in her head, she drifted off...

Screeeeeech! Her eyes snapped open. The gears she curled up on were moving! The green snake slithered between the gears as fast as possible against the threat of being killed. She slid backwards, and pulled the tip of her tail back at the last second. Above her was another gear, one moving away from the others. She froze in fear as the momentum pulled her up to another set ready to crush her head. Either way she was trapped, she saw death approaching—

Something large and pale reached between the gears, and delicate hands wrapped around her body to yank the green snake out of the machine. The world spun around her, and she didn't understand what happened. She was raised to eye level and gazed into the eyes of her savior. Dark, sharp eyes met hers, eyes that belonged to the face of a delicate human woman. The woman wore a long gown of pearl white with gold trim, and patterns of white decorated the cuffs that hung around her wrists. Her hair was pulled up with a golden gear decorating her bun. In all of her years, the green snake had never witnessed a creature quite like this one, with a smile so pure. She held the snake gently, her back protecting her from the wind, but the snake did not understand why.

"Hello, little one," the woman in the white snake gown said. "My name is Bai Suzhen. What brings you so far away from your home?" She spoke not in the language of humans, but in the tongue of serpents, and in that moment, the green snake understood that her rescuer was not human.

"I have not been home in many moons," the green snake replied. "I was captured by a man and sold to another as a pet. He kept me warm and fed, but brought me to this windy place. I escaped my cage, and I want to go home."

"Poor dear! You are so far from the lakes and forest." Bai Suzhen thought for a moment, closing her eyes and nodding. "We are in the clouds now; I cannot take you back to where you belong. But do not despair, for I will give you a gift. I am like you, though I wear a human face. If you want, I can bestow this gift to you."

The green snake stared in awe at the spirit, overcome with grateful thoughts. "I want to go home, and if I must be human to be so, then I will."

She was unsure if she'd like being one of the tall ones, but she had learned that this strange ship was no place for a snake.

Bai Suzhen bent down and carefully placed the green snake on the ground. With a touch on her head, the green snake felt the magic take hold as her body started to change. She felt no pain as she grew taller, limbs sprouted from her, and her tail shrunk. Her scales vanished, replaced by sensitive skin that tingled as a gust blew by. Unlike the white snake, she had no clothes to cover her.

She laid on the deck, shivering as she looked around in confusion. Everything looked so much bigger, clearer, though she could no longer sense the heat of things around her. Her eyes hurt, and she felt blinded by the way the world looked so bright, so vivid that she shielded herself from it. She flicked her tongue, but instead of scents she felt... air? She took quick, shallow breaths; her heart pounded as if it was trying to escape from her chest.

"I..." she whispered, her voice quavered. "Change me back, spirit. This world is too much. I can't!"

Bai Suzhen spoke in a soothing tone, saying, "Listen to my voice and nothing else. You can be human now, and once you return to the forest, you will return to your true form. The change will not be easy, but you can do this. Focus."

"How?" the green snake whimpered. "I cannot move!"

Bai Suzhen reached out to touch her arm, she stroked her as she spoke. "Do not focus on moving; focus on my voice. Steady your breath."

The green snake breathed in deeply through her nose, her tongue flicked again out of habit. There were still no scents, yet with each breath, her heartbeat slowed until it returned to normal. Her eyes fluttered open, and she stared at the floor in bewilderment. Bai Suzhen told her she was seeing color, a concept she could not get her head around.

She sat on the deck for what felt like hours, the white snake beside her, ever patient as she grasped each part of being human. Other humans, from dirty deck workers to pristine men and women, came upon the deck to do their business. Some stopped to ask if she was all right, while the others sent angry glares at the inappropriate display. A few short moments later, a guard approached them, offering to take them back to their cabin. Bai Suzhen pulled the green snake up gently; though she fell down twice more, each time she was never scolded. With the help of the guard, they returned to Bai Suzhen's suite, where the green snake was placed on the bed.

The next few days were spent with the Bai Suzhen teaching the green snake about how to walk, dress, and use her new hands. Magic allowed her to speak, and soon the two became close friends. In order to better blend in with human society, the green snake took a human name: Xiaoqing.

Though there were many things that she didn't understand, Xiaoqing came to like this new world. She began to dread the day the airship would land, for the ship was destined for an newly discovered land, one with fresh trees and clean lakes. Once there she knew the magic would fade, and she'd return to her serpent form.

Such heavy thoughts weighed on Xiaoqing's mind, and one day, after a hard lesson about running, she found that she had to speak. Bai Suzhen, patient as always, had helped her up from her fall, noting the troubled look on her friend's face.

"You are doing fine," Bai Suzhen shushed with soothing words. "We can keep practicing later."

"No," Xiaoqing said as she shook her head. "That is not why I am sad. You have done so much for me, yet when we part ways you will be alone once more. Why do you not return with me instead?"

"I would," Bai Suzhen replied, "were it not for the reason I hide. There is a man with evil in his heart looking for me. If I return to my true self, then he would find me, and take my power with his terrible machine to do unspeakable things."

"This is the first time you spoke of this to me," Xiaoqing said in shock. "Why?"

"I did not wish to burden you. Consider this my gift to you, to return you to the forest where you belong." Bai Suzhen turned away as she spoke to hide her sadness. "Do not worry for me. This man has chased me for many years, he will not catch me. Now I must go for my walk."

While she wished to press the matter further, Xiaoqing knew that Bai Suzhen was done speaking about it. Every night after lessons her friend went off for her walk, where she met with a man at the bridge of the ship. Xiaoqing felt jealous watching them, too far off to hear their words but able to see the smile on Bai Suzhen's face. She did not know who this man was, so insolent to think he had the right to take her friend from her.

Sometime later, Xiaoqing wandered the lower deck of the ship, lost in her thoughts and worries. She enjoyed the warmth as she neared the engine room, and the rusty copper colors of the halls were so much easier on her eyes than the glitzy gold ballrooms where the richer members socialized. In her wanderings, she did not see where she was going, and ran straight into a man. She apologized profusely, and as she looked upon him she realized that he was one of the engine room workers. His body was covered in soot, his short black hair ruffled from hours of work with no care. While most of the other workers remained below deck, she recognized him wandering above, as the man occasionally speaking to Bai Suzhen.

"No need to apologize," he said with a smile. "But you shouldn't be here, miss. It's dangerous if you don't watch your step."

She frowned, her eyes narrowed as she spoke. "I know what I'm doing, but what of you? Tell me your name."

"Xu Xian, miss."

"Xu Xian," she repeated. "If you are such a lowly position, then why is it I see you upstairs talking to Bai Suzhen?"

Even with the soot, the crimson blush on his face was easy to see. "Well…" He stumbled over his words. "I mean no harm to her."

She paused to consider his words. Xiaoqing felt pangs of jealousy, for Bai Suzhen was her only friend in this human world, and here was this man trying to take it away from her. However, she thought back to the nights watching them talk. Bai Suzhen's smile was different when she saw him, though it was impossible to describe. In that moment, Xiaoqing knew they were happy together, and with her soon to leave her friend when they reached the forest, who was she to deny the spirit's happiness?

"She cares for you," Xiaoqing replied. "Your position is not one of weakness. Without your people, we would not fly at all. Next time you go to her, tell her how you feel. There may not be another."

Xu Xian was confused by her statement, though she did not give him a chance to respond, turning around and leaving the area before she changed her mind. She refused to think about it for the rest of the day, instead gathering her courage to state her own feelings, the wish to remain Bai Suzhen's side. At this point in the day Xiaoqing knew that her friend was above deck, she loved to watch the stars. With one last moment to reassure herself, she pressed the button to summon the elevator to go. It felt longer than usual for the gears to crank and the elevator to appear. Oddly enough, it was empty, with most passengers passing through to go to their rooms. She thought nothing of it, entered in and pressed the button to deck level.

The doors opened to the sound of alarms blaring. Xiaoqing covered her ears, wind whipping around her as the ship lurched to the side. Up ahead was Bai Suzhen and Xu Xian, clutching each other for safety against the rail. A shadow descended upon the deck, and above them was the giant form of another airship. She watched in horror as back of the ship opened, and from the hatch a platform was lowered by clockwork machinery. On it was a man, dressed from head to toe in a bright red military uniform, an ambitious smirk plastered on his face.

"I am General Fahai! And I'm here to collect the white snake." The stranger chuckled as he spotted Xu Xian, who had placed himself between the general and Bai Suzhen. "So the great spirit does not defend herself? Pity, I expected more."

"She is not something to be claimed!" Xu Xian proclaimed. "Leave now, and you won't be reported for your treasonous actions, General."

Fahai let out a deep, guttural laugh. "Very funny: a soot farmer thinks he has the right to order me around." He withdrew a pistol, aiming at Xu Xian's head. "Now move along. There are more important matters to deal with than you."

Xiaoqing cowered out of sight. She watched Xu Xian, a simple human, defend her closest friend, while she stood back, a complete disgrace. Her blood boiled with fury, her hand clenched into a fist, and she found her courage. Time slowed down as she ran forward, toward Fahai with her arm outstretched. In a flash, the magic that gave her human form surged forward into her strike, nailing the general right in the cheek, and sent him flying.

BANG!

There came a noise so loud she lost all hearing except for a ringing in her ears, and an unusual metallic smell reached her. She turned to her friend, and her eyes went wide at what she saw.

Bai Suzhen cradled the crumpled form of Xu Xian, crying over him. He had been struck in the right arm, blood coating his clothes and her white dress. Bai Suzhen tried to heal him with her magic, but the bullet was too far in, and blocked her spell.

The General rose to his feet, wiping the small trail of blood off his mouth, and picked his pistol off the ground. Only now where Xu Xian had blocked his path, Xiaoqing stood defiant. He shook his head, and though the strange woman before him glowed with an unusual green magic, it did not deter him.

"Ah," he said, understanding crept into his voice. "You must be one of her pets." He sneered at her, and again aimed straight for the head. "Surely you know you mean nothing to her. The white snake has lived many lifetimes. To have her power is to possess immortality. Move!"

Yet Xiaoqing stood defiant, his words meaning nothing to her. She did not understand what the device he had pointed at her did, only that it would kill her. And in that moment, she knew of no better way to die.

BANG! The wind rushed towards her, and parts of her green dress ripped from the force, but she took no damage from the shot. In the blink of an eye, she rushed towards the shocked Fahai. She pried the pistol from his hand, twisting his hand back until a sickening *snap* was heard. He cried out in pain, grasping his broken wrist.

Turning her back on the injured and now weaponless general, Xiaoqing rushed over to the prone pair, unsure of what had happened, but worried for the fate of Xu Xian. People were beginning to appear from the lower decks, drawn to the scene by the sound of gunshots. A few of Xu Xian's friends rushed to his side. They picked him up together, stating that they would take him to med bay, though, thankfully, they did not think his wound was fatal. That, however, did not stop Bai Suzhen's tears.

"This is my fault," she choked. "he was hurt because of me."

"No," Xiaoqing stated. "That was the general's attack, not yours." She placed a hand on her friend's shoulder, looking her in the eyes. "You have done much for me, now it is my turn to help you. When the ship lands, do not break your spell. I will travel with you, and together we will defeat General Fahai."

"Thank you," Bai Suzhen said, drying her tears as she embraced Xiaoqing. "I knew you could do it."

They were interrupted by the loud cranking of gears; in the commotion surrounding Xu Xian, Fahai had managed to retreat to his platform. He scowled down at the women as the platform ascended. "Do not think you've won this day, white snake," he called out, "for one day, your powers will belong to me!"

Once he was back in the ship, with a loud blast it took off, vanishing into the clouds...

Ayuna's Song

- August Clearwing -
Illustrated by Tawny Fritz

Once upon a time, a group of warring tribes brokered peace into the first proper societies in Elwhane. City-states, scattered throughout the east, divided power and land. They stretched out their long reach in claim of fertile soils and colossal mountains.

Not all tribes were created equal, however, as those who possessed power were accused of unworthiness; slandered for backstabbing and betrayal. They had thrust out their hands too far, and pushed the undesirable tribes to the edge of those fertile lands into the deserts. There, on a chain of islands across the inland sea, the unwanted held their borders.

For hundreds of years the threat of war and constant skirmishes grew to a head as dynasties of bloodlines rose. By the time war came all those centuries later, the children's children of old enemies had forgotten why.

It was within the walls of Langraal, the wealthiest of these city-states, that Ayuna had everything she was capable of dreaming up. Her adoring husband, High King Onwyn, showered her with gowns and jewels and treasures from every corner of their land. And did it ever have such treasures to gift. Silks and gems in every hue of color, paintings from the most skilled artists, portraits in stone chiseled by the steadiest of sculptor hands. More wealth and prosperity existed within their territory than at any time in the long history of the city-state.

Yet, she felt she was about to lose it all.

Ayuna traced her husband's hurried penmanship on the parchment with her fingertips. The ink had still been wet when he folded it; the strokes were smudged in some places. Stray dollops of black smeared where the quill dripped. Despite the callously rushed nature of the letter, Ayuna recognized the hand of her love. She kept a collection of poetry he wrote her before his capture in her vanity. Each one had been committed to memory. Even so, she opened them every night before she went to sleep in a feeble attempt to draw him back into her arms through the pages.

Without a doubt, the hand that wrote those most prized poems penned this most recent message.

Three winters had passed since she received a missive from him. His last letter had been filled with the hope of conquest. He wrote of glory and victory, of the strength of their forces against encroaching invaders from a distant shore.

And then nothing. A full anxious month went by before the news of his imprisonment reached her ears. Another two attempts to breach the stone walls that held him failed soon thereafter, leaving the powers in a heated stalemate.

The words Onwyn spoke on parchment now wavered in their intent, shuddering from cold or injury or worse—she couldn't tell. But the words meant the high king yet lived.

Traitorous tears fell onto the page as she read of her husband's fate. He described a life in servitude and slavery to the lord who captured him in battle.

My dearest love, he wrote, *it is my wish that you should put up for sale all of our worldly possessions so that you might pay the requested sum to this evil man and have me released from this prison of sorrow. The wealth of the nation matters little when its king is shackled between dank stone walls and forced to work the fields each day until his death. I beg you pay the ransom, my heart, and bring me home to you.*

As Ayuna read on, his plea for freedom sank deeper into her soul. The price of one man's life was staggering. Bending to the wishes of the high king's captor would not only leave the palace and their family destitute, but it might well bankrupt their land entirely.

At first, Ayuna felt the letter was a devilish trick devised by the man in whose dungeon her husband rotted, that the high king had been tortured and forced to pen the note as an act of subterfuge. It would prove a bloodless victory for the usurper across the sea. Except that the scrawling on the paper she held tighter with every passing moment did not appear forced. It had instead been written with restrained desperation.

Surely he must have known what he asked of her, she reasoned. Surely he must not have genuinely considered his wellbeing above that of his people. Of his family. Of his young son, whom he had not laid eyes on since the spring of the child's birth.

Ayuna glanced at her small prince, playing by the windows of the library. The child, who did not know his father save in carefully spun stories and anecdotes, remained blissfully ignorant of her dilemma. The boy did not know of the war. He was still far too young to understand the clashes between the politics and armies of kings and queens. Neither did he know of the reason behind his father's departure beyond the veil of maintaining peace in the land.

Oh, how he resembled his father. His hair was light and his eyes the same blue-green vessels of strength and love she knew the high king possessed. Upon seeing her husband in their child, Ayuna decided there must have been another way, a way she was not yet able to fully discern through the haze of helplessness she read.

If you can no longer manage strength for yourself, I shall become stronger for you, she vowed silently.

That afternoon Ayuna slipped away from the careful eye of her advisers. While they were aware of the king's correspondence, she refused their request to know its contents. They had remained silent on the matter as the queen quietly deliberated the paths laid out before her.

Surrender, she felt, was quite out of the question, and so she sought out the Grand Adept, a trusted friend and member of the royal court.

Nikolas was a mage of exceptional talent; skilled at crafting tonics and potions, of the flare of magick his title inherently suggested, but also quick of wit and thought. His expertise flourished from the continued study of his craft in his middle years. When all else failed, Ayuna had always turned to him for guidance.

She called out to him as she entered his office within the palace. "Nikolas, I must speak with you at once."

"I am here, my queen," he replied in greeting.

She could scarcely see him through the bookshelves lining either side of aisle in the room. Taking in the musty smell of old parchment and iron gall ink, she walked further into the mage's personal domain. She heard the scrape of his chair and hurried footsteps, until he appeared from behind the shelves. The subtle blue and gray robes he wore rustled softly as he moved to meet her.

"What do you require of me?" Nikolas asked, dipping his head in a customary bow of respect.

With an ear to bend, Ayuna divulged the contents of her husband's letter. Her face did not betray the storm of emotion churning within her heart and mind as she slowly paced between the bookshelves, explaining her plight. Her gown of deep purple swept the stone floor, and she felt the fabric grow tight around her torso the more she said aloud. Nevertheless, she remained composed and regal in her every movement.

"Please, my friend, I must find the means to save him without bringing our legacy to its knees," she said in closing.

Nikolas thought for a long moment. "High King Onwyn lives then. This is excellent news. However, I cannot see how I might serve you in retrieving him. I'm no soldier, no general; I do not possess the means to plan an escape or a battle to challenge for his release."

Ayuna shook her head. The spark of determination flashed into a roaring blaze within her. "I do not wish for more war, Nikolas. No one may know of this lest it renew the bloodshed. But neither can I bankrupt the land to pay for my husband's release. This venture must be taken in secret."

Her words startled and sobered him as he began to wholly understand them. Nikolas' tone grew cautious as he said, "My queen, you speak as if you wish to journey on your own to rescue him."

"If that is what it takes then so be it," replied Ayuna. "Anything less may summon the wrath of an enemy army to our borders—worse still, it may kill Onwyn with greater haste."

She watched and idea blossom into a smile across his face. "A lonely queen on the road is conspicuous, an easy mark for thieves and highwaymen."

"A disguise of my form," she proposed, quickly picking up on the suggestion screaming in his smile. "One which will last the duration of my passage to and from that awful place."

"Then I know what I must do," he declared. He held out his hand to her. "I shall cast a spell for you. Come."

Ayuna took Nikolas' hand and allowed the adept to guide her, the flutter of hope on her tongue as she asked, "What have you in mind, my friend?"

He led her to the back of the room where a series of stone altars patterned at four corners and in the center. Behind them, the clutter of opened scrolls and scattered tomes laid strewn around his desk. Behind that still, the high shelves of powders, herbs, metals and all manner of liquids hugged the circular curve of the wall. Tall, thin windows caught dust motes floating in the mid afternoon light, and the sturdy wooden door leading to his family's quarters had been left ajar.

"Stand there, my queen," Nikolas directed. He released her hand as she stopped in front of the altar at the center.

After selecting a small amber crystal from a collection on his desk, a bit of dark hair from an unknown source, and a thin wire of silver, he returned to the altar to face her. He set the amber atop the wire, and allowed the foreign hair to fall from his fingertips around the pieces.

"Forgive me," Nikolas said, holding out his hand across the altar. "The magick requires a drop of your blood to attune itself to your form."

With little reservation in her movement, Ayuna offered out her hand, and Nikolas wasted no time. He drew his dagger. Its edge slid swiftly across her index finger, allowing the crimson life to drip onto the flawless golden resin.

Nikolas wove his spell in old tongue, the highly protected fluid and pointed language of the dragons and el'ven people. It was soft and old and wise, and Ayuna could scarcely believe that words alone were capable of summoning such power through her.

The silver wire wrapped itself around the amber. Its immense temperature radiated across her skin from so near. The stray hairs burned away without flame as her gifted blood boiled clear. The wire twisted and spun into an intricate frame, spiraling down one side and into a small loop to encase the amber where it lay. Nikolas spoke the chant until his words filled the chamber near to bursting.

And then the warmth retreated. The chamber calmed its echo of magick and the spell was complete.

He offered out the wire-wrapped gem to her. "This pendant will protect you. Wear it and you wear the face of an unassuming stranger." What once was the source of all heat within the room was now cool to the touch as the adept slipped it into her palm. "May you wear it in good health."

Ayuna's heart beat loudly against her breast. She clutched the pendant close and said, "Thank you, Nikolas. I owe you a debt beyond asking."

"Run, my queen," he whispered in sharp haste. "Run, and rescue your king."

Without delay and with Onwyn's letter still fresh in her mind, Ayuna rushed from the chamber. She discarded her royal gown almost as soon as she slipped the simple tunic and drab pair of dark trousers from the servants' clothesline outside the kitchen. The pants fit snug against her hips. Even while tucked into the trousers, the linen undershirt billowed enough to provide a rather shapeless form beneath her tunic of choice.

The realness of her actions began to settle in while she dressed. Lacing her new magickal pendant onto a chain, she realized there would be no turning back once she left. When she was satisfied with her preparations, she threaded the necklace around her neck and stole away into the city.

She carried with her a satchel containing only the most necessary of items, including a small sum of gold to pay her way. The marketplace bustled with trade and commerce in the late afternoon. This thriving pulse of the city centered in on goods and services, the wealth of the fresh harvest, and the laughter of a satiated populace. All of them had heard of the king's absence, and whispers of his fate traded lips as readily as any other commodity did. They murmured in taverns about his exploits and they pondered his doom, but Ayuna paid no mind to their whisperings.

As she walked the market she noted their full bellies and warm hearths. The smell of freshly baked bread and the sweetness of glazed pastries floated on a sea of flowery perfume from the public gardens around the corner.

Music hummed in the air. The gentle ping of lute strings, a sound as familiar to her as her own heartbeat, strummed softly outside a shop just beyond the main market square. Its minstrel plucked away to a tune befitting the tepid afternoon. The sights and sounds and smells which filled her senses only reinforced her silent promise; she refused to bow to the possibility of destroying their happiness.

Ayuna rounded the corner of the marketplace with determination fresh in her step. Amid the crowded streets a wall of leather and flesh knocked her to the ground with an *oomf*. She had been so enthralled with the minstrel she never noticed the brawny man twice her size, nor his small contingent of companions alongside him.

"Watch where you're going you crazy bastard," the passerby chastised.

Pulling herself to her feet to face him, he pressed on through the crowd without a second glance.

Bastard? How dare he! Ayuna thought. Indignation swelled within her until she recalled the magick. She touched the pendant around her neck.

He had not recognized her. Not as his queen, and most definitely not of the feminine gender. Otherwise, she expected he may have paid her closer attention. At the very least he may have adjusted his manners accordingly. He should have passed her by, excusing himself and stepping aside for a lady as was proper.

Of course, I must appear as a man now.

The pendant *worked*.

It wasn't as if she harbored any real choice in the matter, but as much as she despised admitting it, a man travelling alone such a long distance was far safer than anyone of royal blood—regardless of gender—attempting the same journey. Ayuna collected herself and cast a glance along the road where the minstrel continued playing her melody.

After brushing the dust from her clothes, Ayuna crossed to speak with her. She recalled her lessons on the lute as a girl. In that instant it dawned upon her that, perhaps, the way into the castle of her enemy was not with force, but under the pretense of friendship. Having grown up in a house of sisters, she knew little of martial combat. Furtive stratagems, however, came naturally.

Dipping her voice and hoping it sounded convincingly male, Ayuna said, "Pardon me. I wish to know how much you paid for that lovely lute."

She felt silly for doing so, but it seemed to work, as nary a glint of suspicion flickered across the woman's face.

The minstrel was fair-skinned with colorful ribbons laced through her hair. The smile she wore did not so much dim as relax at Ayuna's question. The luthier who had crafted the instrument must have spent countless hours toiling over its intricacies. A heptagram design cut into the light wood beneath the strings was encased with details so finely carved they belonged on a lady's lace gown. The neck of the lute, rubbed to matte from its fine gloss polish, told Ayuna it was well loved.

"Thirty silver, ser," the woman replied with pride. "A month's wages when the contracts are good."

Ayuna hadn't the time to seek out a lute crafter, not if she wished to move in haste. She brought with her enough coin to manage the trip in relative comfort, and the unexpected expenditure would not be too harsh a burden. With this in mind she offered, "I would pay you forty for it."

The minstrel gave pause to glance between her precious source of income and the disguised queen. "Forty silver is far too much," she protested demurely.

"Nonsense," said the queen. She fished a small purse from her satchel, allowing the polished coins inside to jingle together in an attractive song of their own. "A talented player such as you deserves a new instrument after so much use, and I'm keen to play again myself."

The lute changed hands, though with a little reluctance on the part of the minstrel. After so long together with an extension of her soul, Ayuna could see how difficult it may have been to part with. But she had, and it meant that the queen had found the means by which she might seek audience with the man who imprisoned her husband.

By dusk she reached the outskirts of the city to the west, where she traded coin and song for passage on a merchant caravan the next morning. Along the way she became reacquainted with the lute. Its weight and feel remained as memorable as ever. During the times when the roads smoothed somewhat, Ayuna tested the strings. She strummed an old tune and then plucked away at the chords idly, creating new sounds of her own. When her memory served her the chords to a familiar ballad, she listened as the raucous troupe sung the words on her behalf, limiting her need to disguise her voice. Her playing carried on this way, earning favor with the merchants while otherwise maintaining a quiet, small presence.

The hired guards which kept pace with the wagons seemed to approve as well. Barring any highwaymen who took advantage of the open plains—of which there were surprisingly none—the farmland and flatlands offered little by way of vistas or extreme beauty to distract travelers. On more than one occasion they expressed their gratitude for the entertainment during an otherwise simple and steady road.

Minstrels, storytellers, and bards, she found, travelled across the lands more swiftly than most. Few people questioned the presence of one. It had always been accepted tradition for the artists of the lands shared their culture far and wide. They accompanied pirates and adventurers alike, spinning tales in song to forever immortalize the heroes and villains of their time.

Within a fortnight her journey by caravan came to an end at the coast of the Balten Sea, near to sixty leagues from her home in the city of Langraal. Across twenty more leagues of water lay the small island nation of Saiedor, and Ayuna's prize.

She said her farewells to the merchant caravan, for their destination was some other distant shore. A chartered passage by large fishing boat over the inland sea now drew her eye.

Shadow Market trade may have been highly illegal, but that did not stop many captains of those vessels from ignoring the trade embargo with Saiedor altogether. Especially not when its isle lay so close at hand.

Two days of fruitless inquiries left her frazzled and dismayed, as more of the sea-goers were hesitant to make for the island than she's expected. Then, the glimmer of success in her persistence paid off. A discrete captain willing to book her passage to the island in question made it clear that he harbored no interest in exchanging the reasons either of them had for the trip.

It was a short one by all accounts, covering over twenty leagues in a day provided the wind favored their journey. Three masts of the cargo vessel splayed sails wide as it left the port, catching every bit of air possible for the ship's exceptional size.

Never would the crew of the ship know their part in saving High King Onwyn, Ayuna realized. She secretly promised she would forget their names and transgressions should her quest prove fruitful.

The ship arrived on a misty morning, and Ayuna steeled her resolve as she disembarked. A series of towers lined the coast of the Isle of Saiedor upon their arrival. They rose up through the fog as sentinels along the cliffs, leagues apart from one another. Beacons of torchlight within each warned away wayward sailors from certain death should they venture too close to the rocky shores.

Lute in hand, Ayuna cut a path through the throngs of sailors and merchants on the docks of Shalah, the largest port in the world.

She left the winding streets of the city on foot to press towards the royal palace further north. *Fifteen leagues* further north, to be exact. Her nerves twitched to life with each step closer to the secluded seat of her enemy.

It stood simultaneously as both a self-contained city and fortress. High walls cast deep shadows in the early morning and late afternoon. Built on the bank of a wide river, its construction included a natural source of flowing water for a swift, wide moat. Bridges, as long as the river was wide, ushered travelers into the city's safe embrace. It was no small wonder, she realized, that her forces failed in their mission to free her husband. Ayuna shoved aside her sense of awe; there was no time to admire her enemy's eye for architecture.

Sprawled outside the fortress walls were perhaps a dozen farms. They claimed every bit of land as far as the eye could see in all directions. She took in the sight of foreign crops from recent harvests. Lines of prisoners marched out to the fields to be used as slave labor. Shackles kept some tethered together as their captors' whips rushed them along. Though she could not see him, she knew the love of her life walked somewhere among them.

Her only weapon in her secret war was the instrument she held secure with each step across the bridge.

In lieu of one large marketplace shared by all people, smaller markets were scattered near the gates and throughout the fortress. The closer a group of merchants to the castle, the higher the price tag of those merchants' goods became.

Ayuna walked until she could walk no further. Ahead, surrounded by a second, if thinner, moat, stood the castle itself. Its tall, square features and small windows challenged outsiders to attempt to scale its walls.

She approached the guards alongside a small group of traders and minstrels beckoning the audience of their lord. They crowded close to the large doors on the steps of the castle, hollering for the gatekeepers to take notice of them, which they were most certainly unable to ignore given their boisterous voices.

"What's happening here?" she asked of a guard who was *not* in the process of being accosted.

"First time to the castle, is it," the armed and armored man noted. His voice was thick with the accent common amongst Saiedorians; like chewing gravel. "Well, based on your fellow bards' appearance it seems your lot is hungry to play for someone of importance and not some back-alley tavern or whorehouse."

Ayuna seized at the thought of playing in one of those dens of ill repute. "How does one gain audience with your ruler?"

The guard nodded toward the mass of commoners jumping and yelling. "You're looking at it, friend."

"And that works?"

He scoffed, "Not often. Once a day they'll allow a couple of folks in to be turned away in person, but our orders are clear to keep the vagrants and beggars out."

Then it's a good thing I'm neither, Ayuna thought.

She did not join the fray for entry into the castle, instead choosing to sit on the ledge of the stone bridge and idly adjust the lute's courses. When she was satisfied, she began playing a slow, soft tune the way she played along her journey across her own lands. She let the world around her fall away and blocked out the shouts of the guards as they forcefully turned away anyone who failed to present the required credentials to enter the grounds. Her music spoke for her, a gentle thrum to contrast their impatient fervor.

Patience, she reminded herself. She must not be perceived as a threat, must not do anything which would warrant her expulsion from the grounds.

Calm. Collected. Confident.

Ayuna sat there for the remainder of the cool day, allowing very few moments of silence between the songs she played. Well into the evening, when all of the others had lost their energy to struggle at the doors and the sun had set, Ayuna still sat and picked at the strings. Calluses had begun forming on her fingertips in her travels, and she found she played straight through them. She played until the sun set, until her fingers could strum no more. Her hands ached, raw from the constant attention given to the instrument.

Resigned to find a bed for the night, Ayuna climbed down from the stone wall in search of an inn nearby to rest her head and hands.

But as she crossed the bridge in silence toward the closing stalls of the market, the gravel-tongued guard stopped her. "Ser, wait a moment."

Ayuna glanced behind her as the man approached.

"Your skill and patience have impressed us," he commended. He gestured to his comrades at the gates as if he spoke for the lot. "Please, come in and play for our King Heskel this 'eve."

She smiled through a sigh of relief, having not expected to be welcomed so quickly.

The doors parted to allow her a guided entrance into the castle. An evening dinner was in full swing, complete with boisterous laughter and the toasting of fine wine. The great hall held the whole of King Heskel's court. Delicacies foreign to her senses overflowed the chamber with the smell of how the sea itself must have tasted. Her stomach growled its approval. Ayuna remembered she hadn't eaten at all that day. She was so focused on her task she dared not leave her perch outside, even for the briefest of meals.

As the guard ushered her through the dining hall, she noticed the fashion of the nobility from the court mirrored those of her own kingdom in no way at all. The sticky, moist air of the island encouraged sleeveless or light, sheer garments on the women. The colorful thin fabrics fell across their shoulders in revealing ways. The men wore equally loose pants without a touch of the heavy brocades Ayuna had become used to in her own court.

At the head of the largest table, she saw him—the man who had successfully captured Onwyn. Her palms grew clammy, not from the fear, but from the rage she felt percolating inside of her. She was so close to him. She had walked straight into his den and he had no idea who she was.

Heskel sat at his high-backed chair beside his wife and advisers, a smug and unwitting laugh perched on his tongue. He was a man of modest height. While not difficult on the eyes by any stretch, she felt his presence plain; unworthy of note save the gold drapery denoting his kingly status. He wore his brown hair short and his beard shaved clean and close to his triangular face—another fashion she attributed to the humid climate of his island nation.

At first he did not notice her. His attention had been captured wholly by his inner circle of advisers and friends. Even after she was prompted to begin playing by someone who appeared to be in charge of the meal, he did not look up at her. The music fell on deaf ears for the duration of the feast, until he ate his fill and wished to partake of the entertainment.

Once captured, his awareness of the beauty of the lute she played did not waver. Heskel shushed his companions around the table, listening. He allowed her to perform for hours, until his advisers urged his departure for the end of the day.

Without a word, Ayuna stood with King Heskel and bowed no more than was actively polite.

"Where did you learn to play so well, minstrel?" he asked from across the room. His voice echoed off the silent stone walls around them.

"Here and there, my liege," Ayuna responded simply. Anymore and she might show her hatred of his existence openly.

Heskel chuckled. "I like you, you say no more than is asked. You shall stay and entertain again for us tomorrow at court."

"As you wish, your majesty," she said. She was grateful for the distance if only because she was unable to hide the sly smirk of success from her face.

For three days Ayuna performed at the court as they went about their business. She was made to accompany a minor magician's latest demonstration of wonder. The old man was leagues behind in his own research compared to her dear friend Nikolas, she realized. His magick was little more than common tricks of the eye and sleight of hand. He could not harness coldfire in his palm let alone attempt the level of skill to create or sense such magick as the pendant she wore.

No, this man was utterly novice.

Ayuna played on, glimpsing the insights into the foreign king's political structure. He seemed unaware of her ruse, and fully content to speak to his council of matters which concerned his own wellbeing. She felt the weight of her fear begin to lift. Perhaps, she thought, she may succeed after all. Now, she simply had to slip away to find him in the dungeons sometime in the night, or upon her exit. And she felt that time was fast approaching.

After the completion of the last composition she knew for the third time in three days, Ayuna ceased her music altogether.

"Why have you stopped playing, minstrel?"

She stood from her chair to address Heskel. "Though your hospitality is appreciated, and though it has been an honor to play in your court, I am but a traveler. My life is on the road, good king. It has come time to take my leave of your lovely land and move on to the next adventure."

King Heskel wrinkled his brow in displeasure, but beckoned her forward nonetheless. "A boon for your excellence in your craft and your genuine appreciation of your stay is required from me in that case. Ask your price for your time and you shall have it."

Ayuna's heart fluttered into her throat. She had planned to find a stealthier means by which to extract Onwyn from the dungeons below the palace, but Heskel—in equal parts ignorance and hubris—had given her the greatest of opportunities to benefit from.

"The road is a lonely one, my liege. I seek a companion to travel alongside me. If you might spare someone from your prison, a man you would otherwise be required to feed or clothe yourself, I would be eternally grateful to you."

Then she held her breath, waiting eagerly for his response.

"The men in my prisons are a dangerous lot, good bard. Are you certain this is your wish? Would you not instead prefer gold or jewels?"

She shook her head. "Gold and jewels make for poor conversation and poorer songwriting. The man I choose would be taken far from your shores and never bother your people again. He would be indebted to me for his freedom and act as my personal bodyguard on my path."

"Very well; go and choose your traveling companion then." Heskel waved his hand to a servant nearby. It was a subtle hint to conduct his guest towards the dungeons. "Let it be known in the songs you write of me that I am an honorable man of my word."

"And so I shall, King Heskel," Ayuna said with a dip of her head.

Not that she planned to compose any such ballads. If she had her druthers she would stab him through where he sat. But she kept her desires silent and secret lest she be killed alongside him.

A guard led her down the maze of corridors, and cold hallways, and winding stairs flanked by sconces.

Ayuna covered her nose briefly upon entering the prison. It reeked of waste and muck. Damp covered the stone walls in slimy moss which she dared not brush against. Little sunlight made its way into the hole—and it was only slightly more than a hole indeed.

An expanse of barred cells holding up to ten men in each lined either side; there were dozens of them. So many, in fact, that Ayuna did not know where to begin in her search. Without prompting from her guide, she took a torch from the wall and began her slow investigation.

The men jeered at her passing. They called out for food and water. Every one of them bore the scars of captivity. Hollow cheeks and sunken eyes wore their frustration openly. Some refused eye contact altogether. Others spat at her through the bars of their prison. Her silence spoke for her, enduring the coarse vulgarity only with the purpose of examining them all further. In that moment she was more relieved than ever to be disguised. Ayuna could not imagine the things they might throw at her were she to walk through their broken space as her true self.

She pushed the torch towards the bars as close as she was able; searching for a face she remembered until—finally—one man stood out.

Ayuna would not have recognized her husband save for the keen depths of his eyes. His skin had grown leathery in the elements, his body as weak as his bones. His face smudged with grime. An unruly beard and long light hair made it clear that he had not bathed or groomed himself in months.

But those blue-green eyes of passion and strength beckoned her aid quietly.

"Him," Ayuna said. She pointed at Onwyn through his iron cage. King no more, but soon to be king once again. "That man shall be my traveling companion."

The guard opened the cage. He warned away the others in his cell as he pulled Onwyn free of the prison, then shut up the doors again with a clamor.

Ayuna wished to fall to her knees in gratitude for her discovery. She wished to fling herself into his arms and kiss him and tell him that all was well, that he was safe. It took all of her being to resist tears of joy from escaping her.

The mud-caked visage of Onwyn, too, held back his elation at freedom. He looked between Ayuna—this strange minstrel man, and the guard, as if the whole ordeal was a sick method of torture. As if he might be readily thrown into captivity once more.

He rubbed at his wrists habitually. They were red now not from the shackles themselves, but from the ghost of them.

Had they forgotten about him? She wondered. His letters had mentioned such a high price for his release, yet he was housed with common rabble and seemingly swept from the minds of his captors. And they were allowing her to take him, without questions.

They were free. Almost free. Just a few dozen more steps to the door, perhaps a hundred to the castle gates, and then they could disappear into the city.

"Just a moment," came a stern voice from behind them.

Ayuna froze, feeling Onwyn tense beside her as well. As the stranger neared, Ayuna began to take note of the objector's familiar features. Brown eyes smoldered with a dark ferocity against the tanned skin of his triangular jaw. There was a slight hollow in his cheekbones, and his thick brows knitted together in terse defiance of her path. He wore a red sash across his torso, above his armor. Somehow the chain and plate looked cleaner and more ornate than the rest of the guard. It had been polished and barely scratched by everyday wear or excessive combat.

"That prisoner is not cleared for release," continued the man.

"Captain!" The guard beside Ayuna snapped to attention, his focus forward on the back wall as he acknowledged the intruder.

While the guard remained where he stood, the captain closed the distance between them all.

Ayuna thought fast. After swallowing her fear, she tried to sound convincingly correct when she said, "Your great king has offered me a boon for my services at his court, and this prisoner is the boon I choose."

"That is not for you to decide, bard," sneered the captain. Turning his attention toward his subordinate, he added, "Why is this man with the general populace? He is a prisoner of war with a ransom on his head!"

The guard stammered, as if searching for his tongue in the empty desert of his mouth. In his delay, the smack of the captain's gloved hand echoed as it tore across the guard's face.

Ayuna chanced a glance at Onwyn, only to see a knowing look of urgency rapidly overtaking him. Her own king set his jaw, flicking his eyes between the captain's sword, the guard, and then to Ayuna and her lute.

In one swift flourish, she adjusted her grip on the neck. Rearing back, Ayuna swung the it at the base of the guard's skull. It connected with a loud crack and the hollow twang of the strings against wood. The heavy collection of keys he was holding chimed throughout the prison when they hit the ground. As the guard went down, Ayuna marveled at the lute's strength; not a single crack appeared on its surface.

Once she was in motion, there was little Onwyn could do save follow her cue. The grizzled king lunged at the captain, ripping the long sword from its sheath on his belt before the captain could move to claim it.

The prisoners roared to life around them. Cheers and jeers and the rattling of cages erupted into chaos.

Ayuna dove for the abandoned keys. She scooped them up as Onwyn's foot collided with the captain's breastplate. Crying out, the captain landed with an awkward clamor on the stone floor.

Onwyn descended on the man, the stolen blade poised to bite into him hard. The king pulled the captain up onto his knees and drove the sword downward, piercing between the gap in his armor at his collarbone. The captain's face paled with fright while the vision of death lingered in front of him. He gurgled and grunted against the blood in his throat, the blade skewered through the length of his torso with no remorse.

Then Onwyn pushed him backward to finish dying on the cold prison floor.

Ayuna stared wide-eyed at her husband. She had wanted to accomplish her task without bloodshed. Nobody needed to die, she remembered. As Nikolas had so readily pointed out, they were not generals in battle. Yet, they had given her no choice in the matter.

Onwyn moved to face her again, but before he turned, the door at the end of the hallway swung open. Their ruckus had caused a stir, and now it seemed the remaining palace guards were beginning to stream into the dungeon.

"We must hurry," the breathless king commanded. He was covered with the warm spray of blood from the fall of his enemy.

Ayuna found the largest of the keys in her possession, the one with which she'd seen the guard unlock the entryway. But they needed a distraction, she realized.

And she had a perfect distraction in mind.

Without another thought, she tossed the remaining keys through the bars of one of the cells. The prisoners scrambled for them, instantly searching the hefty ring for the one which might free them.

And then they were running. Ayuna clasped the master key tight in her hand until they reached a door on the opposite end of the dungeon. Praying the key would fit, she threaded it into the lock with a shaking hand.

When the door unlocked to the bright rays of a setting sun, she let out a cry of nervously relieved laughter.

The cells behind them clanged open as well. The guards streaming into the prison were met by the wave of convicts and criminals they'd incarcerated within.

Ayuna and Onwyn took their only chance.

They threw open the door and ran into the orange-red of early evening.

The setting sun cast long shadows over them around the back walls. They followed its trail in silence for some time, until they slipped from the city completely.

Ayuna presented him with her wineskin, which he drank as enthusiastically as he walked in time with her steps. Though darkness descended rapidly, Onwyn showed no signs of slowing down. He was as equally eager to vacate the Isle of Saiedor, she found.

Only when the pair was safely aboard a ship embarking in secret to their shores did Onwyn break his silence. "I have many questions for you, minstrel."

Ayuna smiled, thankful her ruse worked even on him. "And I will answer few of them."

Onwyn considered that. He relaxed against the curved wall of the ship as it creaked along the calm sea waters. His hands still idly rubbed at his wrists. "Then save me the trouble of asking."

She said, "I am but a simple bard seeking company on my journey throughout the realms as I spin stories through music."

"Why me?"

She sat across from him in the small cabin they shared. "Because the pain in your eyes echoed my own," she remarked.

The glint of a tear pricked the corner of his eye, yet he remained composed. "The land you have booked us passage to… what do you know of it?"

"There are many stories of Langraal's territory, all of it spectacular thanks in no small part to its leadership. At least, that is what I have heard."

"Then all is well within its borders?"

"Yes, my friend."

Onwyn's shoulders fell in relief. "Thank the thrones."

Ayuna was surprised only a little that Onwyn had not offered up his title. But perhaps her own secrecy prompted his pause. As far as he knew, she was a stranger from a strange land who appeared from out of the black to pluck him from the Void itself. She could not understand the disbelief he must have felt of freedom, or that he might awaken at any moment to find that he still slept between the dank stone walls.

"You are safe," she assured him.

"No. I will not be safe until we reach the opposite shore of this sea."

Despite his haggard face and tattered rags which only loosely resembled clothing, Ayuna knew her husband still lived inside him. Relaxing beside Onwyn, she clasped the pendant in her hand and contemplated the impossible. She did not care what he appeared as, be it prisoner, pauper, or king. She wished to hold him in her arms and comfort him with her touch. But she knew his pride, and if he knew she saw him in this manner he might collapse from humiliation and shame. He wanted her to know him as a tall, confident man who bowed to no one. And now he sat as a bitter and broken shell of the man he once was with his head bent in reverence and liberation. It would take time, she knew, for his shoulders to straighten and the authority to return to his senses.

The pair stepped off the cargo ship within minutes of docking. Ayuna gladly purchased a new set of warm clothing for Onwyn at the port. They shared a meal of piping hot porridge and a full loaf of fresh bread at a tavern there.

He set about washing the filth from his tangled hair and beard at a stream they passed on their way inland. Slowly, she watched him wash away the animal he felt himself beaten into. Slowly, he became human again.

"This is my home," Onwyn told her as he wiped away the wetness from his face. He had straddled two boulders in the shallow of the rocky creek. She filled her wine skin with the clear running water nearby and enjoyed the coolness of it. He raised his voice over the sound as he stood up. "But I suspect you already knew that."

"Is it?" she asked. "That is quite the happy accident."

He put his hands on his hips and looked around. "I didn't think I'd live to see this place again..." She felt his eyes on her as he trailed off. Then he added, "You never asked what I did to end up the prison."

"No, I didn't," she asserted.

"For all you know I could have murdered someone. My thanks to you may be a knife in your back."

"I doubt that," she told him.

He laughed. "Oh?"

"Neither of us is carrying a weapon. Anyway, you don't seem so dishonorable that you would kill the man that saved you," she said. She capped her wineskin and walked through the cold waters to the shoreline.

"I don't know what power brought you to my rescue, ser, but I shall have you knighted when we reach Langraal." He joined her on the shore, and they continued their journey onward.

That was a problem. She could not be in two places at once. And she wished to greet him at the palace as his wife and queen, not as his minstrel savior.

"Ah. Now I see why you were imprisoned: you're a madman," she jested as they walked.

Onwyn laughed. "A madman—yes, I suppose I am. Though gratitude more than insanity drives this king's hand."

"It was my honor to save a king then. No reward is required."

"You don't believe me," he said.

"If I believed every fool proclaiming himself a king then I'd not be able to walk the realms as I do for the weight of the gold in my purse," she jibed.

"The ransom the captain spoke of was real. Join me in Langraal, allow me to prove my story."

"Your gratitude is enough, kind ser. Sadly, I must decline your offer," Then she thought fast. She ought to lose him swiftly if she was to arrive at the palace before him. Quickly, she lied, "My destination lies to the north, not the east."

There was a pass to the north of their current route, and if she could catch another merchant caravan travelling towards the city as soon as she reached it then she would cut some time off of her travel.

The night she left his company, she played a joyous air on the lute and spoke merrily with him about family. She made up a past for herself, and listened as he spoke fondly of his reunion with his own.

Onwyn fell asleep when the night sky was clear and the stars above lit the darkened paths around their camp. Before her silent retreat, she tied up a handful of silver into a makeshift pouch from his old dusty rags, and left it in his hand. The small purse contained just enough coin to offer him passage close to the city and spare some for a large meal each day.

There, she left him to walk alone.

To Ayuna's delight, she did arrive home before Onwyn. She sneaked into the palace through the same servant's passage she used to escape, and did not stop walking nor remove the pendant around her neck until she reached Nikolas' office.

"Nikolas, I've done it!"

"My queen!" he called in greeting as he saw her. "I'm relieved you've returned! The king is with you?"

She shook her head and caught her breath, discarding the lute and the pendant on his workbench for storage. "No, he has no idea it was me. I must hurry and make ready for he will return soon."

"He doesn't kno—"

Ayuna laughed through Nikolas' words with glee. She grasped his hands in hers with all the effort of thanks they were capable of expressing. "We shall have a celebration yet, my friend!"

"Wait, my queen!"

Without another moment to spare, she took her leave of him. She bathed to wash away the grime of travel and dressed in her royal gowns again in secret.

From her chambers she heard the elation of the palace first trickle and then roar into revelry soon after. The tower bells rang out, heralding the high king's return.

Ayuna made her way from her chambers into the grand foyer of the palace's entrance. She watched from the stairs as his friends, advisers, and son welcomed him with embraces and shouts of joy. Tears were shed by many, and she laughed out a sob at the sight.

Her outburst caught him by surprise, and he looked up towards the top of the stairs to meet her eyes.

Onwyn passed his young son into the waiting arms of a nursemaid and silently ascended the staircase to meet her. His advisers whispered to themselves as they followed close behind him.

"Welcome home, my love," she said.

But his gaze turned foul as he neared her. His joy crumbled at her feet to reveal his ire. "You've betrayed me!" he accused brusquely. "Did you not receive my letter? Did it not ask that you free me? How could you have left me in that place to succumb to death so readily?"

Ayuna's tearful reunion soured. Words felt like glass to both speak and hear. Her breath caught in her throat and she could not make a sound for fear of shattering before him.

His adviser said, "I personally delivered the letter, sire. The queen disappeared shortly after its arrival. This is the first anyone has seen of her since that day."

"You ran away then," he proclaimed.

"No, my love—"

"Get out of my sight, woman," Onwyn snapped bitterly. "You are no longer in my heart, no longer my wife if you cannot follow my very clear plea for my freedom!"

He brushed past her, disappearing into the great hall and beyond, leaving her alone at the top of the stairs as the remainder of the court and servants filed out behind him.

Ayuna walked slowly through the halls, disbelief settling uncomfortably in her stomach. This was not her reunion with her husband. This was not the excited gladness of butterflies dancing. This was a gnawing pain of heartbreak and sorrow.

She did not know for how long she traversed the expanse of the halls. The world fell away around her, and she did not recognize the presence of anyone who passed her by. Aimless was her journey, and disdain her reward.

Only when an unexpected obstruction in the form of her most trusted friend, Nikolas, appeared before her in a narrow corridor did she look up.

"Nikolas. What are you—"

The adept presented the pendant in one hand and her lute in the other. "Show him, my queen. Show him the strength of your heart."

"Nikolas…" She began to protest, and then nodded. He was right— *of course* he was right. Her secret could not be kept her own and still maintain a true love, as much as she willed it to be so.

Once more she entered her chambers to change her clothes and slip the pendant around her neck.

Ayuna found a shady spot in the garden outside of Onwyn's study. There, she sat and played her lute to the flowers and birds. She played the canticles she strummed on the merchant caravan, at the castle of her most hated enemy, and the song she played just for him on their last night together along the way home.

It was somewhere within cadence that the presence of another caught her ear.

She looked up to see Onwyn standing before her. He had cleaned himself up; his beard was trimmed and kempt again. His face was clean and his eyes sharp and keen. Behind him, Nikolas and the high king's advisers kept their respectful distance.

"You are the one from before. I thought I heard your song, I—" The king cut himself short, then approached her and took her hand. "My friend, how did you come to be here? Please, see that I spoke the truth to you, and ask anything of me! Your heart's desire is yours for my life."

"My heart's desire?" she asked, lowering the lute to her side as she stood.

"Yes," he said eagerly. "Ask anything."

Ayuna reached up and wrapped her fingers around the necklace. With one sharp tug the chain snapped and fell free into her palm, revealing her true form. She watched herself change in his eyes as recognition overcame him.

Her somber smile cracked as she replied, "You are now and always have been the one and only desire of my heart, my king."

"It was you all along." Her king fell to his knees and kissed her hands. "Oh, my love! My dearest love," he cried, "I should never have doubted your will. I beg your forgiveness for my brashness. You have shown me courage beyond asking."

The queen beamed a wide, true smile as her sorrow melted into jubilation. She pulled her husband to his feet and kissed his lips in answer; at last she embraced her heart once more.

"A feast!" the high king declared to his assembled court. "Tonight we shall drink and celebrate, in honor of my wife, your queen, for her bravery and devotion."

That evening the realm celebrated the return of their king with the finest of wines and the hardiest of meals. They toasted the trickster queen who so gallantly proved that she would not fall to despair, nor demand the bloodshed of the masses in war, to rescue her lands.

Red Velvet

- Vivian LoDuca -
Illustrated by Ellen Million

Once upon a time, in the faraway, magical town of Austin, Texas, there lived a young woman named Rose. Rose had dark skin and natural hair that formed a cloud-like halo around her face, and a very successful bake shop which she and her mother co-owned. She also ran a delivery service, bringing her mother's home baked treats to all the good men and women of Austin, including the most magical treat of all, *special brownies*.

On a bright and sunny morning in early spring, when the temperatures were still cool and the humidity low, Rose was behind the counter at Red Velvet Rose Bakery, taking down her list of deliveries for the day while her mother served the walk-in clientele. Normally the tinkling of the bell above the door was not enough to distract her from her work, but on this occasion the sound of footsteps that followed was enough to make her look up and take notice.

"Hey, ladies, how y'all doin' today?" a man asked. He was wearing alligator-skin boots and a crooked smile, and his eyes were planted firmly on Rose.

Rose and her mother exchanged a look of mutual disdain.

"Why don't you go check on those cupcakes in the back, Mama? I can take care of this one." The words left a sour taste in her mouth, but that may have just been bile rising up from her gut.

Mama gave her a warning look, but said nothing as she walked through a swinging door into the kitchen.

"I'm glad we have this time to be alone," the man said, leaning against one of the glass display cases. His voice and the way he looked at her, like he was undressing her with his eyes, made Rose's skin crawl.

"I told you never to come near me or my bakery again, Ricky, so what the hell are you doing here?"

"Is that how you talk to your customers? Besides, you know I don't answer to Ricky anymore."

"I would prefer not to talk to you at all, so why don't you just tell me why you're here?"

"Not until you use my *proper* name," he said with a smirk Rose desperately wanted to slap off his face.

Rose crossed her arms and glared at him from across the counter. "What do you want, *Beast?*"

Ricky flashed her a grin and leaned further over the counter, close enough that Rose could smell the beef jerky on his breath. "I just came to see if you had changed your mind. You know, about us." His eyes flicked down to her breasts.

"Rick—*Beast*—" she corrected herself, growing angrier each time she had to use the name. "I told you, there is no us. There never was. All I wanted was a warm body for a few nights, and that body just happened to be yours."

Ricky looked down at his hands, which were fiddling with one of the business cards he had picked up next to the register, clearly not listening to any of the words Rose was saying. "Come on, Rose. You know it was more than that. We had something *special* together."

"Boy, unless you're talking about those brownies I made for you, there was nothing special about it. I liked your arms and your abs and your ass, but even those aren't enough to make up for just how goddamn *stupid* you are." Rose picked up her delivery list and began to fill a large box with cupcakes, tarts, and rolls. "Now I suggest you get out of my shop and on with your life, because I'm about to do the same."

Ricky slammed his fist down on the counter. "Damn it, Rose! Don't talk to me like that. Who the hell do you think you are?"

Rose paused in the middle of reaching for a strawberry rhubarb hand pie, and gave him a long hard look.

"You are the dumbest man I have ever met," she said finally, shaking her head.

Rose's mother appeared from the kitchen, carrying several small boxes bearing the bakery's logo, a red velvet cupcake on a twisted, thorny vine, which she placed into Rose's delivery box. "You better hurry off with these or you'll be late, Rose, honey."

"And remember," her mom said, glancing sideways at the still fuming Ricky, "stick to your route."

"Thanks, Mama. I was just leaving."

Rose packaged the last item on her list, grabbed the pink and red striped box and her keys, and walked out to her car. The bell chimed once more as she was loading the box into her backseat, and she heard Ricky's heavy footsteps behind her. He grabbed her arm and leaned in until his nose was almost touching hers.

"You're gonna be real sorry about this," he said through gritted teeth.

Rose rolled her eyes and shook him off. "I already am," she muttered as she got into her car, not at all sorry to watch him shrink away in her rearview mirror.

Rose's bakery was known far and wide for its delectable treats of all varieties, and had attracted a broad customer base as a result. Not all of them knew about the secret menu, but those who did were Rose's most loyal customers, and these she delivered to on a regular basis. Deliveries consisted of both goods from inside the glass display cases, as well as items from the back room, in order to deter suspicion, and as a good business practice. Rose and her mother were careful, as well as clever.

The first stop on the list led Rose to the gates of a large, private community. She stopped next to the guard house out front and waited.

"Hey, Rose," the guard said, stepping out of the small, white-washed shed. "Gosh, is it Wednesday already?" He handed her a clipboard to sign.

Rose smiled and added her signature below the others: pizza drivers and families of those who lived behind the gates. "It sure is, Jonesy. You know how particular the congressman is."

"You better believe it," Jonesy said, taking the clipboard back from her. "You're all good. I'll see you next week."

He started to walk back into the shed when Rose called out to him. "Wait a minute, Jonesy." She turned and pulled out a small pink box from the bin next to her. "You didn't think I had forgotten about you?"

"Well, I didn't want to say anything," Jonesy replied sheepishly. He took the box from her. "Is it my usual?"

Rose shook her head. "Not today, Jonesy. I made you something special. A limited edition flavor: maple bourbon bacon. It might go well with what you have in your pocket there." She winked at him.

"Mmm, thanks." Jonesy instinctively reached for the flask hidden in a breast pocket. "That's just between you and me, right?" he added in a hushed tone.

"Of course, Jonesy. You know I exercise the utmost discretion." A car pulled up behind her. "See you next week, Jonesy."

Jonesy walked back to the guard house and pressed a button to open the gate. They exchanged knowing smiles as Rose drove through.

Houses in the style of antebellum mansions rose up on either side of her, along with verdant green lawns that Rose was sure were maintained by violating water restrictions during the drought. Luxury sedans and gigantic SUVs were parked in long, curving driveways, and Rose's car was the only one that varied from the black or silver color scheme.

Rose pulled up in front of gleaming white two-storey home with a long curving driveway. A fountain stood out front with two trumpeting angels in long robes facing each other across a pinnacle topped by an eagle. A steady stream of water bubbled out of the angels' trumpets.

The congressman was not known for his subtlety.

The smell of gardenias in full bloom perfumed the shaded entryway as she waited to be let in.

"Rose! How lovely to see you," an impeccably dressed, middle-aged Hispanic woman greeted her. "Please, come in. I'll tell Roy you're here. Go on and have a seat in the kitchen."

"Thank you, Mrs. S," Rose said politely to the woman's retreating figure. She carried the bundle of pink and red boxes across down a long hallway and into a kitchen which might have been straight out of a magazine. Rose shook her head, saddened by the knowledge that this beautiful space was never used for anything beyond letting wine breathe.

"Rose, how are you?" a booming voice called, startling her from behind. "Didn't mean to sneak up on you there." The laugh that followed was even louder.

Rose turned and shook the hand of the biggest hypocrite she knew.

"No problem at all, congressman," she smiled. The man had run on a platform of harsher penalties for drug offenders, claiming they were the most dangerous members of society. His campaign ads stated how marijuana in particular was damaging the moral fabric of society, and in order to protect children and families, repeat offenders should be locked away for life. The ad failed to mention that the congressman's brother operated two of the state's largest privately held prisons. The first time Rose had been approached by one of the congressman's aides for special brownies, she had turned her away, fearing it was a trap. It wasn't until the man himself came down to the bakery that she had agreed to his offer.

"You see," he had told her after his security had cleared out the shop, "I believe marijuana is dangerous for those of weaker minds, but not for those of us who are educated and aware of the risks and effects. People like myself, who are responsible, would never abuse it."

From that day forward, she hadn't questioned his weekly requests, and he became her best customer.

"God bless hypocrites," her mother said each time she filled his very large order.

Rose placed her hand atop the pile of boxes on the counter. "Here's everything for the week, sir. I even threw in an extra slice of peach pie for Mrs. S."

The congressman put one hand over his heart and rested the other on Rose's shoulder. "Thank you, Rose. She'll be touched. Do you have a moment to stick around?"

"You know I love our chats, congressman, but my list of deliveries is longer than usual today, and I want to get off the roads before it starts raining." This was mostly the true, rain was in the forecast, but Rose also had a nagging feeling in her gut that she shouldn't stay too long at any one place today. Ever since her confrontation with Ricky, she couldn't shake the feeling she was being watched.

The congressman nodded. "You're a sensible young woman, Rose. I won't keep you, then." He walked her down the long hallway and back out to the gardenia-scented porch. "You take care, now."

Rose smiled at him and got back into her compact sedan, the only car on the entire street that was not parked in a driveway, and left the neighborhood. One down, five to go.

The next stop was a pastor who was known for his vitriolic sermons on the local Christian radio station. He was anti-gay, anti-choice, and especially anti-Muslim, but god damn, did that man love strawberry rhubarb pies and a good old fashioned special brownie.

"God made everything, and I mean everything, on this Earth. Who are we to say that marijuana, one of God's own creations, is sinful and wrong?" He told her as they sat in his well-furnished living room. Rose nodded along with this familiar rhetoric, the same thing he told her every time she delivered to him. "In fact, I would argue that you and your mother are doing God's own work when you make these heavenly creations."

"Thank you, sir," Rose said modestly, being very careful not to roll her eyes. "My mama will be touched to hear you said that."

Rose's mother hadn't been to church in twenty years.

"Baby, if I wanted to listen to an angry man tell me how I'm living my life wrong, I would have stayed at my daddy's house," she had told Rose.

"I mean it. Here, there's a verse that I want to show you—"

Rose stood up quickly. "I am so sorry, Pastor, but I've got to get to my other deliveries. You know what they say about idle hands," she added in a serious tone.

The pastor bobbed his head up and held up his hands. "You are absolutely right. I know all about doing the Lord's work, so I won't keep you from doing just that."

After that conversation, Rose sat in her car for a moment, staring at nothing, while she cleared her mind.

"Bless his heart," she said to herself finally.

She looked down at her list and saw her favorite customer, Granny Green, was next. As she was leaving the neighborhood, she decided to save Granny's house for last, thinking of it as a reward for getting through this day. As she turned right instead of left, the nagging feeling in her gut grew louder, and she turned up the volume of the radio so their voices would drown it out.

Rose exhaled loudly as she parked outside her penultimate stop. She had already delivered one dozen red velvet cupcakes and one small box to the headmaster of a private Catholic school, who had lamented that there were so few good girls like Rose left these days, and that women ought to take more pride in their domestic roles. Two fruit tarts and another box went to a journalist who told Rose she was conflicted about Rose's bakery.

"On one hand, it's great that a female-owned business like yours is so successful, but I worry that the stereotypical nature of your enterprise sends the wrong message about what women are capable of."

All of these comments Rose took in stride, smiling politely and keeping her responses brief and accommodating. For one thing, she didn't have the time or energy to take these people to school. Instead, she calmed herself by mentally counted all the money each one of them was giving her.

She rang the doorbell of a moderately sized ranch home in a fairly standard middle class neighborhood. Her second largest delivery of the day was heavy in her arms, and she could feel the humidity rising, the sudden change was a sign of rain to come. Out of the corner of her eye, Rose thought she saw Ricky walk past. She jerked her head around and saw only a little girl on a scooter going by, and she chided herself for this unusual feeling of paranoia that had hung around her all day.

"Good afternoon, Mrs. Johnson," Rose said to the woman who greeted her.

"Hi, Rose. Here, let me help you with those boxes," Mrs. Johnson offered, taking all but the two largest boxes from Rose. "I was so caught up planning for parent-teacher meetings and Peter's birthday this week I didn't realize it was already time for the delivery."

Rose followed her into the kitchen. "I thought you might have been having some sort of party," she said. "How old is Peter?"

"Eight," Mrs. Johnson told her with a smile. "And next month Elaine turns six. Can you believe it?"

The progression of time was standard and unchanging, so Rose could absolutely believe this. Out loud she told Mrs. Johnson, "They grow up so fast." Not wanting to get pulled into a conversation about her own plans for children, as Mrs. Johnson had been known to do, Rose changed the subject. "I bet their teachers will be tickled pink when you show up to those meetings with cupcakes."

"Well, I try to send the kids to school with treats for teachers about once a month, as a reward for all the hard work they do," she replied.

"And between the two of us, Peter has a bit of a behavior issue, and I find the teachers are more *accommodating* if there are sweets involved."

This was not the only parent Rose delivered to who used sweets to win over or outright buy teacher favor. Mrs. Johnson was just another woman who was expected to be everything to everyone, but who was never allowed to show any outward signs of the overwhelming nature of her responsibilities. She relied on Rose's special brownies to help her get through the weeks, and her cupcakes to get through the school year. Most women Rose knew used wine for this purpose, but Rose thought Mrs. Johnson had chosen a superior method.

The two exchanged pleasantries for a few minutes more until Rose took her leave. She buckled her seat belt, checked to make sure the only goodies left in the box were for Granny Green, and started backing out of the driveway.

She flicked her eyes up to the rearview mirror and saw Ricky's eyes staring back at hers. She slammed on the brakes and whipped her head around.

The only thing in the backseat was the box with the last few items for delivery, and an umbrella that was rolling around on the floorboard.

Rose swore at herself and took a deep breath. Her heart felt like it was going to race its way up her throat.

"Don't let that asshole get in your head," she told herself. Hearing those words aloud made her feel stronger somehow, and she sat straighter. "Now, let's go see Granny."

Granny Green lived in what was best described as a bungalow, painted in what was now a worn pistachio, with a front porch that was just big enough for a lawn chair, ten potted plants—mostly geraniums, two clay cat figurines, an old birdcage that housed a tomato plant, and a wind chime decorated with owls. Rose thought it was the most beautiful home of any of her clients.

"Well, don't just stand there, come in," Granny Green said, holding open the screen door before Rose had even reached the front steps.

Rose laughed. "Yes, ma'am."

Granny was old, but she was quick, and not to be trifled with. Rose hurried up the three steps to the porch and came inside.

"You can just set those down anywhere you find a spot," Granny told her. As Granny's front porch had the most empty space of anywhere in the home, this was a challenge. Each time Rose visited it seemed that Granny had found at least fifty new *things* to add to her collection. Granny wasn't a hoarder; Rose had delivered to a house like that once and refused to go back, but she just couldn't stand to see something that could still be useful abandoned without a home. Rose parted two stacks of encyclopedias from the 70's and set the two boxes in between them.

"Would you like some tea?" Granny Green called from the back of the house.

"What kind?" Rose asked suspiciously, joining the old woman in the kitchen.

Granny cackled. "Just the regular kind, this time. I know you're still on the clock."

The weather had cleared on the drive over, so Rose accepted her invitation. Truth be told, she would have accepted anyway. Granny loved a good story, and she had a lot of them to tell.

Granny set two glasses of sweet tea down on a cozy table tucked in a corner of the kitchen and took a seat. "Did I ever tell you about the time I got arrested?"

Rose took a sip of her tea and thought about the question. "You told me about the time you were arrested for marching in an anti-war protest in Denver, and another protest in San Francisco, and another one in Little Rock," she answered.

"So I haven't told you about the time I got arrested in college for smoking in the park, then," Granny said mischievously.

"No, I don't think I've heard that one. Smoking what?"

An orange and white cat jumped onto the table in front of Rose, and she began petting him with idle strokes.

Granny frowned. "Oscar, you know you're not supposed to be on the table."

The cat blinked at her and made a show of laying down and wrapping his tail around himself.

"I'll remember that," she told him. To Rose she said, "A joint. In the park in front of the Capitol Building." Seeing Rose's eyes widen, she added, "In Austin, not Washington."

"Still, Granny, that was pretty bold."

"It was a big group of us, and we were protesting. Hell, I don't even remember what we were protesting anymore, but we were rounded up and taken away." She looked wistful at the memory. "Anyway, so I'm sitting in the back of the paddy wagon, and my friend Jean starts singing this song—"

There was a knock at the door. Rose looked at Granny. "Are you expecting anyone?"

Granny shrugged. "No, but that's no reason to be nervous. Just a minute!" She called out as she rose from her chair. From the kitchen, Rose heard Granny open the door and say, "Oh, hello, Officers. What can I do for you?"

Rose's heart started racing, and all she could think was, *Ricky, you son of a bitch.*

Lost in her own head, she missed the next few seconds of the exchange between Granny and the police, but the next thing she heard clearly was, "You'll never take me alive, pigs! Run, Rose!"

"Oh, Jesus," Rose said, running out to stop Granny from reliving the glory days.

It was too late. Granny was on the floor in the hallway, struggling with a bewildered police officer. "You can't arrest me! Not without a warrant! Not without probable cause!"

Rose yelled, horrified, "Granny, stop it! You'll get hurt!"

"Are you Rose Redstone?" A different officer asked her.

"Don't answer him!" Granny shouted from the floor, where she was being handcuffed.

Rose turned to look at him. "Yes, and will you please tell your officer to stop wrestling with an eighty-year-old woman? She could be hurt."

"Rose Redstone, you are under arrest for possession and distribution of a controlled substance," the officer said, spinning her around and placing her in handcuffs. As they marched her out of the house and into one of several waiting police cars, Rose saw that both boxes she had placed on the table were gone.

———————◆———————

Rose waited in the interrogation room. She had already told the police officers who tried to question her that she wouldn't speak to anyone until she spoke with her lawyer, Otis Goodwin. She had no idea how much time had passed since then. Even though Rose had been prepared for this moment, knowing it was a risk she assumed as part of her job, she had been caught off guard. Now she worried she wouldn't be able to get the situation back under control.

A young man in a plaid shirt and work boots walked in the door. "Rose Redstone?" he asked, looking up at her from the papers he was carrying.

"Yes?" Rose said, looking at him skeptically. She had no idea who this hipster was, but he was definitely not Otis.

"I'm Hunter Lovac. Mr. Goodwin is on vacation and unreachable for the time being, so I will be acting as your attorney in his absence." He offered his hand.

"Nope," Rose said. "Somebody better call Otis and tell him his vacation is on hold until this matter is resolved."

Hunter dropped his hand. "Unfortunately, Mr. Goodwin is in Jamaica and will not be able to return for some time. I assure you, however, that I—"

"Listen to me, Hunter. All day I've had to deal with people telling me what they think is best for me, without the need or desire for their comments. Now, the one person whose advice I actually want is out of the country, and in place, they send me a lumberjack for a lawyer. Forgive me if I'm more than a little unwilling to work with you."

Neither of them spoke, each eyeing the other across the table. Finally, Hunter dropped the stack of papers in his hand on the table and sat opposite her. "I can get you another lawyer, one who looks the part, if that's what you're after, but that's gonna waste time that you don't have. Your ex-boyfriend provided more than enough evidence to the police to have you tried and convicted for a long, long time. You're in the belly of the beast right now, but I can get you out of this."

Rose clasped her hands together and set them on the table in front of her. "If what you say is true, and that good-for-nothing gave them what they need, then how do you propose to get me out of this?"

"We can make a deal, give them your list of clients in exchange for—"

Rose held up her hands. "Stop. That's not an option. There is no way I'm selling out any of my clients."

Hunter looked exasperated. "Rose, you don't have any other options right now. It's either make a deal or go to jail."

"What happened to Granny Green?"

"She was charged with assaulting an officer, but the charges were dropped. She's an old pro at this, actually seemed pretty disappointed that she wasn't going to be spending the night in jail. Unlike you," he added pointedly.

"What about my mama and the bakery?"

"Neither one is involved in the charges."

"How the hell is that possible?"

Hunter shrugged. "I don't have those details, but all you need to know is that they're safe, but you're in real trouble unless you make this deal."

Rose waved him off. "If Mama and the bakery are fine, then turning over my client list is definitely not gonna happen. If people hear I got arrested for possession, they might be scared off at first. But once a few weeks pass and no one is coming for them, and they see the bakery is still in business, they'll come back."

"I think you're overestimating people's loyalty to your bakery," Hunter told her gently.

"It's not *just* my bakery they're loyal to," she said. "Those brownies are the best damn brownies in the *state*."

Two officers walked in and made some noise about time being up. Rose stood and held out her wrists. Without looking at him, she told Hunter, "If you're as good as you think you are, you'll find another way to fix this. If you don't think you can handle that, you better send over a replacement tomorrow morning."

———————•◆•———————

The next time Rose saw Hunter, an eternity had passed. Or at least six days' worth of eternity. But as Rose stepped out into the sun, she was grateful that eternity had proven so brief. She turned to look at the man behind her, wearing a different plaid shirt and the same work boots as the day she had called him a hipster.

"All right, I know you're dying to give me the big reveal. Lay it on me."

"Yeah, maybe not right in front of the courthouse," he said, eyeing the building that loomed over them. They walked a few blocks until they were safely out of the building's shadow, to a deli where they could sit and talk.

"Okay," Hunter started,"So you weren't willing to give me a list of names, but I thought there was someone else who would be." Rose raised an eyebrow. "Your mom."

"She didn't tell me—"

Hunter cut her off before she could continue. "I figured if I could explain the situation to her, she might be willing to work with me. She didn't want to talk to me at first, unsurprisingly, but once she realized the how deep into the shit you were, she let me look at the list of clients. I gotta say, Rose, you cater to some pretty powerful people."

Rose nodded as if this were obvious, and Hunter took that as an indication to continue. "I had several people to choose from, any of whom might have had enough pull to get you out, but there was one man who I thought would be the most willing to help."

"The mayor?" Rose asked.

"The congressman. There isn't much evidence linking you to anyone that you deliver to, except for him. All those visitor logs, security footage, the guard himself. If someone enterprising were to put all that together, there could be a lot of damage done. Especially for a man whose campaign slogan was essentially 'drugs are bad.'

"So he and I had a little chat. He made a lot of threats against me, and against you, and your mother, and your bakery. I had to swear to him that both you and your mother had kept his secret, and that I found out from another source, and if he wanted to ensure further silence, he would find a way to get those charges against you dropped. As you can tell by your surroundings, it worked."

Rose shook her head. "No, I don't buy it. The congressman may have wanted to help you, or help *me*, at least, but that's too big a risk. Sure, you're threatening to reveal all these things, but it would be a lot easier to just make you disappear than to explain to the DA why a drug dealer, his most avowed enemy, should be released from prison."

"I thought of that, too, which is why I came prepared. I told him he could get the charges against you dropped by proving the evidence was bogus. To sweeten the pot, I told him he could exchange one drug dealer for another."

"But the evidence wasn't bogus. For once, the conspiracy was real."

Hunter held up a hand. "Please. This is a career politician we're talking about here. Corruption knows no bounds. Besides, I gave him an even bigger conspiracy."

"I'm listening."

"The police were tipped off by your ex-boyfriend. All the evidence was provided by one guy. It turns out, that one guy also happened to be working for the biggest drug ring in Austin. I think it may have been why he came on to you in the first place."

Rose pursed her lips. "I came on to him at a bar, because his ass looked real good in those jeans."

"Be that as it may, he probably stuck around once he figured out who you were."

"Once again, you completely underestimate my skills," Rose told him.

"All right, maybe the whole thing was coincidence," Hunter said, irritation creeping into his voice. "The point is, I was able to provide enough information to the congressman, who in turn provided that information to the police. And that proved the evidence against you was fraudulent and was a cover for a larger operation."

"And you were able to do all that in six days?" Skepticism was written across Rose's face.

Hunter leaned back in his seat. "You aren't the only one who knows powerful people, Rose. I have friends who may be even more dangerous than yours."

Rose snorted. "Okay, sure. What happens when Ricky gets out and comes looking for revenge?"

"I wouldn't worry about that. Turns out he's not very well-liked on the inside, either."

Rose didn't ask if that meant Ricky might not make it out alive, so Hunter didn't have to tell her the odds of his survival were low. Instead, the question and the answer hung unspoken in the air between them. The silence was broken by a tinkling sound from Rose's phone. She checked the message and stood up.

"My ride's here." She offered her hand. "Thank you, Hunter."

Hunter momentarily looked as if at a loss, but regained his senses and shook her hand. "Of course."

An unmarked black car had parked at the curb. A non-descript man in a suit held the passenger door open, and Mama stepped out, her arms held wide.

Rose and her mother embraced, big smiles across their faces.

"It's so good to see you in the light of day, baby," Mama said.

"It's good to see you, too, Mama."

"Ma'am, we need to leave," the man in the suit said.

"Alright, damn," Rose said, holding up one finger for him to wait a moment. She leaned down into the car and held out her hand to the man inside. "It's good to see you again, sir. Sorry about the lumberjack." She jerked her head in the direction of the deli.

"Don't mention it. Besides, I wouldn't miss our usual Wednesday visits," he said, shaking her hand.

"Mama, why don't you slide in first?" Rose said, gesturing to the open door.

Mama obliged and, as Rose turned to follow, she saw Hunter watching her from the restaurant, his eyes wide and mouth open.

Smiling, she tapped out a message on her phone.

As the car drove away, Hunter's phone chimed; one new text from Rose.

I told you my brownies were that good.

Ura and the Turtle

- Malaika R. Goodman -
Illustrated by Iole Marie E. Rabor

Once upon a time, young men knew the heavy weight of honor and responsibility and carried it with pride. Ura, the eldest son of the tribe's chief, was no different.

He sat on the sand as the sea crashed and the white foam lapped at his feet. In the distance, Ura could hear the drums beginning their song of celebration, as he battled with his decision.

Bragged to be the best looking man in the tribe, his thick black hair reached to the small of his back, and smooth tanned skin covered his taut lean body. He had his mother's light eyes and his father's strong chin. His father always said that their only differences were their eyes and that Ura had his mother's merciful and loving spirit.

"Ura, we must go." Jaka, the second eldest of their seven siblings, stood behind his older brother, gently reminding him of his duty.

Ura's role as a male and the next chief was to provide food for his tribe. He hunted, and he fished; anything that could feed his people. This made it bittersweet to pull the net out of the ocean to find this beautiful turtle.

Jaka kneeled down beside his brother and admired the creature. Though twisted and wrapped in the aging brown net, the turtle was relaxed as it looked at them.

"It is a beautiful turtle, Ura. We will have a great feast tonight. The shell will make an excellent shield, and its skin—a lovely dress for our sister!"

Ura looked over at his brother, his mirror image, his twin, younger by just minutes; dark skin tanned from the sun, eyes as bright as the sea and the grass at the same time, and a smile that stretched from ear to ear. That same smile looked tight and grim on his brother's face. Jaka reached towards the turtle, eyes shining with hunger.

Ura shoved him over. "Don't touch her."

Jaka stared at him in shock, and stood to shake the sand off.

Grains of sand fell in Ura's hair and onto his skin as he still stared at the turtle. "See you at the feast," he grumbled at his brother, dismissing him.

Without another sound, Jaka walked away to leave Ura staring into the eyes of his new friend. The heavy burden of being the eldest son began to sink in. He looked out onto the sea and let the somberness of responsibility crash into him.

"It's my responsibility to bring in the food to feed my village," he whispered out into the air. The sting of tears bit behind his lashes. "How can I bring you back to the village, where you will no longer be the beautiful creature you are?"

Its bright green eyes swelled, reaching out to his spirit. The green swirled into the brown of the shining shell dripping with water, hypnotizing him. Before Ura understood what was happening, the net was thrown away, and the turtle had reached the water.

Ura stood on weak knees as the waves began to slowly swallow the turtle, until it twisted its head to look back at him, waiting. His heart beat a cadence, pounding against his ribs as he heard the drums of the starting celebration.

"Go, you must go," he urged his friend, "before they come."

With the nod of the creature's head, time seemed to slow. Once again, he was mesmerized in the beauty of the turtle, yet this beauty seemed strange and new to him.

A dust of sand began to swirl around the turtle, pushing back the blue water until it raged against an invisible wall. Before him, the animal he saved turned to him. It seemed to stand on two feet, and grow.

Ura was too shocked to turn away from her. His lungs began to burn as he held his breath. His heart beat harder and faster, making him dizzy.

She reached one hand out to him. "Ura."

Ura opened his mouth to cry out, and the world turned black.

———————— ◆ ————————

A great horrible screech tore from the air, jolting Ura out of his sleep.

"Calm down," drifted a voice from far off. "Everything will be okay."

The voice was somehow familiar to his ears, though not one he thought he heard every day. He opened his eyes, and in the sky above was a small ball of sun, whiter than the sun he grew up loving. Yet this one did not burn his skin despite being so close, and did not hurt his eyes as much to stare into it. A small ball of fire surrounded by a white sky. He strained his ears for the celebration feast, but heard nothing.

This isn't home, Ura thought.

Again, his heart beat a cadence of his village drum as the pressure began to weigh on his chest. Like when his little brothers would pile on him in fun, he felt the air leaving his body as he tried to catch it. Then a small buzzing noise started to seep into his head hurting it. Slowly, Ura looked away.

"Such a strange sky," Ura mumbled to himself, struggling to sit up.

"It is not a sky, it is a ceiling," the voice said.

Ura didn't understand, but looked back at the 'ceiling'. Then he turned away one more.

The room around him was white, and bright enough to blind Ura as he tried to focus. It was round just like his hut, but the solid walls lacked a single gap to let light in. Tables shiny as the silver of the tradesmen from the north stood all throughout the room.

The room began to tilt and shake before Ura's eyes.

"Please, do not scream again."

Whoever was speaking to him sounded closer, sneaking up on him like a predator. Yet, he buried any fear, refusing to believe he needed to prepare himself for an attack.

"I do not wish to startle you again."

With every word, his heart beat slowed; his labored breath quieted.

"What kind of sorcery is this?" Ura asked without turning. "The words I understand, but a voice with such a strange sound."

Ura sat still facing a door he hadn't seen before as he could feel the presence behind him still.

Something smooth ran across his hand and his hairs stood on end. A glint of light caught the corner of his eye.

I am the eldest son, he thought to himself; *I will not be afraid.*

Slowly, slower than he would admit, he looked up to who stood beside him. Wonderment filled his face, and confusion took his breath away.

"I do not know what 'sorcery' is, but I do not believe this is it. I would like to learn, though. All in good time."

Ura stared at the creature. Small, round, bright green eyes stared back into him, with waves of gold flowing throughout and a circle around each as black as coal after a fire.

"You are my turtle," he said.

A smile appeared from her lipless mouth as she said, "Yes."

Ura slowly lowered himself to the floor from his high makeshift bed to stand opposite the creature.

"I can explain," she offered.

She stood tall, taller than him with arms as thin as bamboo. Her skin shone, too bronzed to be a tan, yet beautiful to Ura. Her neck was stunning, too: longer than any animal he'd ever seen. But it seemed natural as if it belonged perfectly on her body. She stood on two feet and talked to Ura in his language. She was so much like him, yet so different.

She smiled at him, and though it was not a smile like his own, he remained unafraid. Her face grew gentle and soft with few lines. She had a smooth round chin which flowed up into flat cheeks. He looked up to her eyes again, framed by lashes of white. There was a twinkling in them that invited him in; familiar, friendly orbs.

"What are you?" he asked.

"My name is Caxanderil, and I—"

The door burst open. This time Ura didn't fight his instincts and slipped into a fighting stance to face the intruders.

Two creatures with the same skin as Caxanderil strode in. They wore metal plates against their bodies between their clothes and chest, and Ura decided they were warriors. Their bodies were built thick, with chest wider than Caxanderil's. The pair towered over her, looking down as she looked up at them. They stood tense, with hands gripped around items attached at the waist.

The first warrior said something in a language that Ura could not understand. With a sound from his friend, both turned and exited the door.

Caxanderil turned back to Ura. "There is not much time. I will try to explain everything, but we will have to hurry."

She reached out her slender palms and gentle gaze.

"We must go see the king."

———————— • ◆ • ————————

The two warriors and Caxanderil led Ura down a wide, bright hallway. Doors stood on every side of the hall and between them the walls were filled with pictures. In between two doors was an image of a small man with his hand inside of his clothes and a funny headdress upon his head. Between the next two doors, the images showed more men standing together on steps, stabbing another man in his back. The men wore similar clothes to Caxanderil and the two warriors leading the way.

Looking at Caxanderil, he saw that her skin shone past the bright white of her dress, and Ura couldn't help but blush at the memory of how she looked naked at the beach. He admired the way her clothes draped over her strange but beautiful form. Ura's eyes slowly traveled up to hers, feeling heat rush to his face as she caught him looking at her body.

"We know some of your future," she said with a casual smile. "Well...what I mean is your world. B—but your future, too. We know what lies ahead for you," she stumbled over her words. Slender fingers ran over each other as she twitched in her nervousness. Her vision shifted from Ura to the warriors in front of her, and then back to Ura. The closer they seemed to get to where they were going, the more she worried with her fingers.

"They're from the Roman Empire—our clothes, I mean. It's Father's favorite time period of yours. That's a time a good bit after your lifetime. For you, the Earth is still young."

Her fingers flew to the chains draped around her neck attached to a brilliant jewel set into her chest. He counted three fingers and a thumb, one less than his.

"You say very strange things," Ura told her, watching her fumble with the chains to her jewelry. "If this is a dream… I am not sure what it means."

All at once, Caxanderil yanked the jewel away, leaving a crater in her chest, and shoved him sideways into a room.

Ura felt his eyes bulge from his face as he began to realize what she'd done. He watched her slide the door shut, as his heart pumped faster putting him on guard. Caxanderil leaned against the door, catching her own breath.

Ura could barely push his voice out of his throat. "You…you just pulled that from your *body*?"

She looked up at him with a twinkle in her eyes. "You have seen a lot of new and wonderful things tonight, Ura of Sand Isle, and this is what scares you?"

She reached her hand out and slowly walked towards him. He looked down into her long flat palm. The jewel came alive, pulsing in her hand. "It's a small computer made to look beautiful and identify me as royalty. When I set it in, it lets them know where I am, my blood pressure, and my heart rate. They will know if I am scared and come to get me."

"Is that not a good thing?"

"If they are not the one you are afraid of."

Ura wanted to reach out and console her, but he couldn't make himself lift his arm.

"Why would they do that?" he asked her. He looked up to her chest, where her skin peeked from her dress and studied the crater. Ura found his hand moving of its own accord, to brush the chains which appeared to be braided into her skin. "This hurts you?"

For a moment there was a tense silence as Ura ran his fingers along Caxanderil's chain and she looked on.

"It's not bad," she gasped, voice becoming husky.

Ura's hand stilled as he allowed her voice flow over him, so strange but so familiar.

"What am I doing here?" he finally asked.

"Ura..." she started, "I have been watching you your whole life. My job is to help the human race. I don't know quite how to explain this."

Ura's hand slowly slid along her skin, enjoying the feel, before he dropped it to his side.

"My people are the Watchers. We have seen the birth of worlds, and the destruction of them. Our *honor* is to help you grow as a world for as long as you can. And Earth, your planet, is my honor," she said, beseeching him to understand.

Ura stared at her, trying to understand all her words, but he couldn't begin to comprehend what she was telling him.

"What you need to know Ura is I tested you—to see if you were a good man. Three times I came to you; as an injured bear, an enemy, and as a sea turtle."

Ura stared at her wide-eyed as he remembered the bear. After a long day of hunting and finding absolutely nothing, he had stumbled across it, moaning loud enough to alert the whole tribe. All alone, Ura had seen the blood pooled below the bear and the trap wounding it. He remembered being so angry at such a tragedy, that someone had kill something so proud and majestic. So too had he been angry to recognize Jaka's handiwork in the trap itself.

Ura had saved that bear, though it would have been an easy kill. No one had ever known what happened save Ura and the ancestors. Ura didn't remember the enemy, but he could never kill another man, no matter what wrong he committed. Even the murder of a family member would not warrant that kind of hatred from him.

"And when it would have benefited you to kill me, you saved me, as well, and that makes you a good man. However, I broke the rules."

Caxanderil began to pace the room, worrying with the pulsing jewel that started to change colors. "I broke a very important rule, Ura. And that is never to reveal yourself and never to... never to fall in love with those we watch."

She refused to look at him as she continued her pacing, and Ura's skin started to flush and burn. He could not believe the words she spoke. Though everything fascinated him about her duties, he was taken aback by her declaration of love.

We just met, he thought to himself.

"But I do, Ura of the Sand Isle. I did, and you fainted, and I couldn't leave you there. I had to—*had to*—help you. And I brought you here and—oh my ancestor... Father is going to kill me—he's going to kill *you*!"

Ura shot up from where he was slowly melting into his chair, watching Caxanderil ramble.

"No man will kill me; he can try," Ura said, puffing his chest.

Just as the Caxanderil stopped pacing to look at him, the door burst open violently as another pair of warriors appeared.

"The king is waiting," spoke one, coming into the room. "Let's go."

———————◆•———————

Never in his life had Ura seen such an array of color of people, all in one room. Not even when the barbarians from the North came to marry their youngest daughter to his youngest brother. He scanned everyone in the room. Some looked at him with disgust and others with wonder.

But the most intimidating by far was the figure at the front of the room.

Towering over the rest of the people was a chair, much like Ura's father's, but the man sitting in it commanded much more presence. The gray-skinned man, as gray as Caxanderil's hair, sat wrinkled in the chair looking like a ghost, decorated in jewels and robes.

"Explain yourself, daughter," said the figure, filling the room with his voice.

"My lord," Caxanderil said. She bowed low, twisting her body in ways Ura had never seen. "Could we talk in private?"

"Explain yourself!"

His voice thundered through the room making Caxanderil stiffen; Ura fell to his knees, and the creatures around them whispered and snickered.

Caxanderil bowed even lower and pressed her forehead to the floor. Ura stared at his friend and felt enraged at her humiliation, but scared of this man on the throne.

"I wish..." Caxanderil started, closing her eyes. "I wish to marry him."

The room exploded with voices, as Ura snapped his head to her. Arms began to wave through the air as voices screeched, and the figure stood up.

"Silence," he whispered.

Instantly, the room fell silent, though Ura wasn't sure how they all had heard the lord.

"We have a guest. We shall speak his language, and no one will speak out of turn," he said. The king began to stalk down the steps from his raised throne, his long gray hair flowing after him like a bride's veil. "You have disrespected our laws, and by showing yourself to him, you have forever changed Earth. For this dear daughter, you must be punished."

Ura expected an uproar, but no one made a sound as Caxanderil body went limp against the floor.

"You are the daughter of our people. You had responsibilities, and you failed us," the king said. "Stand, Caxanderil of the Watchers and Ura of the Sand Isle, and face your punishment."

Ura's heart broke as he saw Caxanderil stand, body slumped in defeat. He knew how it felt to upset his father, and to be see that disappointment in his eyes. The injured black bear he nursed back to health, the traitorous Northman he showed mercy to, and the turtle today were all a disappointment to his people. And here they were, with Caxanderil facing the same fate.

The king walked back to his throne, his age showing in his shaking limbs and groaning joints as he sat. *So human*, Ura thought, *but not human.*

"Ura of the Sand Isle," the king said, piercing him with his strange purple eyes. "The choice will be yours. You can stay here, marry my daughter, and in time, rule the Watchers. However, eventually your prosperous tribe will die. Or, you can go back to your world, and I can promise you that you will have a family line till the end of your time." The king's eyes shifted upward as he said this, and the leer on his face made Ura uneasy.

"But know this; if you choose to go back to your home... Caxanderil will not be allowed to marry again for the shame of this scandal. Marriage is a sacred right in our world, to be without... is indescribable pain and humiliation."

"Father—"

With a wave of his hand, Caxanderil shut her mouth, and with grim eyes, she looked to Ura.

Ura's heart began to speed and time seemed to slow yet again, as he looked back at Caxanderil. His choices were to save his tribe or to save his new friend this embarrassment. Her green-gold eyes pleaded with him as she began to shake. He had saved her so many times without knowing it, because he loved the beauty of nature's animals, and the flaws of the people around him. But could he save this beautiful creature and doom his family?

"I am sorry. I—I am sorry," he said to Caxanderil, and then to the king. "But I would like to go home."

Caxanderil didn't sink to the floor, and the room didn't erupt into outrage, but something broke, and what Ura imagined was a tear slid down the king's face.

"Caxanderil," the king said in barely a whisper, "take him back."

————— ♦ —————

They walked together in silence as Caxanderil led him into another room adjacent to the court. She didn't look at him, and he didn't look at her.

"Here," Caxanderil said sweeping her hand over the room and pointing out a machine. She walked over to it, pressing the side to make it open up for Ura. "This will take you home."

Ura stepped inside, feeling surrounded by the bright white walls circling around. A white bench was below him, and he sat. The cold from it seeped through his clothes and into his skin. Looking up, he saw the same light he thought was a sun earlier. How much he'd learned in such little time.

"Here," she said again, standing in front of him. "It's from the king."

He lowered his face from the light and looked at her, right below her eyes to avoid the hatred dripping off of her as she handed him a box. "Please—" her voice broke. "Please do not open this."

Ura took the box, staring down at it and away from her, ignoring the brush of their fingers. She walked back to the entrance of the room and behind white panels he hadn't noticed.

"Just relax," she said as the machine around him whirred to life.

Light slid in front of him, back and forth as strange noises sounded off in his ear. Frantically, he looked around him.

"Goodbye, Prince Ura."

———————◆•———————

White lights flashed, blinding him, and when he opened his eyes to say goodbye to her, his breath caught. A warm breeze drifted across his skin. As he looked upon the beach, he knew it was his home.

Ura's heart soared when he saw the sea he had grown to love, but, immediately his elation came crashing down. The blue sea he had known since his childhood days was now dark green and smelled of something he couldn't place, but did not like.

Everywhere he turned were men and women and children. Some as tan as him, some as white as the North men, some as dark as the cocoa beans they traded. Ura's mind reeled as he took in everything around him.

Father must have sent the tribes to look for me, he thought. Nodding his head to himself, he picked up his box and turned to run into the trees to return home.

But the trees were gone.

Ura sank to his knees.

The sand flowed up to a hill to grass. Unfamiliar white and silver square huts touched the sky, and things with strange wheels congregated in front of the strange huts. Ura wanted to cry, but keep it in, knowing his father wouldn't approve. He saw that not one tree was in sight, and the sky went on for miles, and nowhere did he see his tribe.

The sand dug into Ura's shins.

For the first time in his life, he hated the feel of it.

Turning to sit with the king's box, Ura looked at all of the invaders on his beach and began to despise them.

He clutched the box, thinking about Caxanderil and all the times he'd saved her life, hating himself for not being the son the tribe needed and getting into all this trouble, hating the king for lying to him.

The box Caxanderil gave him began to vibrate, and in his despair, he opened it without hesitation.

A soft bud of light sat in the bottom of the box. He could not tear his gaze away from it as it slowly began to swirl. It began to paint a picture in the box, and he felt no fear as it filled and spilled over into his hands.

"Do you see that old man," came a woman's voice from nearby. "The one staring at his box, mumbling to himself?"

Ura's heartbeat slowed, and his lungs began to strain as he found it more difficult to breath. He shifted his eyes to the side as far as they would allow him, and he saw his hands and arms now spotted and wrinkled, thin and bruised like his tribe elder as the light slowly swallowed his limbs.

Can she not see the light? Will she not help, he thought. *I'm dying.*

"What old man, dear?" a man asked.

"That one right there."

Ura continued to stare at his arm, no longer seeing the light that enveloped him, but just himself slowly turning old. His lungs still burned, and he could hardly hear the beat of his slow heart in his ears.

He watched his own skin blow away from his bones in the soft breeze over the sea. With a quick prayer to the ancestors, he made peace with his death. He slowly looked up, made eye contact with a woman and smiled until he couldn't see anything else.

"Oh my gosh, did you see that?"

"See what?"

"The old man, just... he just blew away. His whole body, just... *pfft* with the wind."

The pale man looked up at his wife as he reapplied his sunscreen. "Maybe you had too many drinks last night, Christine," he said to her.

"Hm... maybe I am seeing things," she laughed.

"Daddy look, look," a child called, running up to the pale man. "A turtle in the water!"

The little girl pointed towards the sea, and the couple followed the child's finger. "Look at that, Christine... that turtle is huge!" said the man. "Let's go catch it!"

Maiden Tree

- Elaine Titus -
Illustrated by Michelle Papadopoulos

Once upon a time, the king of Karelia consulted with his royal seers to find his son's ideal wife. He had loved his own chosen queen, and after her death, wished to give his son the same gift of a worthy bride. Word spread that the prince was seeking a mate, and a witch decided that her daughter should be queen, instead. So she and her daughter packed their things into a wagon, closed the doors to their cottage by the White Sea, and set out to lie in wait by the main road. The witch spent her days scrying to discover when the selected woman would appear.

In reasonable time, a maiden with milk-white skin and hair dark as ebony came by, traveling on a heavily laden pony. The witch laid eyes upon her and at once knew her to be the prince's future bride.

"Where travel you, little one?" the witch asked, stepping from the brush alongside the road.

The girl smiled, and said, "I journey to the palace, in answer to this summons I received." With that, she produced a letter bearing the royal crest from her bag.

The witch and her daughter leapt up and pulled the maiden from the saddle by her long hair, muffling her cries with a rag bound round her mouth. The witch's daughter took the maiden's place on the pony, and the witch made her daughter to look like their captive, with a careful spell that perfectly mimicked the pale skin, amber eyes, and shining black hair.

"What shall we do with her?" the daughter asked, nodding at the maid, who stood bound in ropes with the gag in her mouth.

The witch considered. "We cannot leave her here; this is the main road, and she would be found too easily. We shall have to take her with us as your infirm aunt, who fell ill on the journey. I am too tired to deal with her here, but in a few days I will think of something."

So they agreed to put the helpless maiden into the back of their wagon and smear her face with dirt. Then they laid many blankets upon her, emptied her saddle bags into the wagon, and rode on.

The witch held the reins for the wagon, while her daughter rode the pony. The pony, now unburdened, stepped lightly and quickly. They progressed in good time toward the southern border, just as the snow was melting.

Half a day's ride from the palace, when the deep forest began to give way to rocky lake shores, the witch felt her powers had returned to full strength. She pulled the prince's intended from the wagon, still gagged and tied at the wrists, knees, and ankles. With a wave of the witch's hand, where once stood a lovely young woman now stood a slender maiden tree, a birch sapling with silver bark and verdant leaves.

Satisfied, the witch and her disguised daughter resumed their journey. At the gates of the palace, they drew forth the stolen letter from the king, requesting the maid's presence. The guards recognized the royal seal and let them enter.

In three days' time, the prince had met his supposed ideal wife, and was not impressed. She was certainly lovely, but her voice had a meanness to it, and the expression in her eyes was smug. He was not one to doubt the royal seers, and so, he agreed to the marriage at his father's behest. But in the dark of night, his qualms kept him from sleep.

On the eve of his wedding, the prince rode from the palace to seek answers from the moon. Luna was compassionate to mortals, and sometimes granted wishes if the request was worded correctly.

He rode in silence, until he reached the edges of the forest. Under the silver light, the prince sat back on his horse and gazed upward.

"I do not know if this is right," he said hesitantly. "O beautiful queen of night, if you take pity on me, help me find joy. I will accede to my father's wishes. Please grant me a happy life with my beloved."

Amused by his clumsy attempt, the moon chose to shine her beams upon a particularly arresting young birch nearby, so that the leaves glistened.

The prince was struck by the perfect grace of this solitary maiden tree, trembling in the wind. He determined that he must have it in his own chambers, and, seeing as it was a very young tree, thought perhaps it could be borne to the palace to grow at his bedside and glow in the light of the moon each night.

He turned and rode back, giving the command to his guards to fetch him the beautiful silver birch from outside the palace walls and bring it to him. The guards went to the tree and dug it gently from the earth, for its roots were not firmly planted at all. It was then placed it into an ornate pot to sit by the prince's bed.

The next day was the wedding, followed by a feast and dancing. The prince and his disguised bride were borne into the royal chambers to consummate their union. They lay together as was proper, and all the while, the birch tree rustled in its pot, leaves fluttering in the wind.

Afterward, the bride left the prince's chambers to sleep, and the prince lay awake in his bed. He stared at the ceiling, breathing sharply, and tossed about for hours before finally achieving rest.

The birch tree witnessed all this silently, and trapped inside, the maiden wept.

Her grieving continued through the day, disgusting the warrior sun Solaro, who turned his back and sulked in clouds. As day turned to night, her agony caught the attention of the compassionate moon, who climbed into her place in the sky and smiled down upon the sad little birch. And so, when the prince returned to his chambers to sleep the next night, Luna struck a bargain with the maiden tree.

"As long as I can shine upon you, I will make you human again. You may be with him, talk to him, whatever you wish, but once I leave the sky, I will be too far away to help you. You will still be a tree by day."

"Thank you!" the maiden cried. "What must I offer in return?"

"Your secret," the moon said. "You may be with your beloved, but you may not tell him who you truly are. That secret is the price you pay for my blessing."

"I will not tell him," the maiden promised. "Thank you, Luna." And with that, she turned eagerly toward the prince, overjoyed to see her own hands and arms in place of leaves and branches.

She stepped delicately out of the pot and approached the bed. The night air was chilly against her skin, and she realized she was naked just as the prince stirred.

The maid scrambled to pull the bedclothes over herself, which unfortunately kept her tethered quite close to the bed.

The prince opened his eyes, and beheld a gleaming silhouette at his bedside. He sat up, whispering in the dark, "Who is there?"

"My name is Breza," the maid replied.

"How did you get in here?"

"The moon brought me."

The prince was silent for a long moment, then reached for her. His fingertips grazed her jaw. In the darkness, he could barely see her face. He remembered his plea to the moon, and his hand trembled to touch her.

"Come closer, Breza," he said. The maid clutched nervously at her meager coverings, and took one more step until her thighs were flush against the side of the bed.

"Why are you shaking?" he asked.

"I am cold, your highness."

He shook his head, his silver-pale hair tousled from sleep. Standing, the prince took little care for his own nudity as he grabbed a thick coverlet from the chest at the foot of the bed and threw it around her shoulders. Grateful, she clutched it closer around her to conceal her body completely.

"I am Andrei," the prince said softly, smoothing the coverlet over the girl's slender frame. "You look as if you are made of moonlight. If I move too quickly, will you blow away?"

That shook her out of her nerves a bit. She giggled. "No, your highness."

"Andrei." His face broke into a smile at the sound of her laugh. "If we are to be this intimate upon meeting, let us be intimate with names as well."

"Andrei," she said, looking up into his blue eyes. They stood quite close, but not touching.

The sound of his name on her lips pleased him. "That is better. Now come, sit by me. Tell me how the moon brought you here. It must be a fascinating story."

He gestured toward the wide expanse of the mattress, holding out a hand to help her climb up.

They lay side by side through the night, conversing easily and laughing often. She stayed tightly wrapped in her coverlet, and he lay facing her, drinking in every nuance of her voice, her face, the glow of the moon in her hair.

Many things were discussed, but she kept her promise, and did not reveal her identity. As the moon began to recede into the horizon and the sun peeked over the opposite side, Breza felt her skin tightening to bark. She hastily said her goodbyes and asked the prince to turn his back so that she might leave without revealing herself.

He complied, smiling to himself at her modesty, and when he turned around the maiden was gone, and the sunrise warmed the leaves of the birch tree in its pot.

The next night, the prince claimed an illness so as to keep his new bride from his bedchamber. He had been walking and talking as if drugged or half-dead all day, and no one questioned him. He hurried to bed and could hardly close his eyes for the excitement, hoping that his moon maiden would return.

Despite his eagerness, he fell fast asleep before sunset and woke to Breza's soft touch. This time she was already wrapped tightly in the coverlet, and she climbed into the bed next to him, with only her small pearly-white feet showing. When he stretched out an arm and gathered her close, she lay her head on his chest. They spoke quietly until the first gray warnings of sunrise, when she took her leave, once again asking him to shield his eyes.

On the third night, he rang the kitchen for some rye bread with jam, claiming that his stomach was upset. The servants, concerned at the prince's prolonged illness, sent many trays of pirogs and pastries, berries in cream, as well as coffee and buttermilk. When the maiden appeared, they spent hours stuffing themselves full of treats, leaning on their elbows atop the bed like sultans.

Breza had not tasted real food in many days, and crammed several things in her mouth all at once. She closed her eyes and savored the taste of each bite before reaching for more. Andrei, accustomed to nobility, laughed to see her with butter and crumbs smeared all over her cheeks. Her response was to wipe her jam-coated hand in his blond hair.

Shocked, the prince paused for a moment, before dipping a finger in yogurt and poking it toward her face. Breza giggled and bit his finger tip, licking it clean.

They both froze.

Andrei moved slowly, tilting his hand to cup her chin. Her golden eyes wide, she did not move, until the prince touched the pad of his thumb to her lips. All breath left her body.

He shoved the trays aside, so that they clattered against the bedpost. Heedless of the mess, he hauled her closer, his heart leaping when he felt Breza's arms encircle him. He was not quite gentle, and his hands shook as he slid fingers behind the nape of her neck and pressed his sticky mouth against hers.

Through the dizzy joy of the prince's embrace, she felt the prickle in her scalp that signaled the setting of the moon. Her full belly hardened around the food in her stomach, and her skin grew tighter and more coarse.

"I must go!" she gasped, pulling away.

He did not loosen his grip. "Stay, just a little longer. Don't go now."

She shuddered. If she didn't get her feet back on soil, she would transform right there in his arms. "I must. I have no choice. Please."

Andrei hesitated one more second, then loosened his hold. Breza scrambled off the side of the bed, lurching toward the pot in the corner. "Don't look!" she cried, glancing over her shoulder.

The coverlet lay abandoned on the bed; it would take armies to avert his gaze. His eyes were dark as lakes as he swallowed, his voice thick. "Why must you leave me?"

Her vision swam with tears. She had but seconds left.

"I'm sorry," she whispered, and stepped into the decorative pot. The change happened so quickly it hurt, and she stood inside her bark prison and mourned.

The prince gaped in disbelief at the silver birch. But no matter how he gripped the trunk in his hands, shook it, shouted, or begged, it remained a tree.

———◆———

The next night, Breza refused the moon's offer of transformation. Andrei sat poised on his bed, staring at her papery bark, and she did not know how to explain without betraying her promise of secrecy. They both remained immobile, as if the prince, too, was enchanted. When the sun rose over the forest the prince gave up his vigil, and fell into an uneasy sleep.

The second night began the same, with the maiden hiding, while the prince watched and waited for her to appear.

Many hours passed, until the prince walked close to the tree in its pot. He gazed upon it wonderingly, touching the places on the trunk that were scarred from his frenzied grip, stroking the branches like a lover's hair. Finally, he leaned close until his face was shrouded by her leaves.

"I'm sorry," he whispered. "Please come back."

Several minutes passed, while he breathed into the shadows of the tree. Then he startled as he felt Breza's arms close around him. Her skin was warm and soft, and he was quick to respond, gathering her against his body.

For once, she was not shy of her nakedness, and leaned into him. "I... I cannot..." she struggled with the words in her mouth, drawing a first breath into new lungs.

"You are safe here. Whatever has happened to you, I will save you," he promised, gliding lips across her cheek and forehead.

She drew back, and he grudgingly released her. His fingers still ached to tangle in her hair, but he could see that she was trying to speak. "I can't tell you, and you can't save me," she said. "This is my burden. It is the suffering I bear to be with you."

He was unsatisfied, stretching out empty arms to beckon her. "I would ease your suffering. Tell me how."

In the darkness, he could not see her face, but her hands crept up his chest. "This is a blessing from the moon," she whispered. "It is all we have. Do not waste it."

In consent, he cradled her against him. When their lips touched, it ignited a fire that quickened his heart and body. He was elated to discover that she met his kiss with equal ferocity.

It took mere moments to lift her into his arms and carry her to the bed. Her breath came faster as their bodies slid and caught. Adrian rolled onto his back and pulled her on top of him. She could feel every inch of him, and blood burned in her cheeks.

"I will not hurt you, or frighten you," he promised, but his voice was shaking. "Do what you would like. But I must have you close to me."

They coupled the rest of the night, and every night thereafter, only stopping when sunrise threatened the sky. The prince lived for night, sleeping well past noon so that he could spend long hours with Breza, touching her, listening to her laugh, and sharing tender words.

He cared nothing for his duties, and in his absence the new princess stepped in, learning from her father-in-law the ways of running a country.

She sat in at council meetings, and joined the king on presentation days, when the common folk visited with concerns and requests. She became known for her eagerness to speak on the prince's behalf. Unlike her husband, however, she was apathetic to the needs of farmers and fishermen. She much preferred granting the petitions of clergy and gentry, saying the peasants offended her nose. Her opinions, often declared loudly in the hearing of the royal subjects, grated on their ears.

The king responded by encouraging the princess to restrict her audience to the royal court, with whom she was becoming a fast favorite. They spent hours drinking honey wine and entertaining each other, for they delighted in her cruel wit. In this way she flourished, gaining influence along with popularity among the nobility.

The witch was pleased, believing that all was turning out quite nicely, until months went by and her daughter had yet to conceive an heir to the crown.

When questioned, the princess explained that the prince had not asked for her since their wedding night. She stayed away because of his seeming illness, and then began to enjoy keeping to her own large, well-appointed bed. She had no desire to hound him for his attentions, happy as she was to be performing his duties in his absence.

Her mother boxed her ears thoroughly, and hissed that she needed to find her way back into the prince's bed, or she would not sit on the throne for much longer.

Servants in the palace were the first to talk, questioning the prince's health. Word was that he ate enough for two men, but rarely left his chambers, and showed no interest in his royal office. It had also become known that the prince did not seek his new bride's bedchamber. Seeing as the prince was hale and hearty before his wedding, this disinterest set many tongues wagging.

In time, the rumors worsened, and it was whispered that the prince was under an enchantment, kept in his room so that no one would see him wasting away while the princess stole the kingdom. The princess was called grasping, then barren, before finally the palace was full of whispers that she was a sorceress holding the prince under her spell.

The witch, upon hearing these rumors, flew into a rage. She determined that she would follow the prince, and see for herself who was laying an enchantment on him and endangering her daughter's hold on the crown.

That night, the prince was coaxed down to the dining hall by none other than the king himself. He ate little, spoke less, and sat with his eyes darting about the room. As soon as the king stood from his place at the table, the prince sprang to his feet and excused himself, claiming that he felt unwell.

The king looked saddened and did not challenge him, but the witch narrowed her eyes with suspicion.

When the prince mounted the stairs to his room, the witch gripped her daughter's elbow and tugged her into an alcove, whispering a plan. "I will follow him to his room and cast a spell to awaken his passion. When you enter a few moments later, he will be inflamed with desire and take you into his bed. We will repeat this each night until you are with child. If someone comes in to counter our spell, I will discover them."

The princess made an expression of distaste, but upon seeing the fierceness in her mother's eyes, she complied. Keeping a safe distance, the witch crept after the prince on silent feet. The prince, preoccupied with who would be waiting for him in his room, did not notice.

And so the witch, slipping through the door, beheld the prince embracing his birch maiden. She crouched behind the dressing table and peered at the lovers with fists curled like claws. An incantation manifested in her mind, and the pressure of casting in silence meant that she was still spinning the fabric of the curse when her daughter arrived.

The princess exclaimed in shock, which became a screech of fury as she flew across the room toward them.

The witch lost the words for her complicated spell and emerged from her hiding place, exasperated. A single sharp word stunned the prince where he stood, so that he dropped to the floor. The princess laid hands on Breza and began to yank out chunks of her shining dark hair, while the witch snatched a paring knife from a discarded tray on the nightstand. The two women fell upon Breza.

The prince lay at her feet, insensible.

The moon, gazing in the window, quickly withdrew her magic so that Breza's skin hardened to wood again. Her soft hair became leaves, and her kicking feet were tangled roots on the carpet. The witch and her daughter did not relent. Within minutes, the lovely girl intended for a prince was on the floor in a pile of broken branches, shreds of bark, and thick black sap that clung to her attackers' hands as they fled.

After a few minutes, the prince recovered from the spell and sat up, to find himself alone in the room with a devastated mess of wood and leaves. He had no memory of the assault, and was stricken to see his love in pieces. He gathered the shards into his arms, shouting for the palace guards.

When the guards arrived, they found their frantic prince holding a bundle of sticks. He raved about an intruder who stole into his room and destroyed his tree. The guards, puzzled, promised to search the palace and left the prince as he placed the pile of branches and roots into the large planter in the corner.

Moonlight caught the tears on his cheeks as he buried his love's remains, tenderly putting dirt over them. He begged and prayed in the empty room as he planted the branches which still retained leaves, placing them upright in the soil and bathing them in cool water. "I will save you," he whispered. "I will protect you. I will keep you with me. No one will ever hurt you again."

He only left his room to join the guards in their search. It proved to be fruitless, as the gates were locked and the doors were barred for the night. The witch and her daughter covertly washed the sap from their hands, scrubbing their hands raw when the stain would not fade.

———————◆———————

Breza lived in a world of pain. Neither a tree nor a woman, she felt every injury and wished only to retreat from it. The broken remnants of her outer shell were far too damaged, and her spirit could not bear it.

Luna bathed her in light, whispering words of encouragement. "Andrei loves you. He is fighting for you. It was good that you came to him."

"He could not protect me!" Breza cried. "He promised, and he failed."

A cloud drifted over the moon's face. "He was not at fault for this."

Breza, embittered, did not answer for a moment. "Perhaps. They transformed me, and would have left me there. I could have stayed a tree. I chose to be with him, and I paid this price. They took everything from me."

"Not everything," the moon whispered, and it was the rustle of the wind in the argent forest. "Your destiny will always be yours, unless you surrender it."

"I have no destiny! I was a turnip farmer's daughter. Then I was a birch tree. Now I am nothing." Breza curled upon herself and felt despair close in around her.

"The seers found you. They saw that you belonged with the prince. You were destined to rule," the moon said. "You think I offer my blessing to just any peasant girl? I was aiding the future queen."

Breza fought back her agony for a moment, trying to think clearly. "The queen?"

"Yes. The king sought a paragon. The prince's true love. A compassionate ruler. And the most powerful soothsayers in Karelia chose you."

"Chose... me." Something inside Breza began moving again, and she stretched out to feel the ends of her shattered wooden confines. Everything ached, but it lived. She could still inhabit it. A heat began to build at her core. "They chose me. I am the rightful princess. I was to be queen. I was born to stand at Andrei's side and rule this kingdom. I was born to love him and guide him and bear his children. It is my destiny."

"Unless you surrender it," Luna repeated.

The heat grew, and Breza reached for it, pressing it to her heart and letting it burn. "They have taken so much," she murmured, feeling the pain swell to anger. "I will not let them have it all."

Moonlight sparkled on the remnants of birch as a gentle shower began, soaking the soil around her. "Oh, no? What shall you do, little maiden tree?"

In answer, Breza unfurled roots to absorb the rainwater, and pulled every ounce of strength from her leaves. The twigs coalesced as one, and a tiny seedling began to grow. "I will keep my destiny. I will take back my prince. I will take back my kingdom."

The moon rejoiced, sending her rain through the night to feed her, until Solaro, the sun, could return and nourish her with his warmth. The mated pair watched and fed her for weeks, as she fought to live and return to her world.

———————◆———————

The witch and her daughter were unable to remove the black stains on their hands, and took to wearing gloves daily, regardless of the weather. The palace staff, already accustomed to gossiping about the two interlopers, seized upon this with suspicion. Rumors and theories continued to spread, breeding unrest in the capital and beyond.

The prince never ceased in his hunt for Breza's attackers. He mounted a search across the kingdom, fanning out from the isthmus and extending across the lakes, to the icy northern borders of Karelia. Andrei was awake again, his thirst for justice lighting a fire in him that nothing would quench. He spent his days on his horse, checking the tenants' farms and fishing hamlets for news of the palace intruder, taking notes on matters that his subjects wanted him to discuss with the king.

Following one particularly long journey, the prince reluctantly returned. The autumn wind had knives in it, and the threat of the first snowfall drove him home after many weeks away. He handed his father the extensive list of concerns and requests from around the kingdom, and fell into his bed in utter exhaustion. He did not notice the lovely young birch that once again flourished in his chambers.

Breza saw Andrei enter the room, and longed to reach for him. He looked so worn. But it was day, and Luna was too far away to help. She had no magic to take her true form.

Then she felt, through the sunlight on her leaves, the warrior Solaro. "Child, who fed you these months? Who warmed you and guided you upright? You have overcome much suffering, and shown great courage. Your strength is beyond that of other mortals, and this I must reward. I would accept you into my perennial court, to live for centuries under my light, but you foolishly wish to return to humanity. Take to your feet and go to him, if you find him worthy."

Breza felt dizzy as breath returned to her lungs. Her ears were deafened by the sound of a sudden heartbeat. Flesh once more, she basked in Solaro's warmth, her heart singing its gratitude.

Then her bare feet stepped out of the pot and carried her to the prince's bedside. She swept the white-blond hair from his brow, warming his skin with her fingertips.

He stirred immediately, turning his face into her palm. Eyes still closed, he reached for her. "My love," he whispered. "I knew you would return to me."

"I belong with you," she replied, and at last it was time to tell her secret. She quickly related the details of how the witch and her daughter captured her, transformed her to a birch tree, and made the daughter into Breza's likeness. "It is they who destroyed me. They saw us together, put you into a magical sleep, and tore me to pieces."

He pulled her to him. "Then, for their sakes, I hope they flee before I can find them."

Discovering them was not difficult. The princess and her mother were seated in the council chamber, listening to the royal advisors confer with the king. The prince came in without ceremony and confronted them both. He demanded that they remove their gloves, and when they reluctantly did so, the black stains on their hands gave truth to Breza's charges. "Seize them, for attempted murder of their future queen."

Guards apprehended the witch, but when they laid hands on the daughter, she shrieked in the way her subjects had come to abhor. "Do not touch me! I am the princess of this kingdom!"

"How can that be? For I am the princess," Breza said calmly.

"You are a pretender, trying to steal my crown," the daughter spat.

The prince placed his arm around Breza's waist. "I think I know my own wife."

The guards looked from one woman to the other: one scowling, radiating avarice and hauteur, the other sweet and lovely in the arms of their prince.

They carried the witch and her daughter away without another word, though the women clawed and kicked as they were escorted to the High Tower for questioning.

The kingdom's wisest mediums and soothsayers were called to the palace. They conferred on the identity of the true princess, and named Breza as the prince's intended bride. The witch and her daughter were banished from Karelia, their hands forever stained with the mark of their crimes. Breza and Andrei were married soon in a quiet ceremony, and the king was overjoyed to receive a new grandson and heir with the birth of spring.

The kingdom's new princess, blessed by the moon and honored by the sun, spent the rest of her mortal life at her husband's right hand. They ruled with wisdom and compassion for decades, as did their children after them. When Breza died, she returned to Solaro's court, to continue to serve her kingdom, and a ring of birches slowly grew around the royal palace.

Centuries later, when the birch queen was but a legend, a great fire swept the kingdom, devastating the forests. The birch trees withstood the fire, protecting the palace and surrounding farms from damage.

The birches watched over their land forever after.

BELOVED OF THE SUN

- C.L. McCollum -
Illustrated by Kym Schow

Once upon a time
there lived a woman wise,
who dwelled within the forests
of Rus' northern climes.

Her dearest friends were animals
and the brightness of the sky.
The stars and moon all knew her name
and spoke to her by and by.

But it was the sun above,
whose warmth caressed her face,
that stole her heart each precious dawn
and wrapped her in his rays' embrace.

As summer turned to fall
and his winter jounrey threatened,
she begged him to stay beside her,
but his grand progress beckoned.

As days grew cold, she was more alone,
and despaired for his return.
But on the darkest Solstice eve,
the fates granted her a boon.

Within her came a spark of heat,
and at her core, a child moved.
A miracle she could dream not ask,
but in this, his love was proved.

All through winter, the child did grow,
and she dreamed of flame and heat
and hoped for spring to hasten him home
so his child and he could meet.

On that first bright day of spring,
she lifted her face for his kiss,
and in the forest bore his child;
the daughter already her bliss.

Bright of hair and fair of feathers,
flame gave the girl her form.
And the woman smiled to see
the wonder she had borne.

The child took flight on wings of fire,
a gift of her father, the Sun.
The daughter's story would live on,
but the woman's now was done.

And the Petals Were Long Gone

- Mitchell Lehnert -
Illustrated by Katherine Guevara-Birmelin

Once upon a time, in a small home in the hills of the Europan countryside, lived three sisters. Their father, a merchant of various knickknacks and trinkets, left them for a month on a voyage across the solar system to sell his wares. Before he left, he asked the girls what they wanted as small gifts on his return.

The eldest, Elyzia, who had bright hair, bright eyes and milky white skin, asked for clothes, as she took care of her younger sister and never had a chance to shop for herself while caring for their home. The middle child, Meela, with dark hair, deep set shadowy eyes and olive skin, asked for jewelry, as she missed getting to wear all the extravagant rings and necklaces she remembered her grandmother wearing back on Earth. The youngest, Belle, with mousy hair, hazel eyes, and alabaster skin, did not want to be selfish and ask for such possessions. She instead asked for a rose, as she could never get any to grow in their garden on Europa.

Their father bid his daughters farewell and left in a hurry, embarking into the night sky in his sparkling space ship, the *Jeanne Ciel.*

It was almost two months before Elyzia began to worry. "Do you think he's forgotten about us?" she asked during dinner.

"Who knows?" Meela said. "I wouldn't put it past him."

"That's rude, Meela," said Elyzia, glaring at Meela.

"Oh and asking if he'd forgotten about us isn't?" Meela rolled her eyes.

"You two quit bickering. Father will come back; he always does." Belle smiled weakly and went back to cutting up the meat on her plate.

"I'm just saying, he hasn't been gone this long since Mom... It's already been two months, and I would like to go do something other than watch over you two." Elyzia sighed and picked up her tablet, flicking her fingers around until she was looking at pictures of her friends. "I'd like to have a life, too."

Meela sighed, "Whatever. You don't have to watch us. We're almost adults. Belle is turning eighteen next week and I'm already twenty. There is no reason you have to follow us around like a mother hen."

Elyzia winked at Meela, "I do when we have no ship or port to get us around. Not to mention; who else is going to make sure you're doing your studies for school?"

"Please. You know I'm doing it even without your bickering. And probably getting better grades than you ever did." Meela picked up her plate and stood dramatically, tossing her dish into the sink.

"Hey! These are mom's wedding china. Be careful!" Belle said frowning.

"Stop being so sensitive, Belle. They're old anyway." Meela looked around the house and flung her arms wide. "This entire house is just a ghost of Mom. It's like Dad doesn't even want to remember she died."

Belle's eyes welled up with tears, and Elyzia looked over at her, reaching out and grabbing her hand. "Don't listen to her."

Meela started down the hall toward her room. "Oh yeah, don't listen to me. The wicked sister! Blame everything on me."

Elyzia shouted so Meela could hear her, "No one is blaming you, Meela! You just don't take anyone's feelings into consideration, and it's rude!"

"Great. I'm not trying to help this family move on! Thanks, sis!" Meela slammed her door, making Belle jump.

Elyzia growled down the hall and looked back at Belle. "She's such a brat."

"Why do you stay here?" Belle asked.

"What?" Elyzia said.

"Why do you stay here with us? You're already an adult. You already have your schooling. You could get a job, and be on your own. You don't have to stay with us."

Elyzia frowned and sat down at the kitchen table with her sister. "Because I love my family. And it's not fair that father keeps leaving you two alone. Once he gets back, I'm moving to Nova."

Belle sighed, "You always say you're moving to Nova."

"But I mean it this time!" Elyzia said, putting her hands on the table.

"I just wish you wouldn't let us keep you tied down. Just go be free and explore the worlds. I know I would." Belle stared out the windows, picking up a small inhaler on the window seal and inhaling two puffs of vapor from it.

"And soon you will. Just focus on your studies. And you can go live anywhere you'd like." Elyzia kissed Belle on the forehead and went to her room.

Belle spent all evening staring out the window of the kitchen, waiting for her father. Her eyelids grew heavy and her focus began to wane. Even the brilliant glow of Jupiter in the sky could not keep her attention before the gentle waves of sleep took her.

Belle dreamt of a brilliant world, filled with roses and birds; a beautiful field and grass in colors she never dreamed grass could be. It wasn't until Belle felt the vibration of the ship's entry jets outside that she awoke from a world that smelt like orange marmalade.

The *Jeanne Ciel.*

Belle snapped back and looked at the bright lights shining through the window. "He's back!" She jumped up and ran out the back door.

The *Jeanne Ciel* touched down gracefully. Belle waited for it to complete the landing sequence. Jets and exhausts hissed and coughed, and she watched the flickering of lights in a uniform pattern she was all too familiar with.

The bay door roared, and the hydraulics clicked as the pressure released.

Belle worked her way around to the ramp as it gently pressed into the ground. She smiled in the bright Jovian light but no one came out of the ship.

"Father! We're so glad you're back!" Belle called out.

Nothing but the sound of cooling metals filled the air around her.

"Father?" Belle looked up into the ship. There were lights flashing and blinking in their usual process after entering the atmosphere and landing, but no sign of her father coming out of either the bridge or the living quarters into the cargo bay.

"Hello?" An uncomfortable knot twisted and pulled at Belle. She followed the uneasiness into the ship.

The cargo bay was empty. All her father's products were gone. The boxes were empty, and there was no sign of his most recent products.

"*Jeanne Ciel?*"

There was a flash of pale blue light and a small holographic panel appeared in front of her face.

"Hello, Belle."

"Hello, Jeanne. Where is my father?" Belle looked over the panel. She didn't know much about the controls that appeared in front of her. Her father had tried to teach her many times how to control the ship using the panel, but Belle was never interested, not when the ship's AI could handle all commands. It was safer than her pressing something she wasn't supposed to. Not like the one time she almost flew the ship into the gravity well of Jupiter and nearly crashed into the gas giant.

"Your father is not on the ship. He sent a remote command for the ship to return back to Europa." *Jeanne Ciel's* AI spoke with a cool female voice. Regardless of the AI's calm demeanor, Belle felt the knot in her stomach expand and explode into fear.

"What do you mean he's not on the ship?" Belle flicked through the control panel, looking for the flight record or any sort of coordinates she recognized.

"Your father is not on the ship; his exact location is not known. He is too far for my system to locate his coordinates for pull."

Belle was lost within the internal computer of the ship. She checked the current fluid status and flicked her fingers to reset the commands back to the home screen. She realized that the *Jeanne Ciel's* AI was very specific when it came to answering questions. Taking a moment, she collected her thoughts and rephrased her question.

"What was my father's last recorded location?"

"His last known location was on the ship, *Étoile Filante*. Belle, you cannot access your father's personal logs. I will return you to the Home screen."

Belle exhaled loudly. She attempted to enter the restricted space in the ship's control, but the panel flicked back to the home screen. Maybe there was another way around it?

"*Roses are red.*" She whispered. Belle felt a vibration in her wrist from her reactive implant's keywords. Most everyone had a reactive implant that allowed them to connect with various networks. It was how the *Jeanne Ciel* recognized her. They were also used to browse the internet without having to have a device, use virtual reality devices and make other technologies in the world sync up to a person's individual preferences.

After she issued the command, Belle saw virtual rose petals fall out of the sky. Each one glowed a pale red. In front of her a much larger control panel appeared. None of this was holographic, instead her reactive implant pushed visual signals directly into her mind. No one else could see what she saw.

She stepped forward and raised her hands, browsing through the various menus. She tried to remember how to contact her father through it. He was not very good with his reactive implant and preferred to communicate through holographic or his tablet. Belle tapped her chin and flicked through the menus. She found her contacts, then her father's profile, and then saw nothing. He had his implant turned off, as usual. But it was worth a shot.

"*Violets are blue.*" Belle said. The rose petals around her faded away as her reactive implant vibrated to signal it was being booted off. "*Jeanne Ciel*, I am going back into our house and will return for more information. Please do not lock the ship when I exit and wait for my return for further instruction."

"Understood."

The panel vanished as Belle whipped around, running out of the cargo hold and down the exit ramp of the ship.

"Meela! Elyzia!" Belle screamed as she ran through the house.

Both her sisters darted out of their rooms.

"Belle? What's wrong?" Elyzia grabbed Belle's hand.

"What's happening?" Meela yawned. "Are you crying?"

Belle glared at her sister. "Yes. Father's ship is back, but he isn't. *Jeanne Ciel* told me he was on another ship or something. Come on!"

"Wait, what do you mean... Belle!"

Before Elyzia could say another word, Belle was out the door and running back to the ship.

"Why would the ship come back without you?" Belle thought out loud as she ran back up the entrance ramp to the ship.

"Welcome back, Belle," the ship's AI greeted her with a pleasant hum.

"Hi. Did my father leave anything else for us? Some information or clues or whose ship that was?" Belle looked through the empty boxes of the ship for something. A note, a receipt of purchase, maybe an item she had overlooked.

"Your father left three gifts on the bridge."

Belle stopped and looked over toward the door to the main control room as her two sisters ran in.

"Belle!"

"He still sent our presents. Like he said he would." Belle, without looking at her sisters, ran to the door to the bridge. The room was small with the main control panel and various smaller screens that flashed ship information and statistics. The LEDs that lit the room were varying shades of blue and red. Across the floor, an assortment of pathways were illuminated with a soft white strip of light, and on the ceiling above was a dome that contained the ship's computer core where lights danced across the glass, alternating between hues that reminded Belle of a sunset on Earth.

Three oversized plush chairs sat in the center of the room, with the control panels in front of them. On the center panel were two perfectly wrapped boxes, and a rose tied with a red bow.

"Why?" Belle said, staring at them in awe.

"Why what?" Elyzia was standing behind her, with her arms crossed, a frown on her face.

"Belle! Where is Dad?" Meela said, walking into the room. "Ooh, are those ours?"

Meela smiled and walked past Belle and went straight for the gift in front of her.

There was silence except for the ripping of wrapping paper.

"Are you kidding me?" Belle protested.

Meela turned around, pulling a golden necklace out, admiring the sparkling gem hanging from the chain. "Right? Neptunian diamonds. How did he get a hold of one of these?"

"No. Meela. Our father is missing, and you are so self-absorbed that all you can care about is a piece of jewelry?" Belle looked at the ground, her hands clenched into fists as she felt tears falling from her cheeks and onto the metal floor below.

"What? What do you mean he's missing?"

"You are the most selfish little jerk!" Belle ran forward and grabbed the necklace out of Meela's hand.

"Hey! That's mine!"

"You don't deserve this. You don't deserve any of us. Get out. GET OUT!" Belle screamed, running into the cargo bay and throwing the necklace out.

"Okay, princess. God!" Meela ran after the necklace and left the ship.

Elyzia walked up, holding her gift in hand and Belle's.

"Here." Elyzia handed Belle the rose. It was dipped in a thin coat of preservation resin that was hardly noticeable, except for tiny specks that looked like fresh morning dew.

Belle grabbed the rose and held it tightly in her hands. The stem was filed down perfectly with no signs of where the thorns had been. "There aren't any thorns. Don't roses have thorns?"

"Father was always trying to protect you, even when you were a baby. You were so sick then, and I don't think he ever got over it." Elyzia shrugged and looked around the ship, "Wherever he is, he should come back soon. Don't worry about him. He probably just wanted to get us our gifts. *The voice of the sea.*"

Belle heard Elyzia's reactive implant vibrate. "I already tried. He isn't there."

Elyzia sighed, "I figure I'd try. *Speaks to the soul.* Well let's see what the ship knows. *Jeanne Ciel?*"

A control panel appeared in front of Elyzia, who navigated it with ease. "Hello, Elyzia."

"Please estimate your trajectory from your last ported location before your arrival on Europa." Elyzia reached up and grabbed the corners of the holographic screen with both hands, stretching it out till it was almost three times its normal size.

The ship showed Europa, then Jupiter, and then zoomed out farther.

"*Jeanne Ciel*'s last known ported location was with the ship, *Étoile Filante* within the Kuiper Belt, approximately 2.37532167 AU from Pluto's orbital position of Earth date March 6th, 2201, 14:37 GMT." *Jeanne Ciel* paused as the map showed the ship's course with the *Étoile Filante*, which was marked with a nine pointed star symbol that Belle had never seen before.

"Okay." Elyzia chewed on her tongue as she thought.

"*Jeanne Ciel*, can you estimate the *Étoile Filante's* current position based on its previous location and trajectory?" Belle asked.

The ship AI processed for a moment and then spoke again, "Based on the *Étoile Filante*'s previous movement, its current location is likely…"

Jeanne Ciel stuttered and the lights on the ships dimmed.

Belle looked to Elyzia. "*Jeanne Ciel?*"

The control panel flickered a few times and was replaced with a large black square. A pair of red eyes appeared, and a voice roared through the speaker system of the ship.

"Greetings." The voice made the hair on Belle's neck stand straight up. "This message is to the poisoned brats who find the *Jeanne Ciel*. Your father has been taken by my ship for his recklessness and thievery. The ship has been returned to you as a peace offering, but your father will not. I have implanted a virus within the ship's AI that will prevent you from locating the *Étoile Filante*. Move on with your lives and—"

"Girls! Don't come! I'm fi—"

"Restrain the human." The dark voice broke calmly over that of their father. There was muffled struggling and then a loud crash.

"As he said," the voice continued, "your father is now under my jurisdiction and will be imprisoned for his crimes. Do not come searching for us, or you will find yourself in the same prison as your father."

The voice faded away into thick laughter that reverberated around the metal panels.

The control panel hummed back to its normal configuration, and the three stared at one another. Belle felt the exploding fear return to a knot in her stomach. It was the eyes. The pure madness in them and how they darted back and forth, not directly looking into the eye of the camera.

"Was he even… human?" Belle whimpered.

"I… I don't know." Elyzia's eyes filled, but tears did not fall down her cheeks.

"Are there aliens?" Belle asked.

Elyzia looked at her sister and tried to talk but nothing came out. She took a deep breath and shook her head. "I don't know."

Belle had never seen her sister so clueless. She always knew what to say, even if she was unsure. Coming up with a plan was her strong point. She was the rock that held her family together. If anything scared her more than the creature that peered at them through the video, it was seeing Elyzia completely unsure of herself.

"We have to go find him," Belle said.

"I don't think that's a good idea," Elyzia said.

"But if he's there! With that… that thing! We can't just leave him." Belle felt her chest start to burn. She took a few deep breaths and tried to calm herself.

"Belle, we can't. We…" She looked back at the control panel and the trajectory of the *Jeanne Ciel* and that back to your sister. "Are you sure?"

Belle gave a thinly veiled smile. "No. But we have to save him."

"It could be dangerous. That monster looked… its eyes…" Elyzia tried to find the words.

"Vicious. I know. But that's why we have to go." Belle reached out for her sister's hand.

"You're right. Let's go." Elyzia waved her hand to vanish the panel and grabbed her sister's hand, squeezing it and smiling.

The two set off to begin the take off sequences for the ship.

"The ship's food replication should last us for a three month voyage." Belle was on a large panel on the left wall of the ship, flicking through the checklist of supplies and replaceable equipment the ship might need.

"How is air and water filtration?" Elyzia asked as she logged into her own account on the *Jeanne Ciel*. The ship's panels quickly re-adjusted to her personal settings, and the LEDs around the bridge changed colors to a deep purples and light blues.

Belle tilted her head and shook her hand a little. "Water looks like it could last us two months, air about three. If we can stop on our way, we should replace both filters."

"Waste management is good, too?" Elyzia was already plotting a course to the Kuiper belt and calculating.

"Yup!" Belle finalized her check list on the panel and looked over to Elyzia, smiling. "I thought for a second that I'd have to go alone."

Elyzia stopped her work and turned around smiling. "You think I'd let you go alone? You're crazy. Go check the cargo bay and secure what needs to be secured. Check to make sure the living quarters aren't a mess, either. You know how Dad gets."

Belle nodded and ran out of the bridge. The cargo bay was mostly empty boxes and containers, except one crate labeled 'Trinkets.' It was all tightly secured for zero gravity conditions. She ran past the cargo and to the small lift that led to the living quarters. She pressed a few buttons on the circular pad. The gate in front of the pad dropped, locking in place to prevent anyone from stepping on mid-lift. Belle felt herself vanish. For a moment she was nowhere but in between. Like a moment between being awake and asleep. After a split second, she materialized into the lift pad on the top level of the ship.

Belle was surprised at how clean it was once she arrived. The 'living room' was spotless. All the entertainment devices were neatly packed, and the books and periodicals that their father loved so much were all in their appropriate containers. Even the virtual reality unit was perfectly packed with all sensors and cords tightly wound.

Belle shrugged and moved onto the kitchen and dining area which was also immaculate. No dirty dishes, the usual trash had already been placed in the waste receptacle which had already been emptied.

"*Jeanne Ciel*?" The holographic panel appeared in front of her. It was no longer the deep blue as it was before, but now vibrated through various shades of purple.

"Hello, Belle," the AI responded from the overhead speakers.

"Who cleaned the living quarters?" Belle moved into the bedroom. The four small single sized beds were tucked away, and there were no clothes strewn about the floor.

"The living quarters were cleaned before the departure from the *Étoile Filante*."

"By who?" Belle asked again.

"The living quarters were cleaned before the departure from the *Étoile Filante*," the AI repeated.

Belle frowned and waved her hand, dismissing the control panel and the AI. The virus was still implanted. There was no way she'd get any answers until she or her sisters were able to remove it.

As she pulled out each bed, she noticed they had already been cleaned and made. The sheets were pristine and the corners of the thick comforters tucked in a uniform manner.

"*Jeanne Ciel*?" the panel quickly reappeared in front of her.

"Yes, Belle?"

"Is there anyone else on this ship besides me and my sisters?" Belle held her breath.

"No. There are only two reported life forms on the ship currently."

"Oh, thank goodness. Just checking." She waved her hand and pushed the beds back into their compartments.

The bathroom was also clean, as though someone had scrubbed it until it sparkled.

Belle walked back out into the living room and turned around, staring at the living quarters, tapping her fingernails against the bar that separated the kitchen from where she stood.

What caught her interest was a silver tray in the kitchen, with large cover. Belle raised her eyebrow and walked toward it. There was a small flower, one she had never seen before, next to the covering, on top of a lacy napkin. Belle put her hand on top of the covering and took a deep breath. She lifted it up and on the center of the plate was a bloodied finger with her father's wedding ring still on it, with a note that read, "Do not come for the rest."

Belle screamed and dropped the covering. She rushed back to the lift and made her way back to the cargo bay.

At the entrance of the *Jeanne Ciel* was Meela, carrying three large bags.

"Meela." Belle sobbed and unlocked the safety gate to the lift and approaching her sister and wrapping her arms around her.

"I know. It's okay." Meela dropped the bags and hugged her sister tightly. "I heard the message. We're going to find him."

"No. Meela. His... his finger." Belle quickly explained what she'd seen, choking back her tears.

Meela did not cry; she did nothing but listen to her sister tell her what she found in the living quarters. She nodded and smiled, holding strong. "I'll take care of it. Don't think about that. If we're going to save Dad, we need to bring some stuff with us." She motioned to the bags on the ground, "You need your medicine; Elyzia needs some clothes to change into; I need to bring my study equipment. And there is no way we can make it to the Kuiper belt without some entertainment. Dad's VR is so outdated."

"I'm so sorry that we got mad at you." Belle wiped away the tears streaming down her face and hugged her sister again, tightly.

"No. Belle." Meela pulled her sister off and grabbed her by the shoulders. "I'm a jerk. Dad works hard for us; Elyzia sacrificed everything to watch us. It's fine. We need to find Dad. He deserves that much." Meela hushed her voice. "You know Elyzia got a job in New Rome a year ago and turned it down?"

"What?" Belle felt her tears retreat.

"Yeah, she turned it down because Father was going on that trip to Tau Ceti and was going to be gone for six months. She knew that I wasn't going to do a great job of watching over you, especially in your last year of primary school." Meela smiled a smile that Belle knew well, an easy grin that hid a frown.

"I can't believe that. Elyzia always talks about wanting to get out, to be free. Why does everyone think that I need so much attention all the time? I'm fine being alone. When I get done with my studies, I'm going to be out on my own and take care of myself." Belle smiled, clearing the tears that were left in her eyes with the sleeve of her shirt.

Meela pushed a loose strand of thick brown hair behind Belle's ear. "I know you will."

"Belle, did you—Oh, Meela. I take it you're coming with us?" Elyzia walked out of the bridge with a control panel hovering next to her.

"Yeah, I heard everything; I already packed us all up. Good thing you're organized." Meela smiled and motioned to the three bags at her feet.

"Did you pack Belle's medication? Clothes? Toothbrushes? Credit cards?"

"Of course I did. I packed everything we need. If you want to be our overbearing captain for this voyage, go crazy and go through what I packed to make sure." Meela picked up one of the bags and walked to the lift. "I'm going to unpack my things."

The lift gate locked, and she vanished out of sight.

Elyzia grumbled to herself. "I should make a checklist first to make sure we have everything we'll need."

"I can check everything," Belle said.

"I'll do it. Did you check the living quarters? Everything okay?" Elyzia asked, pushing her control panel out of the way while she unzipped the purple bag with her name embroidered on it.

Belle felt her throat close up. "Dad." She swallowed hard. "I found Dad's finger."

"What?" Elyzia asked.

"Whoever took Dad... they left a note and his—his finger."

Elyzia looked past Belle at the walls of the ship, deep in thought. She chewed on her bottom lip for a few moments and then nodded. "That's why we have to go. Was there anything else strange?"

Belle inhaled deeply and pushed the memory out of her mind. "Yes. It was very clean."

"How clean? Like Dad clean or us clean?" Elyzia asked, not looking up.

"No, like, really clean. Imagine if you were given a week to clean because Meemaw and Pops were coming to visit from Earth." Belle unzipped her own bag, and was glad to see her medication right on top along with her personal tablet and three of her favorite books.

"Dad wouldn't have cleaned. Maybe he hasn't been using the living quarters. Sometimes he'll just pass out in the bridge or put himself in cryo down below if he doesn't feel like dealing with the trip." Elyzia replied.

"There is no way. Dad would have at least used the bathroom or the VR for a day or two. He always does. The VR machine was put away. The bathroom looks like someone scrubbed it, and the waste receptacle had already been emptied." Belle finished looking through her bag and zipped it up, throwing it over her shoulder.

"That is strange. I'll take a look at it. *Jeanne Ciel?*"

"Yes, Elyzia?" the AI chimed.

"Please begin a full diagnostic check. I'd like you to shutdown and boot into mode Elyzia after you've completed, authorization Elyzia omega four three seven." She placed her hand on the control panel which flashed a bright white light around her hand, before reverting back to purple.

"Authorization accepted. Diagnostic test will begin in twenty seconds. Estimated run time, five minutes. *Jeanne Ciel* AI will be temporarily unavailable during Diagnostic and reboot process. Do you wish to continue?"

"Yes." Elyzia walked over to the lift with her bag. "Go double check the house, turn off all the electronics, and lock up. Send a message to the Youngs down the road so they know we're going to be off world and to watch the house. Oh, and turn on Betty so she can feed the animals."

"Okay!" Belle walked out of the *Jeanne Ciel* as her sister vanished up the lift.

It took only a few minutes for Belle to scan their home and all its rooms for items they might need. She grabbed her favorite pillow, Meela's silk robe she liked to wear before bed, and Elyzia's personal tablet. She threw them all into a canvas bag and went to the back of the house. Next to a small shed was a tall cylindrical tube with a small glowing panel next to it.

"Betty?"

The glowing panel projected out, similar to the way *Jeanne Ciel* projected out its controls. Betty's panel glowed blue, and a cheerful voice replied, "Hello, Belle. How can I be of assistance?"

"We are going off planet for an undetermined amount of time. Please enter 'Caretaker' status." Belle scrolled through the holographic panel, checking various settings and making sure that Betty was fully operational.

"My records show that the chickens will require additional feed in thirty six days. Shall I order more?" The tube opened up, and a robotic creature rolled out. It had many appendages with various tools attached to them. Its height adjusted to match Belle.

The lights around Betty adjusted to a much duller shine to fit the time of day. Belle looked up and watched Betty run through her personal diagnostic.

"Yes, that's fine. Use the family's credit account. Send the *Jeanne Ciel* a notification when any purchases have been made."

Betty processed the information and dinged, rolling back into her tube. "My records show it is still the early time before our orbit reaches stabilized sunlight. Duties will begin in five earth hours and twenty seven earth minutes."

Belle smiled and waved away the small control panel. She turned on her heel with the canvas bag over her shoulder and her pillow under arm and rushed back to the *Jeanne Ciel*.

The ship lit up brighter than before as it was preparing for takeoff. Valves and exhausts hissed and expelled fumes preparing for its departure. Belle walked up the ramp and looked back, staring at her home. Her father would be so proud of his daughters.

"Don't forget to call the neighbors!" Elyzia yelled from the open bridge door.

"Oh yeah!"

"The virus should be gone," Meela said as she walked past Belle in the cargo bay.

"What! How?" Elyzia asked.

"Eh, it was just hiding in some encrypted folders that Dad stores his inventory lists in. It was actually stupid easy; I'm surprised you couldn't find it. I also beefed up the firewall to prevent them from injecting *Jeanne Ciel* again." Meela waved her hands, and her personal control panel, which had been adjusted to her personal settings and was now a rich gold color, vanished.

"Nice! You're so smart, Meela." Belle clapped as she headed to the lift to retrieve her tablet in order to send their neighbors a message.

Meela winked and joined Elyzia in the Bridge.

Belle's tablet was in a drawer next to the bed she had been assigned. Her name glowed in the panel above it in pink letters. Belle quickly typed up a message to their closest neighbors, informing them of their absence, but advising them not to worry since Betty would be caring for all the chores and animals. She added that if they could please just keep an eye on the place, she'd greatly appreciate it.

"Belle," *Jeanne Ciel* chimed calmly, and a pale pink panel appeared in front of her. Belle smiled, knowing that Meela had taken the time to customize it for her.

"Yes, *Jeanne Ciel*?" Belle sent the message and placed her tablet back in the drawer, turning her attention to the panel.

"Meela and Elyzia are about to initiate take off. Would you prefer to be in the bridge or in the living quarters?"

"I'll get to the bridge!" Belle quickly walked to the lift which rushed her back to the cargo bay. The large door was now shut, with the secondary entry way sealed tight with a red locked symbol on the center.

Belle walked into the bridge, and the door shut behind her. Elyzia was in the center chair, with Meela to her left. Belle to the last chair to Elyzia's right and sat down. She strapped herself in and then flicked her control panel so it ran into the large screen in front of her. It expanded into a much wider screen, the same as her two sisters.

"Ready?" Elyzia said with hesitation in her voice.

"Yup." Meela nodded.

"Ready!" Belle said.

———— ◆ ————

The journey from Europa to the Kuiper belt took over two weeks. In that time, the sisters had been through at least six fights, Meela had locked Elyzia out of the living quarters twice, Elyzia had programmed *Jeanne Ciel* to call Meela 'Buttface,' and Belle had threatened to throw both of them into an escape pod and send them to Pluto if they didn't stop.

But in that time they had also shared so much about themselves with one another and cried together that Belle couldn't help but feel like she had grown even closer with her sisters.

"How much longer do you think, until we reach the ship?" Meela asked as the group finished watching a movie in the living room.

"I'm sure the ship will tell us whenever we reach it. It should be sometime today." Elyzia sighed, standing up and stretching from the long couch.

"Ugh. I just want to find Dad and get back home. Not that I haven't *loved* this sisterly bonding." Meela immediately flopped over so she could lay down where Elyzia was sitting.

"*Jeanne Ciel*?" Belle asked.

"Yes, Belle?"

"Based on your trajectory, how much longer until we reach the *Étoile Filante*?" Belle asked, as she shoved the last handful of popcorn from her bowl into her mouth.

"Estimations show that we should reach its estimate coordinates in twenty minutes."

Belle felt a knot in her stomach appear. "Is anyone else getting nervous?"

"Yes," Meela said frankly. "I've been nervous since we reached the Kuiper belt."

Elyzia smiled at her sisters, crossing her legs. "It's going to be fine. We'll be able to pull Dad right out and get back home before you know it."

"Are you sure?" Meela asked.

"No. She isn't," Belle said.

The overhead LEDs began to flash red. "Already?" Meela sat up.

"I have detected the *Étoile Filante*," The AI said.

They felt the ship groan as it fell out of dive, and the girls ran to the lift, appearing in the cargo bay. They rushed to the bridge, all three trying to fit through the door at once, and stared past the three dimly lit control panels.

"*Jeanne Ciel*," Elyzia said.

"Yes, Elyzia?"

"Please display the *Étoile Filante*."

The large false window which displayed the outside of the ship, zoomed in ahead of them. They were passing a large asteroid and around the back side, as it spun infinitely through space was a large deep blue ship. Across it was an antique shooting star painted on the side, which looked as though it had seen better days.

"*Jeanne Ciel*," Meela called to the ship, her control panel appearing. She flicked through various windows and walls of coded text in a matter of seconds.

"Yes, Meela?"

"I need you to activate the lift. Pull Dad into our ship from his current location." Meela threw her control panel at the windowed display. It zoomed even closer to the *Étoile Filante*, and a small circle appeared and began to spin around the ship, searching for their father's location.

"I am unable to comply. The *Étoile Filante*'s firewall prevents anyone from being pulled via lift technology. However, it is possible to launch into the *Étoile Filante*," the AI said.

"Okay. Launch me inside." Belle said, rushing back to the lift.

"Woah! We can't just throw you inside the ship, Belle. Besides, I should go," Meela said, following behind her sister.

"What makes you think you can go?" Elyzia crossed her arms.

"Well, I'm the crazy sister so I should do the crazy thing. That's sound logic, right?" Meela ran over to the lift pad and stood on it, staring at her sisters.

"No way. I'm the eldest; I'm going." Elyzia walked over and tried to pull Meela off.

"You can't use that excuse anymore!" Meela went to grab the gate closed but grabbed Elyzia's long braid in the process.

"Ow! Did you just pull my hair?" Elyzia gasped, reaching for her scalp.

"It was an accident!" Meela frowned.

"Oh I'm so sure. You are such a brat!" Elyzia and Meela started to grapple with one another, hands clasped, trying to push or pull the either.

"Stop!" Belle shouted. "This is ridiculous. Dad is trapped on this ship with some... monster. Ugh. Why didn't we call the authorities?"

"Because Dad is a smuggler, Belle." Meela grunted, still trying to push Elyzia off the lift. "Stop!"

"You stop! I should go! Dad only trusts me!" Elyzia said.

"So? Have you helped him run before? No. You haven't. Have you had to work a job with him? Lie to drug lords right in their faces? I didn't think so. I did. I did it all, because why would he want to taint pure Elyzia and Belle." Meela finally pushed Elyzia off the lift pad and grunted loudly.

Belle felt her fears started to push her over the edge. She gasped for air as she tried to push the tears back inside. Hadn't she cried enough? She sat down on the cargo bay floor and let her anger flow freely.

"Belle..." Elyzia started.

"No," Belle interrupted her sister as the two stopped fighting. "I'm done. I'm done with the two of you fighting with each other. We're sisters. We're adults now, not kids. There is no reason for this." She pounded her fist down on the ground. "Dad trusts all of us, Meela. He trusts you with work. He trusts Elyzia with taking care of all of us. Who knows how many other pieces of Dad are already missing. For all we know he could dead, and this is for nothing."

"You go," Meela said softly.

"What? No! She's sick!" Elyzia stepped off the lift and squatted down by Belle.

"She's not weak. She's stronger than both of us. She's the one Dad trusts to hold this family together. If anyone is going to get him, it's Belle. Not us." Meela stepped forward. "*Jeanne Ciel.*" The control panel appeared. "I need you to launch Belle into that ship, preferably where Dad is."

"I am unable to locate your father; however, based on our previous encounter with the *Étoile Filante,* I can place her location in the dining hall of the ship, which was your father's last known location."

The lift lit up and Belle stood up.

"Are... are you sure?" she looked over to Meela and then to Elyzia.

"Find an escape pod and launch yourself out. We'll pick you up as soon as we can." Elyzia smiled and took a step back.

"I can do this," Belle said, hugging both her sisters quickly and then jumping onto the lift.

Belle had been launched plenty of times before. Using the lift from the various sections of the *Jeanne Ciel* was one thing, but being launched through space was something else entirely. She felt herself in space, floating for a moment. Some people liked to say there was more in the time when you are nothing but molecules. That you were closer to the Universe as a being. That you were experiencing the beginning of what was, your own personal big bang. Belle felt bound to it, to the stars, to the void. She could see nothing and everything in that few seconds. She was thoughts, an idea, a person smashed to pieces. She tried to smile but realized she had nothing to smile. And before she could figure out how to show her emotions as a series of atoms, it was over.

She felt an eerie rush as her body reformed on the *Étoile Filante*. A chill ran down her spine as she regained control of herself. It was dark, very dark. Dim track lights ran the floor to show the pathways, but there were no overhead lights.

The dining hall was completely empty. The tables were all pushed together and set formally with a series of forks and spoons on each side of decorative dinner plates.

Belle looked over them and raised an eyebrow, confused at why someone would use fine china on what was more than likely a scientific study ship.

There was something covering the floors, which seemed to catch the light as she moved. Belle bit her bottom lip and thought for a moment. Would her reactive implant connect with the *Étoile Filante*? She hoped maybe her link to the *Jeanne Ciel* was still not lost. If it wasn't, maybe could find her father on the *Étoile Filante*'s network.

"*Roses are red.*" She felt a small vibration in her wrist and saw petals appear on the dark floor. They glowed dimly. She flicked through the settings to the wireless connection option. She saw the *Étoile Filante*'s network. It was possible that it could fry her reactive implant or, if it was infected, it could cause another slew of problems that could reach her visual cortex and make her see a million kinds of things. She felt like she was burning in fire, drowning in water, covered in thousands of space cockroaches. It was a chance she had to risk. If it meant finding her father, she could take whatever this network could throw at her. She just hoped Elyzia's firewalls held. She reached up and clicked on it.

A small hourglass appeared in front of her, flipping up and down with small pink crystals falling through it instead of sand. Belle watched it fell quickly from one end, flipping over and over until it flashed a small 'Connected' notification.

Belle flinched and waited. But nothing happened. It simply welcomed her to the Titanian Deep Space Research Vessel of the French Republic, *Étoile Filante*.

"Oh. That's good," she whispered to herself.

She checked the ship's registry and found her father's name right at the top; it listed him as "Guest" and noted his current location as "Guest Quarters C on Deck Four." Belle looked down the list of other passengers. There were dozens, with at least fifty listed with their location as "Cryo" with a small vitals status of: "Alive." Two of these passengers were listed as "Non-responsive." The last person on the list was Captain Rodolphe Dupont with a location of "Bridge" and his status as "Unknown."

Belle quickly closed out of the passenger registry and pulled up a map of the ship and started to walk.

The ship was massive. Belle figured with a crew of fifty it might be pretty large, but she had severely underestimated the size from her first viewing of the outside. She couldn't tell much of its condition, in the low light of the corridors. She was sure at least fifty *Jeanne Ciel*'s could fit inside this ship.

She stopped and looked to the directions guiding her. It looked like the ship worked via lift, similar to the *Jeanne Ciel*. But she didn't want to risk using them. If she was being monitored, it would be very simple for a tapered lift to trap her molecules somewhere until whoever was running this ship decided to free her.

Belle quickly pulled back her command screen and looked for the closest stairwell. While they were hardly used, every ship had to have one for emergencies.

There was one at the end of the hall. She started to jog. If she could just make it up two floors, then she would reach the guest quarters.

She pushed against the door that the map labeled as the entrance to the stairs and felt it easily pop open. She was home free, until the alarm that the stairs had been opened started to go off.

"Really?" Belle said loudly over the shrill sirens and flashing red lights over head. She realized that she had triggered an evacuation alarm by opening the door. She went into the stairwell and up the stairs. The track lights on each step remained on solid as lights above her spun with the obnoxious screech.

As she reached the fourth deck and opened the door, the alarm turned off.

She heard voices from the stairwell below. "Who would have set off the alarms?" the voice was deep and more annoyed than curious.

"I'm not sure, but we'll need to figure it out or else the Captain will shut another one of us down," a higher pitched tone replied.

Belle grabbed the door and slowly slid it back into place, instead of letting it free fall back into the frame.

She started to run. The ship's floor was an overly plush carpet that absorbed the sound of her feet. She thanked whoever designed the ship in her mind as she sprinted down the hall to her left and down a small half stair.

The door to her father's room was marked, as the registry said it was, "Guest Quarters C." She tried the doorknob and felt it was unlocked.

"Dad! It's me, it's Belle. I'm here to—"

The smell was perhaps worse than the sight. He had probably been dead a few weeks, but he looked peaceful. His neck had been snapped, and his head hung awkward and unnatural on his shoulders. His eyes had been closed, but his mouth was still gaping open, his tongue crusted over, and long since dried. His boy was slumped in a square arm chair. His hands placed on his lap, crossed over one another.

Belle wanted to scream. Wanted nothing more than to get away from that room, crawl out of her skin and out into the openness of space, let the void embrace her entirely. But she couldn't. She couldn't find the words or remember how to make sounds.

There was a noise behind her; she turned, tears flooding from her face. Two androids smiled at her with holographic faces. Belle tried felt the urge to run and tried to get away but one reached up and tapped her forehead with a device coming out of his finger before she could do much of anything.

Everything went black.

The void around her seemed to linger much longer than it did when she was launched into the *Étoile Filante*. She felt dizzy, confused. It was like her entire body had been rendered completely useless. She heard voices in this void. They spoke in hushed whispers.

"Do you think it is the daughter of the merchant?" one with a thick French accent asked.

"Well, of course she is," a much kinder feminine voice replied.

"The Master said that his daughters would not come," squealed a high-pitched voice.

"The Master also said we'd all be booted back to our bodies by now. But that virus hasn't let go of the ship yet," the female voice replied.

"Or let go of The Master," the thick French accent added.

"Can you blame him? We've been like this for... what... thirteen years?" a very deep voice said.

"Has it really been thirteen years?" the female voice drifted.

"I miss being human," the high pitch voice sighed.

"We all do. The Master most of all." The high pitch voice said quickly.

153

"We will never be human again."

Belle recognized the last voice and felt her heart beat increase. She still couldn't move. Silence lingered until she felt another shock similar to the one that had immobilized her before.

She opened her eyes and looked up. In front of her were five androids, all staring at her. Their heads were nothing but screens of eyes and mouths. Some had more eyes than others, but they all looked at her, gazing in curiosity at her.

"Back away from her." She remembered again the deep voice and felt herself trying to scream, but there was something around her chin keeping her mouth shut.

"Brave daughter tries to save her father. I admit your attempt was amusing. If he was alive, you might have made it out, even with tripping the alarm system." The creature that stood before her was dripping with mucus as it stepped into the light.

Horrible sores covered his body, which might have once been human. His arms and legs looked swollen. The skin stretched too far. Belle thought she was looking directly at exposed muscle but she couldn't be sure. Wild hair flowed down from the top of his head, and jutting out of his forehead were three strange horns, twisting like a ram's. His mouth was wide, and his teeth oversized. He wore a traditional white and blue captain's uniform like those she had seen on Earth, but it was ripped to shreds, his boiled skin exposed from almost every angle.

He stomped closer to her, his feet cloven and bursting out of leather boots, and the androids stepped away with spider-like legs.

"Belle. What a pretty name," he said with a smile.

Belle said nothing, not only because she couldn't, but because she was paralyzed by the sight of the beast.

"Do I frighten you?"

The androids stepped back further.

Belle nodded.

"Good. Now. Your thieving father, foolish enough to think this was an abandoned vessel, launched himself here and tried to steal whatever he could."

Belle felt the tears well up. Her father. The recent memory of his rotting corpse flashed across her mind.

"I tried to be kind and send his ship back to his daughters. But when we got word that the *Jeanne Ciel* had left Europa, your father couldn't have been more afraid. He killed two of my crew and then tried to come after me. So, I put an end to him."

The captain stepped back, his feet clacking against the metal floor beneath him. Belle looked around and assessed her location. She was astounded to see dozens of robots and android on the rafters above her. Their virtual eyes staring at her, most concerned, but some wild with joy.

"Some of my crew disapproves of how I run this ship." The beast looked up at the crowded eyes above. "Others encourage it. We've been here a very, *very* long time."

Belle tried to breathe and came up short. She closed her eyes and took two deep breaths. When she looked again she saw even more looking back at her. Hundreds of eyes peered down now.

She realized she was in a cargo bay, tied to a chair with something wrapped tightly around her head to prevent her from opening her jaw. Her eyes moved wildly around, searching for something, anything to help her get out.

"I don't anticipate we'll ever be free from this." The beast motioned to his own horrific body. "While my crew lives within these robotic machines while their bodies sit in cryo, I have to live in my own horrible prison. But we'll be free soon. *But on my own terms.*" As he shouted, spit and thick phlegm flew onto Belle's face.

There were cheers in the rafters. "Oui!" and "Hoorah!" echoed through the cargo bay. Belle swallowed hard, still finding it hard to catch her own breath. She wondered how low the oxygen levels were set on this ship.

"I very much like who I am now, thank you very much. I don't *need* anyone's help. And I don't *need thieves* or the *spawn of thieves* to come onto *my ship* without an *invitation*!" He shouted more, his voice echoing across the cargo bay. He stepped forward and grabbed her jaw, pulling himself closer to her face. "I've got a present for you, my beauty. My toy. *Étoile Filante.*"

"Oui, Monsieur?" a cool male voice responded.

The command words summoned a black control panel in front of the beast. It was much older than the *Jeanne Ciel*'s operating system, but it was similar technology.

Behind the captain a large display clicked on, and Belle saw the asteroid she and her sisters passed before finding the *Étoile Filante*. She then saw the screen zoom in on the *Jeanne Ciel,* and she felt her eyes widen.

"Oh yes, we detected your ship before you even launched yourself inside." The beast scoffed. "*Étoile Filante*, how many life forms are on that ship currently?"

"Deux femmes, Monsieur," the ship's AI responded.

"Good. Destroy it."

"Oui." The AI began a sequence on the display.

The beast waved his hand, and his control panel vanished. "*Adieu aux petits poulets.*"

She watched the *Jeanne Ciel* suddenly start to move. Like a fly, it buzzed around. She knew the ship had likely sensed the oncoming attack and was attempting to evade it.

Bile rose up Belle's throat and tears fell as she watched a small green light appear and then vanish. The *Jeanne Ciel* exploded without a sound.

Emptiness was all that filled her. It felt like the void was collapsing in on top of her. She inhaled sharply through her nose and screamed. The inhumane noise that came out of her pierced sharply through whatever kept her from speaking. She screamed again, this time with rage. She wanted to rip whatever was human out of the Beast and rip it apart with her own bare hands. She tried to kick but her entire body was tied directly to the chair.

The beast reappeared and looked down at Belle. "You shouldn't have come."

Belle screamed at him again. She grunted loudly, her feet and hands flailing as tears flew from her wild eyes.

"Your father was a horrible man, but he was smart. How long do you think he was stealing in order to survive? To provide for your family? I bet a lot longer than you'd think."

With a raise of his hand, the remaining machines left the room. They walked or rolled out single file to various doors. The eyes above her seemed to flicker out one by one as rafters above her emptied. Only the eyes of those truly compassionate or mad with lustful destruction remained.

"And now for you," the beast continued. "I don't need another mouth to feed. I've long since run out of uses for a girl of your... age. And you have bad blood. It sinks into your heart and your mind and corrupts you from the inside out. I've got enough corruption to deal with in my own heart."

The beast sighed as Belle tried to break free again. He looked over at the large cargo bay doors behind him. "It will be fast, so I hear."

He turned around and left.

An alarm sounded again, and Belle heard the loud crash of locks and metal doors securing. There was a hiss of pressurization, and she felt a dull pain in her skull. She tried to reach inside of her to find something, anything that would help her break free from the chair she was tied to. But her bindings were secure.

Belle did the only other thing she could think of. She prayed. She prayed for the first time since her mother died. Since her father walked in and told her that Mom was gone forever. Now it was her. Belle was going to be gone forever.

Before she could even process if this were a dream, a cruel prank, or harsh reality, the cargo bay doors open and a fierce wind whipped through the bay as the air was pulled out into the vacuum. Her chair flew back toward the door, and it, along with her, was sucked out into space.

The first sensation was how cold space was, and then there was the pang of the void. She had no time to compare it to anything, to relate the feelings to a past memory. She saw ice in her eyes, and then saw nothing at all.

Dying, she thought, was easy.

How Virginia Dare Slew the Waffle Dragon

- Gerald Sallier -
Illustrated by Karin Van de Kuilen

Once upon a time, there was a small village at the edge of a forest by a lake at the foot of a mountain in the Kingdom of Eurocentricia.

Once upon an earlier time, the forest teemed with all manner of treefolk and fae. Once upon a later time, the city council annexed the forest, the lake, the mountains, and a good deal of a nearby estuary during a resource grab and indirectly killed three species of elf.

This did not bother the humans, as is often the case with humans and once upon a later time.

It was in that great mountain, where, once upon a time—somewhere between earlier and later, a ravenous man-eating dragon built a nest of sheep bones and gold coins in a cavern near the mount's base. Once upon a later time than once upon a later time, this hoard of treasures began to vary in worth as the GDP of the varying kingdoms fluctuated.

This did not bother the dragon, which is often the case with gold hoarding dragons and the boom-bust cycle of market capitalism.

For, once upon a time, the mayor's Great-Grandmother, then the Mayor, had created a method to profit off the dragon—since she had to find some way to recoup such a loss of sheep and gold. She opened up the kingdom's first amusement park, with fun liability-waived rides, greasy fried mutton pops, and an annual competition to slay the dragon.

No one could, which for some reason did not discourage the competitors. Or the dragon.

Generations later, once upon a time after once upon a later time than once upon a later time, the award lay unclaimed, and the dragon flew undefeated. The current mayor of Dragonton, named for the dragon which had terrorized their community for nearly a century, eyed the beast's treasure with avarice. She sent one of her officials to find a young local urchin who worked and lived in the stables to vanquish the wicked dragon once and for all.

Which would make this time, where that lovable vagrant girl is in the back end of stable 4B and slopping the horses while talking to a magical rock she found in a ditch, the time when our story begins, and thus, the actual and official 'Once Upon a Time,' once upon a time.

———— ◆ ————

"Oy! And when ay woke up, ay 'ad the stink o' mead on me person," Virginia said with a laugh as she heaved a shovelful of slop into the near-filled slop barrel. "Didn't know where ay was or how ay ended up there, but ay toweled off me bum and—"

"*Insolent, sinning trollop,*" the tiny hunk of sulfur hissed at her atop a barrel. The young Virginia had set the good saint there while performing her last task of the day. "*Why must you insist upon assailing my ears with tales of your delirious whoremongering?!*"

"Wot?" she said, cupping one hand around her ear as though this would allow her to more easily hear the yellow rock. "You'll have to speak up, Mr. Stein. Ay've got me nose clipped tight with me clothespin."

"*How you can stand to clean this stable of filth while tolerating the feces caked upon your own soul? And my name is Augustine. You would do well to remember a Saint, whelp.*"

"Ah, forgiveness, Mr. August," she sighed, wiping her hands clean on her stained apron. She smeared her tawny hair across her sweaty forehead and curtsied. "You know ay always try to keep meself on the path of the Lord when ay'm shovelin' 'orseshit."

"*And yet you stand here reciting a charming tale about your bacchanalian infanticide.*" The little hunk of sulfur possessed by the vengeful spirit of St. Augustine sighed. "*One can only imagine there was nude dancing and a raucous, ethnic drumline.*"

"Tweren't no pagans involved," she replied, stiffly. "What was ay 'sposed to do?" Her voice turned grave. "No, best it 'tall be over with in a haze. ...Drunk on mead and stumblin' troo the back alley behind the pub. Someone takes you by the 'and—he, he guides you out into the darkness. Before you know it, yain't sure if you can get out of 'is arms. You're... you're pinned in... And when 'e lays you down in the gulley underneath the bridge, no one can 'ear yeh."

"Virginia?" A young man finally decided to ask. He was well-groomed and bespectacled, dressed in a frayed three-piece suit, and had been watching the ginger urchin girl wax philosophical with a rock for some time now.

"Eh? Oo's askin'?" she asked, one fist arched down against her hip while she slapped the other against her knee.

"I am. Are you Virginia Dare, the stable girl?"

"Yussir," she said with a curtsy. "Virginia Dare, ah'm the one wot slops the 'orses an' mends the stables."

"I am the mayor's assistant, and you are to come with me immediately."

Virginia's face sank. "Oh no, ay won't be doing that." She took one step back. "Ay think it's best you leave."

"*Wench!*" St. Augustine shrieked from atop his slop barrel. "*Now you speak out of turn to a man who is your better in all accounts? Virginia, I know that I've been harder on you today than usual but... perhaps you are too far gone, after all.*"

"No, that ain't so," Virginia said to the rock.

"I'm sorry?" the young man asked, equally confused and alarmed.

"Ay didn't do nuthin' wrong," she insisted.

There was a brief silence.

Virginia sobbed, "But you said them angels ain't watchin' over lessen' we deserve it!" She turned on the mayor's assistant. "And ay ain't gotta see the Mayor if'n ay don't want. Wot's your name?"

"Roderick. Virginia—"

"The mayor don't need to see me, and ay don't need to see 'er. Now, if'n yeh don't mind, ay've got more 'orse shit to shovel with me good friend there."

"The rock. That rock. The rock right there."

"'E's a Saint. 'Least 'e says 'e is."

"Riveting. Unfortunately, you and the... *saint* will have to come with me. You've been selected for a special award—direct from the Seat of the Mayor."

"Maybe later, after ay finish. Got a 'ole round o' stables left to muck. Best try again tomorruh. Definitely should be done with the rest o' these stables by next week. By the end of the month, ay'm yer girl, ay am."

"I'm afraid you'll have to come now. She's a very... *exacting* woman."

"Oh, is she?" Virginia asked.

"*Put me in your pocket,*" St. Augustine demanded, "*and march down to the mayor's office at once or suffer the wrath of the next life!*"

"Right," Virginia sighed, while plopping the sulfur chunk into her apron pocket. "Best be off to the mayor, ay guess. Should I leave a note with Mr. 'Orshackles?"

"The stable manager has been informed," Roderick gruffly said as he grabbed her arm. "Now if you'll just follow m—"

Virginia violently wrenched her arm away from the mayor's assistant and glared, eagle-eyed, at him.

"I'm... I'm sorry," he said, in such a rush he couldn't fully process what wrong he had committed.

"No..." she said. "It's okay."

"Well," he said. "After you?"

———————•◆•———————

The mayor's office began as a village complaint box, left in the middle of the town at the intersection of Main Street and 'The Other Road' Boulevard. There, Dragonton began as one old woman and a battered wooden shipping crate with a slot on the top and a sign that read, simply,

"Granny Mayor's Department of Gritches and Snitches" on a three-legged stool in the center of town.

As the complaints and missives from the villagers grew in number, so too did the box until it was finally so large that the then-mayor set up her own desk inside and received her constituents personally. She also set up a human-sized cage for her interns, but no need to dwell on that for now.

When a townsperson wanted to submit their inquiry with the Mayor, they simply climbed the stairs built on the side of the giant box and dropped their forms in the slot over the Mayor's desk. This tradition carried on for generations until the current Mayor nullified it altogether and insisted everyone simply walk through the door. She also cancelled the internship program and turned the cage into a low-end menagerie.

But that's unrelated to what happened to the complaint slot, through which the town spinster had just dumped two bedpans, covering the Mayor's husband, who was sitting where the current mayor insisted they put the scribe's desk during the remodel.

The Mayor sighed, let her quill drop to the desk, and finally asked, "Yes, Mrs. Welshire?"

"Mah plumbin's broke!" the old woman yowled through the opening in the ceiling.

"I've explained this multiple times, Mrs. Welshire. I don't know what plumbing is. No one does. "

"Then figure it out!" the old woman replied with a stomp.

"Do you think I like it?" the mayor countered. "Do you know how hard it is to get these suits tailored by a cobbler?"

"Am I..." the Mayor's husband stammered. "Am I... covered in...?"

"Not now, Kevin," the mayor snapped. "Will that be all for today, Mrs. Welshire?"

"I'm thinkin on it!" shouted Mrs. Welshire.

The mayor nodded and returned to her work.

"Dear," her husband began again, "am I covered in–"

"Yes, Richard, of course you are. She emptied her bedpan. You can either stay there under the hole, or you can get in the cage with the imported Turkish condor. At least then all my regretful investments would be in the same box."

"Yes, dear."

At that moment, the door to her office swung open, and her assistant entered with Virginia following close behind.

"Wastrels! Vagabonds!" St. Augustine shrieked from Virginia's pocket. *"Boasting of their sloth in the open streets while the streets of Heaven—"*

"'Ush, Mr. Stein," Virginia said. "Remember the sermon."

The mayor arched an eyebrow and pointed to her assistant. "Who is she talking to?"

Virginia curtsied, nervously. "St. August Stein."

"Who?"

"A rock in her pocket," Roderick sighed.

"Great," the mayor sneered with considerable exhaustion, "she's *that* scarred. Virginia, why don't you have a seat?"

"Naw, ay'm good over 'ere," Virginia replied.

"Then I'll come to you," the mayor said with considerable frustration. She pushed her swarthy, nordic frame away from her desk and walked over to Virginia. "Have you ever killed a dragon, Virginia?"

"Not that ay can recall, yer Mayoresty."

"Well then, today's a perfect time to start. Are you aware that this town has a dragon problem?"

"Ay've 'eard."

"Lies!" St. Augustine screamed. *"Does your sinning not stop at your seducement of the greater sex?"*

"I'm sorry?" the Mayor asked. "Did you say something?"

"Naw, din't say a nuthin' yer Mayoresty."

"Good," the mayor said as she returned to her desk, opened a drawer, and returned with a bundle of official scrolls under her arm. She unfurled one on her desk, scribbled a few notes on the bottom, and then handed it to Virginia.

"What is it?" Virginia asked, throwing another nervous glance at the Mayor's husband.

"Um...er.. hi, Virgin... yer," he mumbled.

She did not reply. Instead, she looked at the scroll and then back to the Mayor.

"Well?" the mayor asked with a toothy, forced smile as pressed as her suit. "What do you think?

"Ay can't..." Virginia whispered. "Ay can't read."

"Oh, well… um…" the mayor rifled through her desk, looking for something even she couldn't describe.

"Oh!" Virginia exclaimed. "Ay'll ask 'Is 'Oliness.'"

She pulled the Saint from her pocket and held the scroll up for him to read. "Uh-huh. Uh-huh. Really? Wow, never won anythin' in me life before."

"Come again?" the mayor asked. "Oh, yes. The Scroll. You see, Virginia, you have been nominated 'Hero of the Year.' Aren't you excited? Hero! …Of the Year! …Yay!"

"You illiterate tart! What chance do you think you have of slaying a dragon?"

"A dragon," Virginia gulped.

"A dragon?" the mayor chuckled. "What dragon? All I hear is 'Hero! Hero! Hero! Look at Virginia go!' Right, dear?"

"Um," Kevin muttered, "yes."

"A wreckin' hammer, a gunpowder flower, a rising star—zing-zang-zoom straight to the white glowing orb of light that God put in the night sky so we know when to go to sleep and plant corn," the mayor continued. "Right?"

"Right," St. Augustine agreed.

"But," Virginia said. "Ay can't kill a dragon, ay'm just a girl. A girl 'oo… 'oo can't even protect 'erself at night. Ay'm just… just askin' fer trouble—"

Before Virginia could finish, three feral cats fell into the Mayor's office and landed square on her husband's head.

"My eyes!" he shrieked as the cats ran over his shoulders, head, and finally down his back and out the door. "I thought I moved away from the hole!"

The Mayor rolled her eyes and called out, "Mrs. Welshire?"

"I got too many cats!" Mrs. Welshire hollered back.

"We didn't have you scheduled for a cat appointment today."

"I'm makin' one!"

"Have you considered," the mayor let out an angry grunt. "Have you considered getting rid of them?"

"Tried to starve 'em. Wait 'em out. Let 'em eat each other and raise the survivors as me own chirren," Mrs. Welshire explained matter-of-factly.

"I see," the Mayor said.

"That was a tit buster, though! They just up and et me granbaby. Now I got twelve problems!"

"Why twelve?"

"I got eleven cats!"

"Fine," the mayor sighed. "We'll send someone out with a flower basket."

"That'll do nicely," Mrs. Welshire hollered with a softer tone.

"Anything else?"

"Orchids. Granbaby loved orchids."

"Virginia," the mayor sighed again, louder this time to make sure the room heard her. "I am a very busy woman, as you may have gathered while eyeing every possible escape point in my office since you walked in. Aren't we a skittish minnish, huh? What is that, I wonder? I certainly don't! So, is there anything else you need explained or can you get on with solving our town's pesky dragon problem?"

"But ay cain't kill anythin'!" Virginia leaned in so that only the Mayor could hear her. "The saint says murderlin's uh sin—and Jesus'll fly on down from 'is diamond palace n' the 'eart o' the sun and smite me somethin' wicket, 'e will!"

"Riveting. Well, I'm more or less certain dragons don't have souls while I am the *sole* governor of this town, so..."

"...so?" Virginia asked after a beat.

"Oh, that wasn't just going to finish itself for me? It means it's a freebie! No soul means no murder and no murder means no sin! It doesn't count. It'd be like killing a... killing a bug."

"Or plumbing!" the Mayor's husband interjected.

"I mean, what is that? My cobbler certainly doesn't know, I know that," the Mayor chuckled with a shrug. "Can't kill what doesn't exist— so go kill that dragon!"

"Right," Virginia said in resignation. "But wot if'n ay croak?"

"Oh, we've already planned for that!" The mayor clapped her hands together. "Show the lucky girl, Roderick."

"Oh, well there's the, uh," Roderick reached into his coat pocket and produced, "Martyr of the Year Plaque and Certificate–"

"Ay cain't read," Virginia reminded him.

"—with a solid oak and papyrus finish that would look marvelous in any home—"

"But ay don't got no—"

"—and a commemorative wristband that says 'Virginia Strong,' and glows in the dark. Her Mayoresty drummed up a warlock from the town mage prisons to get that little trick to work."

The mayor cleared her throat threateningly.

"Apologies, your Mayoresty. And, finally, this." He held up a quill with a tiny woman inside. When tilted upside down, the woman in the quill turned into a naked dragon. "Sexy, right?"

The Mayor and Virginia shot him a look, then the Mayor took Virginia by the shoulder and led her to the door. "Listen, Valerie."

"Virginia."

"It doesn't matter. It really, really, really doesn't matter. But I have more appointments for the day so if you could kindly shamble on up to the dragon's cave down by the river and snuff it out once and for all, we'll see about getting you some of that beast's treasure, huh?"

"Oh, no," Virginia said. "Mr. Stein says money is a sin, that's why ay 'ave to give it all to the church. They know 'ow to clean money right."

The mayor cupped Virginia's face in her hands and cooed, "Of course they can, you adorable little... I want to say girl? Now hurry along and we'll see about finding something to reward you with if you get back—gah, when you get back."

"A 'ome?" Virginia gasped. "A family?"

"Possibly, we'll see what that wizard can muster up. I've got some extra brooms and hog fat around here somewhere."

"Oh, thankee, yer Mayoresty," Virginia clucked as she stepped in closer to the Mayor.

"Okay. Good. Don't touch me, don't touch me!" She brushed off her coat. "Nothing personal, it's just too difficult to get horse slop out of imported linen. And dry cleaning is just atrocious this far out in the boonies."

"What's dry cleaning?" Virginia asked.

"How should I know? I don't even know what plumbing is! But I do know that we'll be waiting here for you when you get back, *hero*."

Virginia smiled and hurried out the door. Once it had slammed shut, the mayor slowly walked over to her desk and sat down.

After a few minutes of silence, her husband finally asked, "Dear, do we really have to send her off to—"

"Oh, I'm sorry, were you about to question my judgment?"

"No, dear, I just–"

"Roderick?" the mayor asked. "Could you leave my husband and me alone for a moment?"

"Of course," Roderick nodded, "your Mayoresty."

"And fetch the town mole, we'll need him to send some parcels to the King."

"Yes, your Mayoresty."

And with that, Roderick left.

The mayor stood and walked over to her husband. "Now, was there something you wanted to say to me? Something you wanted to ask?"

"No... no dear."

"No, I want to hear it. Out with it."

"It's just... no one's ever been able to kill the dragon. We just leave sheep out there every year to keep it happy."

"So you do want to question my judgment. Fine—how about we question *your* judgment at the Dragonton 'Boy That's a Lot of Gourds and Sheep' Festival after you had three meads and stumbled out to the streets looking for lady-boys and a swift handie—"

"Dear, please—"

"Don't talk over me. You, plastered off honey and what we charmingly pretend isn't recycled Viking piss, tumble into a darkened alley and—without any forethought whatsoever—force yourself upon the town urchin."

"But, honey, we haven't... been together in so long—"

The mayor slapped her husband across the face. "Do you see the calendar on my desk? Does it say 'Christmas Morning?' No. It doesn't. Boxes aren't big enough. And it's not snowing!"

"I didn't know what I was doing, I wasn't thinking about—"

"Of course you weren't thinking! You were drunk! You were asking for it!" She slapped him again. "What would you expect, dressed up like the back half of our Harvest Centaur costume? The girl works in a stable! How can she *not* trust horses—but you, you should know better!"

"But I—"

Kevin winced abruptly, expecting a third slap. Instead, the mayor straightened her bun, marched over to her desk, and sat down.

"So, now I have to send her off to be charbroiled by a dragon before anyone can catch wind of this scandal, and I have to tell my constituents how my feckless husband decided to force himself on a homeless child. So—if you don't mind—I think it's best we leave running the town to the one with actual leadership skills while you stay under the deposit slot. Mrs. Welshire has another appointment this afternoon to discuss her nephew's urine jars."

"…yes, dear."

———————— • ◆ ————————

The dragon lived in a cavern at the foot of Waffle Mountain, by the river outside the town of Dragonton. The stream carried small chunks of debris from the mountain's guts and, eventually, filled stream's basin with some of the dragon's treasure. Prospectors from near and far tried to fish out what little gold they could find, only to be scorched, flayed, eaten, digested, and then left in the river by the dragon.

This did not bother Virginia as she made her way out of the forest and into the clearing at the cave's entrance, where the prospectors looked about the same as the rocks at this point.

"Just a little further, Mr. Stein," Virginia said with a huff. The sweat stung her eyes and the grit of the earth chaffed her skin. "Nuthin' beats a nice walk in the forest, eh? Better'n' them horse ends, ay'd say."

"*Yes, by all means, carry me along as you hike up your skirt for all of nature to see. Seducing the Mayor's husband wasn't enough?*"

"Tain't no bears in these forests since the Emperor 'unted 'em dead, Mister Stein."

"*Then the Lord will send wolves along your path and that will be that. Of this, I am most certain. I can feel it as though it were written upon my heart like the natural order of the Universe. Take me out and wash me in the river at once; I fear taint from your sin and am overcome with a need to be baptized.*"

"But, Mister Stein, we be doin' that every night for over a week now. Ain't ye clean yet?"

"*Baptize me in the loving purity of Christ, you incredulous whore!*"

Virginia washed the sulfur pebble in the river, grabbing the water with one hand then letting it dribble out over his Holiness.

"*Yes, yes. Good, Virginia. Very good.*"

"Ay don't understand what ay did wrong, Mister Stein."

"*Stifle, child,*" the rock whined. "*I feel His glory approaching.*"

"Ay just wanted to go back to me stable Mister 'Orshackles lets me sleep in. Ay din't belong there. Then outta nowhere came this 'orse…"

"*And the moral compass has swung full circle. Keep washing.*"

"Ay knew it wadn't a real 'orse—but it was such a good costume, ay 'ad to get a closer peek. You spend as much time as ay do lookin' at a 'orse's back end, you come to admire fine craftsmanship. It was the mayor's 'usband. 'E's 'apposed to be a nice guy. Ay must've dun somethin', must've made 'im think ay wanted 'im tuh… tuh…"

"*Of course you did!*" St. Augustine shrilled. "*Why else would a woman walk around alone at night?*"

"Ay don't," Virginia had begun crying, "ay don't know wot you mean, Mr. Stein—"

"*Stop looking at me like you deserve redemption—you don't deserve to be clean, Virginia! You aren't allowed to enjoy this!*"

"Ay didn't mean tuh—"

"*Avert your gaze, trollop! AVERT YOUR GAZE!*"

Virginia squinted her eyes and turned her head. She held Augustine of Hippo over the creek, screaming, "Ay wodn't lookin! Ay wodn't lookin'! You tol' me to!" She slapped the surface of the river with her free hand, sobbing, "You tol' me to!"

"Virginia?" Roderick called from the forest. He ran out into the clearing, leading three sheep with a rope. "Are you alright?"

"Ay…" Virginia looked at her hands and slowly picked herself up. "Ay guess ay… got all wet 'n there."

"Yeah. Yeah, I guess. Is that the dragon's cave?"

Behind Virginia, the gaping maw of the dragon's cave beckoned. Occasionally, a low rumble slithered out from the entrance and settled on the edge of the brook. Near the entrance a wooden sign read, "There be dragon(s)."

"Huh," Roderick said, reading the sign. "That looks ominous."

"Ay... yeah... yeah, ay 'reckon 'twould be. You got a lot 'o sheep there for a mayor's assistant. Two over the unlicensed limit, eh?"

"It's okay; I got a permit. It's why it took so long to catch up with you. But you can't go in there."

"An' why not?"

"Because it's a dragon."

"*Virginia! Order that wretched man hence and venture towards your redemption!*"

"No, ay've got to do this," she said.

"Why? What would compel you in any way to actually go in there and confront a dragon?"

"Ay..." she sniffed, wiping her eyes. "Well... now that you mention it—"

"What's this?" a low, thunderous voice asked from the cave. "Another knight here already?"

There came a trembling of the earth and the sound of a mighty weight being dragged across ancient rocks. A crimson scaled head, golden eyed and thrice-horned, emerged from the cavern, fire belching from its eight nostrils and four slavering jaws.

"What's this on about then, eh?" the dragon said. "They plopped a li'l pollie here instead."

"Whazzat?" another voice asked from the darkness.

"Seems they sent a li'l pollie here tah slake our hunger this time."

"They left a little girl in front of our cave?" A second head, this one pointed and single-jawed, hornless and round like a serpent's, with scales like ice, came out and said, flatly, "Well, that's a bit macabre."

"Would it be?" the red dragon countered. "I mean, after they get past five feet tall, they all look the same to me."

"I see your bigotry against mammals isn't in dispute, then," the blue dragon sighed.

"You guys say something?" a third voice asked from inside the cave.

"Okay, Virginia, we're leaving," Roderick said.

A fat, green scaled head with one eye and a massive tongue slithered out to join its brethren. "Hey guys, did you guys say something? Oh look! There's people! Hey, people. You guys see there's people?"

"Yes," the other two dragons said in unison.

"Roderick," Virginia said. "Ay don' think there's just one dragon."

The three heads lurched forward and the three-headed dragon of Waffle Mountain stepped out into the light.

"Ohh, this one 'ere is a clever one," the red head clucked. "We rarely see a clever adventurer. Usually it's all 'for kingdom an' country,' this and 'innocent blood must be repaid,' that."

"Oh, and how they go on," the blue head chimed in. "Bandying on with their swords out, 'Your gold belongs to the people!' Well, come on then, I suppose you just run around the countryside tearin' into people's home and stealing their furniture on the daily."

The green head propped itself against the cave entrance by bending its neck. "I like the sheep! Sheeps is like people."

"I swear to god," the red head started.

"No, it's okay," the blue head whispered, "let it out."

"I can't take that asshole sometimes," the red head sobbed.

The blue head sighed. "What are you doing outside our cave? You don't have any weapons? Are you here to fight us or did you just come to die—because we are not about to become a suicide center."

"You know," the red head said, "that could be why a lot of them have come here."

"Oh my god," the blue head gasped. "You mean—we've been... oh man, wow. Wow."

"That boy has sheep," the green head exclaimed, it's fat tongue bobbing from its mouth. "Three sheep. Three. Sheep!"

"That's true," the blue head agreed, and said, turning to the red head, "Can sheep be suicidal? Do we have any numbers on that?"

The red head belched fire from one of its mouths. "I got this. Stand back, kid."

A gout of fire rocketed from the dragon's maw and engulfed one of the sheep. Roderick leapt from where he was, lost his grip on the rope, and let the other two sheep escape.

Except that those two sheep stayed exactly where they were, idly chewing grass.

When the flash of heat and blinding light subsided, a blackened lump of hairless, not-quite-as-lucky sheep fell to the grass.

The blue head cheered, "Twenty-two, precisely!"

"No," the green head said. "There's two sheep now."

"No, I wasn't counting the," the blue head sighed. "Mother always said you were punishment for my—never mind, now I've lost track."

"One," the green head counted to itself, "One and a burned one, and that means the other one is…"

"Oh, for the love of—look! Over there! Griffons are courting pixies!"

"What?!" the green head shouted as it darted around to mouth of the cave to peer into the forest. "The deviants!"

"Good," replied the red head, "that usually distracts him for a while."

"I'd say we've got about five minutes," hissed the blue head.

The green head called out to the words, "Don't think I can't see you snorting their wings in there!"

By this point in the dragon(')s' conversation, Roderick and Virginia had crept near the edge of the clearing.

"Sorry," the blue head said, finally turning to face its human guests. "It's been five years since he kicked the stuff."

"It was a rough time for a while there," the red head said with a chuckle. "But pixie dust just ruins your body.

"Yeah," the blue head said. "You wouldn't know it by looking, but he's actually the youngest out of us."

"Oh," Roderick said, nervously, "Your heads come in at… different… times… that's… that's something I didn't know."

"So what do we do about the uh…" the blue head whispered, "you know."

The red head sized Roderick up, "One apiece, I guess?"

"So that one breathes fayre?" Virginia asked, pointing to the red dragon's slavering jaws—slavering with fayre—er, fire, naturally.

"Indeed," the blue head replied.

"So," Roderick asked, reluctance weighing down his voice, "what do you do?"

The blue head proudly stiffened its neck, "I breathe ice!"

The blue head reared back, took in a deep gulp of air, then jerked its head forward violently. It squeezed its eyes shut and began retching every two seconds until a flat, white pillar began to slowly exude from its mouth.

"Is that?" Roderick asked. "Are you actually…?"

"Give him a minute," the red head said. "Been a long hibernation for 'im. 'is polly left 'im, you see."

The blue head let out sputtering, choked gurgles as a rounded pillar slid out its throat. Finally, after about ten minutes, a six foot long cylindrical tube of ice plopped onto the ground, and the blue head collapsed in agony.

"Oh god, it hurts! It hurts!" it screamed. "Why? Why would any kind of god design this?!"

"Breathes ice," Virginia observed.

"You okay?" the red head asked.

"Sure," the blue head replied, arching its neck like it was trying to start something. "My throat teeth were just stuck."

"It's been a while," the red head said, covering for its blue head. "Takes a bit to get started. You want me to?"

"Oh, no," the blue head replied. "I've got it now." It grinned and a sick whirring erupted from its throat as a spray of crushed ice pelted Virginia and Roderick.

"Agh! Ah!" Roderick shrieked, "This is mildly irritating! Virginia, follow me!" Roderick pulled her and Augustine behind the nearest, largest old tree.

"Why is it attackin' us?" Virginia tried to ask over the howling flurry of ice surrounding them.

"*Because of your sin, Virginia! For women, the very consciousness of their own nature must evoke feelings of shame!*"

Virginia threw the saint into her apron pocket.

"*Woman is man's helpmate, a function which pertains to her alone. She is not the image of God but as far as man is concerned, he, by himself, is the image of God.*"

"What was that?" Roderick asked.

"Nuthin'," Virginia sighed.

"*The word and works of God are quite clear, that women were made either to be wives or prostitutes. Remember your place, girl.*"

The dragon's icy breath had frozen the front half of the tree solid— and it was beginning to crack. Virginia feared that this would be the end when, from out of the forest behind her, a glint of silver whizzed past her face and *fwacked* across the dragon's blue face.

"And the next one's goin' 'tween yer legs!" Mrs. Welshire came barreling out of the woods, followed by exactly eleven gnarly housecats that pounced on the bedpan-conked blue head. "I've run with spice merchants, I know how to throw it down!"

Three tabbies and an old calico rampaged down the beast's neck while the rest of the cats took turns tag-teaming the eyes and ears—yes, dragons have ears, just not great ones.

"Mrs. Welshire?" Roderick gasped as Virginia helped him to his feet. "Why aren't you at your grandson's memorial service?"

"Turns out he wasn't 'et!" Mrs. Welshire said. "Goblin King took 'im. Raised the boy as 'is own!"

"Good fer 'im!" Virginia cheered. "'Ear that Mister Stein?"

"I thought the cats ate him," Augustine replied.

"Boy came back this afternoon," Mrs. Welshire replied. "Thirty years old now. Got his own place. Couldn't be prouder."

"Wait," Roderick said, "the cat ate the Goblin King?"

"Excuse me," the dragon's red head clacked out of its upper mouth.

Mrs. Welshire was beside herself with pride, "Time dilation did the boy some good. My daughter's beside herself."

"Oh!" Roderick said. "It was her grandson."

"Could do without all the goblins living in my house now, though," Mrs. Welshire added.

"Well, that's understandable," Roderick said with a nod.

"Excuse me!" the dragon bellowed.

The dragon's green head whipped back around from the side of the cave. "What? Oh, hey, they got Simon. Simon, you got cats! Cats are like sheep!"

"So what," Roderick sniffed, "does that one breathe lightning?"

"Why would it breathe lightning?" the red dragon asked, perplexed.

"Well, you breathe fire and that one breathes ice, so..."

"So what about fire and ice makes you think the third one is lightning? What kind of logic is that?"

"I breathe good," the green dragon asserted. "See?" It began to inhale and exhale, loudly.

"He..." the red dragon began, "...he breathes... good. He's a... good breathing dragon."

"My head's the wind element!"

"We tell him that, keeps him happy. Everyone knows the Chinese were right, and air doesn't exist. Now then, let's discuss me burning you and everything between me and you." The dragon's red head belched a volley of fireballs from its three mouths.

Virginia, Roderick, and Mrs. Welshire stood still as the blasts flew past them and into the forest. One hit a tree, another hit a rock, and the third hit a deer, then a tree, then a rock.

"Yeah," the red head chuckled. "Aim's not so great with four mouths."

Roderick took Virginia by the arm, "We have to get out of here!"

Virginia yanked her arm away and punched Roderick's nose. "Ay'm not goin' anywar!"

"Fine!" Roderick said after a personal break to check his ego and slightly bloodied face. "We can just die here. That's tenable."

"Ay... uh..." Virginia helped him up. "Nuthin', you okay?"

"Yeah, yeah I think I broke my fall."

"If you two songbirds could warble it up already, we gotta scoot!" Mrs. Welshire held a bedpan prone, spun, and shot it at the green head. "The cats are dispersin'!"

"*Now, Virginia!*" St. Augustine shouted. "*Sacrifice your whore body for the good of all!*"

"Run," Virginia said. "Ay'll 'old 'im off."

"What?" Roderick laughed. "No, that's insane. We're not in serious danger, we just need to carefully walk back to town and avoid poorly aimed fireballs. I'm frankly amazed no one's been able to kill this dragon so far from the go we're having of it."

"*Now, Virginia!*" St. Augustine shrieked. "*Cast yourself into the flames!*"

A fireball careened behind her and splashed against an upturned rock. Another shot off towards nothing in particular.

"Boy's right," Mrs. Welshire observed. "We'd best skedat 'fore the cats get bored. They're a fickle hound, cats."

"No!" Virginia sobbed, "Mister Stein's right. Ay... Ay..."

Roderick snatched the rock from Virginia's hands."This? This is just a stupid rock! It doesn't say anything!"

"*Stifle the boy, whore! Leap for the dragon's maw!*"

"That's it!" Virginia shrieked. "You wanna fight the dragon so badly, you can do it, Mister Stein!"

Virginia snatched the rock back and threw St. Augustine at the dragon. The tiny lump of sulfur landed in the red head's left mouth as it recoiled, a new fireball already charging in its maw. In a puff of green light and a flash of fire, the dragon's red head exploded in two, the leftmost half evaporating in an inferno of viscera and light.

"Fah~hoke!" The red dragon's head collapsed in an agonized, bloodied heap. "Gah! God!" It gasped, *"Ssssiiiiissssssss, hyawh,* gawd it fuckin' burns! *Ow, agh,* my head… *Ugh,* ah…" The red dragon's head sized up its wounds—the entire bottom half of its head blown clean off and gushing blood. "Oh man, oh yeah I'm a goner… agh…. Uh… I… oh man… this is…" The dragon's claws pawed idly at the ground. "I just gotta… I need to lay down for second, I just…"

The dragon rolled over on its back, the blue head mauled to death by cats, and the green head laughing for no discernible reason.

The red head chewed on the ground for a second and reached for a nearby tree, smearing blood across its trunk. "Oh, here it is, it's get—it's getting' hazy…" The red head flopped upright and gurgled. *"Glaghlurghl,* I just… whooo, whoa guy, I just… I hah—ho, huh… I just need to close… close my eyes, everyone. Just gotta… whoa, just gotta close… my… eyes…"

Finally, after one more retch of blood from the red head, the dragon lay slain.

"It's okay!" the green head said. "I'm still fine—oh, nope, there it goes, feelin' woozy. Here I go, night everyone! Bye-bye. See you next week!"

And, thus, the dragon was slain.

"We did it!" Roderick cheered, "We did it! Virginia, everything worked out—"

Virginia jerked away.

"Oh, right," he said. "Okay, so I guess we didn't really… yeah, that wouldn't… that wouldn't make sense. Why would that be better because you threw the rock into the… that would be moronic."

Mrs. Welshire sized Virginia up. "Somethin' happen to the stable girl, Roderick?"

Roderick opened his mouth to reply when the earth began to shake and his feet fell out from under him, quite like a metaphor.

"Oh, come on," Mrs. Welshire spat, "if it turns out that dragon was just a baby and the mother's the real dragon comin' up to 'et us, I swear to goblin god, I'll—"

The ground continued to shake as the Town Mole burrowed up from the ground with an official parchment. "Are you Virginia Dare?" it asked.

Roderick and Mrs. Welshire pointed to Virginia.

The Town Mole cleared its throat, "By order of her Mayoresty I hereby swear and guarantee that Virginia Dare, the Stable Girl, slew the Waffle Dragon indubitably!"

"Who are you?" Mrs. Welshire asked after an intense beat.

The Town Mole threw a handful of confetti in the air. "And with that, I take my leave!"

"Is it over?" Roderick asked with one eye closed.

"Ay think so," Virginia replied. "Ay do believe so."

And so they returned home. Virginia went back to the stables where she received a 0.5% raise and a second stable to add to her first. Roderick remained under the mayor's employ, and the mayor was re-elected even though that came much later and had little to no bearing on the events of this story.

The Town Mole returned a week later with a boat, ready to fulfill his lifelong dream of owning a boat. Mrs. Welshire finally worked up the gumption to kick her son and his goblin horde out, and the Goblin King continued to steal children and dance the night away as though that was behavior becoming of mythical royalty.

And, as the people in these stories so often do, they all lived happily ever after—except for the Mayor's husband, who was mistaken for a moose by King Bourigard Fitzgerald IV while drunk in the woods and shot five times in the back.

Which would make that the real ever after.

For every ever, forever.

After.

Generations in Gingerbread

- Stephanie Gaudin -
Illustrated by Jessica Douglas

Once upon a time in a tiny forested English village, there was a small bakery that always smelled of gingerbread, and had lush clover patches growing along its path. Hibiscus flowers dipped in sugar shone like the crown jewels across the rough hewn counter-top. Pastries and breads filled the hand-woven baskets on her shelves, herbs hung in bunches from the rafters, and a spinning wheel stood in the far corner with a basket of fresh wool next to it.

Cailleach came from the kitchen cradling the glass jar of lollies that had just finished cooling. She smiled wistfully as the jar bumped with a tiny baby kick from within her womb. After she placed them on the shelf, it was time to tend her small garden. It wouldn't be much longer now, and she would have to leave her garden to her husband's care and the care of some of the ladies in town.

It wasn't much of a garden, but it was all theirs. The garden was about the height of a tall grown man, and about as wide as their wheelbarrow turned sideways. The full little garden was lovingly bordered in stones brought from Ireland. It had taken her and Carlin nearly eight years to enclose the garden and lay the floor of the smokehouse with the same type of stones. Their home and store still had packed earth floors that were swept before dawn every day and after dusk. Upstairs in their bedchamber, Carlin had built them a raised bed frame, and she had sewn a mattress they filled with wool they had traded for, feathers earned from the butcher in exchange for doing all his plucking, and soft tree moss they found in their travels. She was already filling a mattress for the baby bed with wool and scraps of fabric.

The upstairs was the same size as the shop below, though the fireplace upstairs was smaller than the one downstairs and had a solid iron bottom. There was a log stand built into the iron so that it could share the chimney with the fireplace below in the kitchen without the ash falling into the cooking food. The kitchen fireplace held an iron hook to hold pots over the fire with a very wide chimney tapering into half its size as it hit the second floor. There was an iron stove that sat against the same wall with its black pipe taking the smoke into the chimney, as well.

A single doorway lead out into the shop which was a large, open room with hand built shelves lining three walls. Upon the shelves stood hand woven baskets filled with breads, cakes, and tarts, as well as teas and other wonderful treats. Behind the single counter stood a shelf with glass jars that held spun and pulled sugar sweets. Herbs hung from the rafters with colorful bits of yarn and fabric leftover from projects or from old clothes.

Cailleach's long red hair was now in a single thick braid down her back, and had been since the day she married Carlin. When she was a child, she used to spend hours practicing braiding on her mother's hair, knowing when she was wed that was how hers would be, too.

Cailleach wasn't greatly showing yet, though those closest to her had already noticed. She knew her body well and could already feel the tiniest of flutters and kicks from the babe in her belly. Carlin was thrilled, beaming so bright and wide Cailleach was afraid he'd hurt his own face. Her husband was nesting, as the squirrels do in the fall. As a result of his manly desire to provide for the upcoming growth of his family, their smokehouse couldn't hold another animal. He had already sold two bucks and a boar to the butcher, earning a little money to put aside. He wanted to stay near home closer to the end, to be there when the baby came.

She heard the little feet scurry across her threshold with a weary mother's steps heavy behind them. Cailleach pulled a ginger root from the soil, knowing exactly who had come in and how badly it was needed. She gathered her basket of harvested herbs, and rose to greet her customers inside the store. Dusting her hands upon her apron, she set the basket just inside the wide doorway, slipped the ginger into its pocket with a smile, and greeted her guests. Sophie marveled at the candied flowers as her mother whispered softly in Cailleach's ear about trading work for half of their bread money this week. Cailleach noticed how thin they had both become.

"Oh love, don't worry about it. We are doing well right now. When I need help, you just promise to come by and help me, eh?" Cailleach grinned and reached for her largest loaf to gift to her friend.

Esmeralda noticed the way one hand lingered near her belly. "Oh, síle, are you—" she gasped.

"Mama, may we get a sweet flower?" her daughter interrupted. The sad mother's face began to pale even more, before she could answer she was saved by Cailleach.

"Of course you may, darling! Your mama has already paid for one. As well as this." She placed the ginger into Esmeralda's hands. "To make some tea, just for Mommy," Cailleach chuckled, turning her attention back to Esmeralda as Sophie did a happy little dance and picked herself a flower. "Put a few small bits into your kettle, let it boil and steep as you would any other tea. It revitalizes and stimulates the fire within." Cailleach's voice was earnest now, as she gave instructions to help her weary friend in the traditional Irish way. Esmeralda tried to refuse the generous gifts, but found herself being drug out the door by a very excited little one nibbling on a vibrant pink candied hibiscus flower.

Later that night, long after the sun had sunk below the horizon, Carlin's deep booming voice was soft and tender. "You can't keep giving things away my dear. We have our own little one to worry about now." Carlin's strong calloused hands gently stroked her belly through her cotton shift.

"I know, but you have prepared and provided so well for us, and they needed it. I cannot let them suffer and go hungry. I know they have struggled since her husband took ill last spring." He could only smile at her kindness and kiss her soft lips. He blew out the candle beside the bed and pulled her into his arms in the darkness.

Cailleach realized what she had previously thought to be a single blessing growing inside her, was actually two. She felt each child move independently of their sibling now, and could often identify a hand or foot pressing against her from inside. She was winding her freshly spun yarn to continue knitting winter garments for the babies. Carlin was outside working on the babies' bed. Esmeralda helped tend the garden for bread, and Sophie helped tie the herbs into bunches to dry once the necessary ones were harvested. There was enough meat to last them a year, their vegetables were doing well, and some even went home with Esmeralda and Sophie so as not to go to waste. Cailleach was always careful to sneak them to Sophie without Esmeralda knowing until they had gotten home.

"What are we going to name them?" Cailleach smiled and looked up questioningly at her husband as she continued rubbing her belly.

Carlin suggested warmly, "Hansel and Gretel?"

The baby bed was in their bedchamber, its soft little mattress lovingly embroidered with a small gingerbread house and as a memento of their parents' travels. Cailleach finished the infant sized sweater she was knitting and placed it on top of its mate in the baby bed as she clutched her belly. The contractions were getting stronger now, and closer together. She had delivered a few babies herself back home, and knew it was probably time to send Carlin for the midwife. As the wave of pain passed, she pushed herself up from the rocking chair that had just been finished a few days ago and placed in their room. Waddling carefully down the narrow staircase into the kitchen, she smiled softly as she saw him place the bread dough in the oven that she had left to rise and forgotten about. Just as he closed the oven door, another wave of pain overtook her and made her gasp. Dashing to her side, he got her settled on the kitchen stool as the relief washed over her.

"It's time to run to town. I'll be fine until you get back." Placing her mother's teakettle on the grate over the fire, she began ladling in some water from the bucket on the floor. "I'll make some labor tea. Go and bring her back."

Hiding her pain, she turned her back and tossed some herbs and roots into the water. Knowing labor would be coming soon, she had preblended and kept them in a jar on the kitchen table.

As dawn broke over the horizon, little Gretel broke free of her mother's womb with a fierce roar clearing out her tiny lungs. Within a few minutes, her brother Hansel made his solemn-faced debut. He didn't cry, but looked around with wide eyes and began to take in his surroundings. They were like night and day from the very beginning

———◆———

Esmeralda and Sophie continued to come daily even after the twins were born, learning the names of roots and herbs, and going into the woods with Cailleach and the twins to harvest wild ones to make teas, salves, and other medicines for the townspeople.

Though the Hansel and Gretel were nearly two years old now, she vividly remembered every moment of her pregnancy and the birth of her babies. She knew that her mother would be proud of the woman she had become. With a deep sigh, she tied off the braid in her hair, just after dawn broke. As she had since the day she was born, Gretel awoke at dawn and demanded breakfast. Carlin kissed Cailleach's neck softly, making her start.

"Did we wake you, love?" she whispered. She turned her moss-colored eyes to meet his impassioned gaze.

"No. Is breá liom tú." He growled with a mischievous grin.

Fire flashed behind her eyes for a brief moment, her fear nearly palpable. "Carlin, I love you too. Please, you make me miss home so. I don't know what others would think if we were to speak our language. We never have."

They had argued about it many times over the years. He saw no reason to hide who they were; they had worked so hard to preserve their heritage, carving knots into their doors and furniture, bringing stones all the way from home, bringing hard-to-find herbs with them, all one long trip at a time. He didn't understand how she could be so proud and so secretive of her heritage all at once.

He scooped up Gretel and carried her down for bread and butter, rather than arguing. The utter despair in his eyes as he walked away nearly broke her heart. She noticed Hansel laying down silently with his eyes wide open.

"What do you think, little mister?" She pulled him into her arms, and he hugged her tight with those little baby arms as she carried him down to breakfast. Hansel had brownish red hair like his father, and it was completely straight. Cailleach made the porridge as they nibbled on bread and butter with some weak ginger tea to help wake their bodies from sleep. After breakfast, she left the children playing in the store, building with scraps of wood and cloth left for them in a basket. Cailleach pulled Carlin into the kitchen and stared into his eyes.

"You are right. There is no reason to hide. But the people here do not know our language, and I fear they will think we are talking about them."

A visible wash of elation, adoration, and relief over-washed him. "Is breá liom tú! We will only speak it when we are alone or with the children!"

By summer, the children were more fluent in their parents tongue than they had been in that of the locals up to this point. In addition to teaching Hansel and Gretel to speak the words of their homeland, Carlin also taught them to craft, hunt, and smoke meat as his father had taught him when he was their age.

Their mother taught them the names and uses of all the herbs and plants, as well as how to prepare them, how to bake breads, and make sweets. And as a family, they built gingerbread houses and villages for fun. Oftentimes they would give them as gifts to the townsfolk, though occasionally they would trade them, and even more rarely they would eat them as a family treat.

They were making less gingerbread houses now than they had in the past. Supplies were becoming more difficult to come by, with village raids, skirmishes, and the beginnings of a war breaking out in England.

"Mamaí, is féidir linn a imirt le Sophie lasmuigh?" Hansel was so soft-spoken, she could hardly tell him no.

"Of course you may play with Sophie. If you see your father coming home, let me know so I be prepared. He should be home before sunset. You and Gretel stay close to home. It's not safe to wander far!"

Gretel had hair the color of the red sunset, and perfect angelic curls that bounced as she ran out the door. Every aspect of her perfect children seemed to be balanced evenly. Where she was playful and spirited, he was somber and stoic; he calmed her and she made him laugh and play.

Carlin snatched up his children and rushed into the door. "Ní mór dúinn a fhágáil. Anois. Go tapa!"

Startled, Cailleach latched onto his arm as he pushed past her and jerked up his hunting bow. "What do you mean we have to leave? Why so quickly? Where are we going?"

In this moment, she noticed the sweat drenching his body, the way he was clinging to the children...

She nodded and took the babies from his arms so he could grab a loaf of bread and followed him out the back and into the woods. But they were too late. Like many of their neighbors, they had been surrounded.

———————◆———————

Only smoldering ashes remained of the town and the outlying houses.

Esmeralda's husband, James, had never fully regained his health, but was still strong enough to sacrifice himself to save her and Sophie. He'd shoved them in the small root-cellar Carlin had dug them in exchange for all of Esmeralda and Sophie's help at their shop the past summer, just before their attackers arrived.

They listened as he was tortured and their house burned above them. Then, they waited, side by side, for two days. Once they were positive it was safe, Esmeralda pushed on the clay slab covering them. Ashes, dust, and sand rained down causing them to cough and shield their eyes.

When they emerged, the town was in ruins. Charred stone and bits of timber where so many homes used to proudly stand, bodies strewn throughout the streets, blood soaked dirt with deep sword cuts, and the haze from smoke still hanging in the air.

Running to Cailleach and Carlin's home, they saw all four bodies curled together, as if their love could protect them. In the ashes Sophie noticed the embroidered gingerbread house from the twins' bed. It was singed, but somehow had survived the fire. She placed it over the burned hands of the family she and her mother had cherished so much.

Esmeralda fell to her knees, the shock leaving her body in racking sobs. She pulled Sophie to her in the warm ash, the smell of burnt flesh and wood still filling their nostrils. In the tear choked voice of utter despair, Esmeralda told Sophie, "We will go on. We will live with them in our hearts and we will be safe."

———————•◆•———————

Esmeralda and Sophie did not to the village after that day they escaped the root cellar. The town had been resettled now. It had been some thirty years since that devastating raid, and Esmeralda wanted to go home before she passed. Just one last time, to say a final goodbye. She was ill and didn't have long left. The deep sadness in her eyes had never really left, but these days, it appeared the same way it did when it was fresh. A vast ocean of despair slowly overwhelming the small woman from inside.

They checked into the inn and began asking questions about the town from the owners. It had been resettled about twenty five years prior, when some travelers found the overgrown remains of the previous town. There was a place outside of town they were cautioned to avoid, one with stones foreign to the area and a few charred chunks of wood with intricate and elegant knot work. The villagers believed it was the home of an Irish witch, and that it was now haunted by her vengeful spirit.

Esmeralda smiled when she heard that, clearly confusing the nervous townspeople. She had begun to guess that she knew something they didn't. That, perhaps, some part of her friends had survived after all. Even if it was no longer as kind as the people she had known.

Ignoring their protests, she and Sophie set off out of the town proper in the very direction they had been warned against.

There, in the woods, stood a gingerbread house. It was real gingerbread speckled with cinnamon and sugar and trimmed with icing, and she could hear the sweet voices of her friends. There was no mistaking that accent. Sophie stayed at the path and waited as her mother went inside.

Sophie heard her mother shout "Hansel! Gretel! Cailleach! Carlin! Oh my friends!"

She ran up the path just in time to see her mother's body collapse. And yet, there her mother stood, thirty years younger, smiling at her.

"Oh my dear Sophie, we're home!" A translucent younger mother exclaimed as Sophie knelt beside a lifeless body.

Hansel and Gretel were playing on the floor, and decorating the inside of this gingerbread house were the candied hibiscus she remembered eating as a girl.

"But, how? This whole house... How did you... What is all this?" Sophie asked.

Cailleach's face darkened as she answered, "Draíocht, child. Witchcraft. After they took our family and friends, you left us a token of pure love that had been blessed. We awoke to live here in our gingerbread house.

"Every time one of the settlers with the blood of our attackers in their veins ventures inside, we take their souls and entrap them in the candies that decorate the outside of our eternal home. They took our lives from us; we will take their very souls. You are free to come and go as you please, my dear girl. Your mother must remain here with us."

Sophie promised to visit her friends and mother soon, but she had to live her own life, to teach her own children all that Cailleach had taught her and her mother.

And with that, the house and everyone faded away, happy and smiling, leaving Sophie standing with her mother's lifeless body on a bare patch of earth. The air still smelled faintly of gingerbread, and a single candied bright pink hibiscus flower was nestled in Sophie's young hands.

Sophie traveled for decades, passing through the town every few years, and always came back from a walk with the same candy. From a walk the woods, where the villagers feared to wander and nobody dared settle. They townspeople whispered about it, but not a single person had the courage to ask her. Everyone but Sophie who had ever traveled that way never returned.

Eventually, she settled in the little town, married, had children of her own, and then grandchildren.

Every month, on the day of the full moon, she walked into the woods and came back with her sweet treat, as she had done for so many years. When she was old and gray, she told her husband and family goodbye.

She walked out into the woods, and did not return. By nightfall, her sons had gone looking for her, but they didn't know her secret, where to look, or even why she walked here.

Her youngest granddaughter, Esme, did. She had followed her grandmother many times, though she knew she shouldn't. Once, when when she was five, her grandmother had caught her and told her the story of those who lived there so many years ago, what had happened to them, and the wonder that still went on in that place. She was twelve now, and much more stealthy. She slipped away to the magic house she had watched appear for her grandmother month after month. When she arrived, Esme found her grandmother's body. It looked like she was sleeping, with a smile on her face.

Somewhere in the night she heard a funny accented voice call, "Hansel, Gretel, Sophie! Time to come in, it's getting dark."

Esme's pert little nose twitched, and she closed her eyes as she smelled gingerbread and felt her grandmother's touch on her cheek for a split second. She opened her eyes to find a hibiscus flower, bright pink, and coated in sugar and sparkling in the moonlight like the very stars themselves.

And it was then that Esme knew in her heart that she would pick up her grandmother's tradition, and share the story; the story her grandmother began telling her that very night.

"Once upon a time..."

Snow & Red

- Kristi Luchi -
Illustrated by Wendy Martin

Once upon a time in a galaxy light-years from here, Earth ceased to be the home of humanity. No one knows why they left it, and the reason for their move isn't important to our story. Our story takes place on a small planet in a small settlement named Tolstoy. Those who resided in Tolstoy were concerned only with living their lives, and not in the machinations of the larger city nearby or the more populated planets circling around their own star.

One pair of girls in particular spent their days in their own private world: the twins, Snow White and Rose Red. In their youth, their interests were focused mainly on their mother and each other, and it was not unheard of for them to go days without leaving each other's side. Snow, a fair haired and blue-eyed child, and Red with her fiery hair and bright green eyes were a common topic of conversation among the villagers.

The girls grew as the years went by, retaining their sweet natures and blossoming into young women. At the time of this story, they are well into their twenty-first year, still living with their mother and tending the house and not interested at all in the husbands that those same townspeople thought they ought to be finding.

———— ◆ ————

One winter day found Red out in the woods hunting while her sister was in the kitchen preparing dinner for her family. Red's responsibilities kept her mostly outside, which was where she very much liked to pass her time, while Snow was content to be in and around the house, with her extra time spent helping her mother with repairs in the shop. She was slicing potatoes when her sister popped her head through the door.

"Got a deer for ya. He's a big one, too." Red gestured out the door to where a large deer was tied to the back of her hover bike. She kicked the dirt from her boots and brushed the forest from her breeches before coming in and sitting at the table. Her weapon, a sleek laser rifle with a worn grip and a matte white finish, was settled across her knees.

"Good, we need it," was Snow's only comment as she looked up from the stew. Red looked ready to trek back out into the woods where she could keep her own counsel and feel the fresh air on her face. Snow smiled and turned back to the pot.

"Soup should be done in a half hour." Giving it one last healthy stir, Snow swung the pot back over the fire, and they retired to the bathroom to wash up. It didn't take them long to get cleaned up from the day. Though, when their mother arrived, her hands were still grease-stained.

Jeanine was a Sci-tech and the only mechanic in all of Tolstoy. She spent most of her days tinkering between whatever machinery she was currently drafting and repairing the townspeople's robots. It was mostly a trade for goods service, though there was an assortment of individuals, the mayor for instance, who paid in credits.

After dinner and while they were all settling down to their nightly routine, a loud pounding rattled the solid door.

"Don't sit there with your mouths agape," their mother scolded. "Get the door, Red. It's snowing too hard and is entirely too cold out there for someone to stand and wait. We'll offer them the fire and a comfy chair. Snow, go and get a blanket."

Each went to do as commanded, but when Red opened the door, she screamed at what she found there.

On the other side of the door was a man, half robot and half human, beaten and injured. His sandy blond hair hung over his eyes, and his face was bloody and bruised. One eye, blue as the sky, was wide open, but the other was swollen shut. Red, having never seen a cyborg before, shut the door in his face. After a quick word from her mother she opened it again, keeping her reaction much more controlled this time. With the blanket her mother had bade her to fetch, Snow came from the room to his left, and without missing a beat, reached out and took his battered and mangled hand into her own. She wrapped a blanket around him and led him to the chair across from their mother in front of the fire.

"You poor thing," their mother clucked. "What's been done to you?" Memories flashed before her eyes, long and forgotten circumstances of a world and a war that seemed to exist a lifetime ago.

Snow started gently poking at a wound on his head, testing it for tenderness and weighing the need for stitches. She decided against them, saying, "When the swelling goes down, it'll be closer together. Really, it's just a side effect of the bump."

He shivered when he spoke. "I—I need a place to stay. It's too cold outside and—"

Jeanine, who had been studying him closely, interrupted his words. "Hush now and let Snow look at you. Of course it's too cold outside for sleeping. The snow won't let up until midday, I'll wager. I offer you the warmth of the fire for as long as you need it, and the healing and company of my daughters, Snow and Red, only if you promise to do no harm."

They exchanged a long and meaningful look before the man nodded.

"I promise." His voice, now stronger than it had been a second before, was deep and resonant in the quiet of the room. Snow moved from examining his head to his eye, dabbing gently at it. Then she moved onto his jaw, where there was a long and deep gash. She could see metal instead of bone through the abrasion.

"This one will need stitches. And you'll want Mother to look at it to make sure it's not damaged before I clean it up." He raised his eyebrow at her, but her mother replied instead.

"I'm a Sci-tech. Seen a lot of people like you before." Thinking of the veterans she'd cut her teeth on as a young trade school graduate, Jeanine finally set aside her knitting and stood from her seat. She examined the cut and felt along his jawline, but there weren't any fractures or nicks that she could see. "Whoever put you together made you out of good steel, boy," was her only reply before she resumed her seat and her knitting.

He was still and silent for the most part, extremely alert to everything they did around him, watchful even when she gave him the local anesthetic before the stitches. Barely a wince out of him.

"Where are you from?" Red wasn't one to beat around the bush and had no delicacy with words.

His looks alone would set him apart. Not that blond hair and blue eyes were uncommon; her sister Snow was of the same coloring, but the climate on Tolstoy was a mild one with long but pleasant winters. His skin was tanned with warm olive undertones that weren't common on their home planet. His eyes darted toward her, but he didn't respond.

"You must hail from somewhere," she pressed. "People like you don't just pop out of the woods in the middle of the night with no story to tell."

Still, he remained silent. Red, willing to let it go for the moment, got up to get him a glass of water from the kitchen and wondered who he was running from.

Snow found herself concerned with his quietness and wondered why he wasn't talking and what had happened to him.

Jeanine was only curious as to when he would fall asleep. She was the only one to find her answers that night. While Snow was tending his mangled knuckles, and just after she finished wrapping his hands in gauze to protect the cuts from infection, he drifted off into a slumber.

———————— ◆ ————————

The weeks went by, and the man became a fixture around their small house at the edge of the woods. Neither sister was sure if he was waiting for the parts that Mother had ordered, or if he was simply relaxing and hiding from whoever had hurt him. Some days he would accompany them as they walked through the woods, and others he would stay in the shop with Jeanine. Every day that passed, he became less reserved, until finally he told the girls his name: Bastian. No more information was forthcoming, though; he still wouldn't tell them anything about his family or his home.

During their long conversations after dinner and throughout the day, Bastian would very carefully avoid topics that would reveal too much about himself. He kept instead to the topic of the girls and their lives. Bastian was very afraid of something or someone, that much Snow could tell.

Thinking that maybe their mother would have more luck with him, the girls went off alone into the woods for the day. In her shop, Jeanine sat down across from Bastian and motioned for him to position his hand palm down beneath the magnifying glass. They were quiet for a long time while she opened the panel and examined the complicated jumble of wires and rods that made up his hand.

"I've said it before, and I'll say it again: this is good steel, boy. Where did it come from?"

"Johann Enterprises," Bastian replied quietly.

"Hmm." Jeanine reattached a bit of wire where it had come loose from one of the rods. "Flex your first finger." With that small success, she moved on the other three knuckles on the outside of his hand. She worked to replace the wire on the next knuckle.

"Why so much metal? And don't bullshit me, boy; I've put veterans back together who have less alloy running through their bodies than you do."

He was quiet for a long time before answering and Jeanine let him go at his own pace when he decided to speak. "I was born with a degenerative bone disease. When I was old enough, my parents operated to have the affected bones removed. At first, it was just one of my legs, then the hand, then the whole arm. Each year, they updated the parts and pieces to match the growth of the rest of my limbs. I've lost so many bones, I'm more machine than man now."

Jeanine nodded, guessing on the price such a venture would cost and tucking the knowledge back into her memory for later.

"That's a lot of surgeries. You're hearty and whole, otherwise?" She asked, replacing the rod that connected both of the last knuckles to the wrist.

"They cured the disease when I was fifteen. It's been erased from my DNA, but I can't grow back the bones I've lost." His voice trailed off, and Jeanine was aware that no more information would be forthcoming. She rewrapped the last two wires in his knuckles and carefully closed the compartment. Bastian leaned back and rubbed the back of his hand.

"Snow loves machines. Always wants to know what makes them tick. When the girls were little, I used to bring them in here and teach them what I was doing. Never had too many vets who needed work on themselves, but there are plenty who have other work for me. Red mostly sat and played or day dreamed of being outside, but Snow soaked it all up like as sponge. Snow sees beauty in all the mechanisms she treats." Jeanine paused and let that sink in for a moment before changing the subject.

"That hand should be good as new now. Sorry I had to wait so long for those parts to come in. Feel any better?" Bastian nodded, and gave it a good flex.

"Is there anything you need any help with?"

"Now that you mention it…"

———————◆———————

As the girls walked through the woods, they held quiet conversation about the weeks since Bastian had come to them. As they walked Snow gathered wood fit for kindling while Red kept her longbow at the ready. The rifle was strapped to her back, but Red hunted smaller prey with the bow when she could. They were following a small game trail when a sound from a nearby clearing drew their attention.

Red sank to the ground, the cold of the snow seeping slowly through her breeches while her sister carefully set her bundle of sticks into the hollow at the bottom of a familiar tree. Situating the pack that hung around her hips, Snow reached into the folds of her dress to grasp the handle of a knife she kept hidden there.

The twins moved closer. The noise, which Snow now recognized as the hum of an engine, seemed to lessen and give way to the ranting and screaming of a man.

His voice, rough as rocks tumbling down a mountain side and just as feverish, came to them clearly. "What the hell is wrong with this thing now? I swear if you've managed to ruin my ship, I'm going to have your fucking hide."

More ranting and swearing was accompanied by a loud banging and, after the sound of a compartment hissing open, there came a high pitched whining sound Snow immediately recognized. She took off toward the sound.

Red jumped up and took off after her sister.

"Dammit, Snow!" she hollered ahead of her. "Why is it I'm always chasing you into some hell or another that I'm going to have to bail us out of?" She kept the arrow at the ready, quicker on the draw than she was on the pull, and kept an eye out for anything and everything as she came to her sister's side. Snow, ever their mother's daughter, picked through the contents of her little deer skin pack while she walked, gathering the items she'd need by feel while she scanned the area in front of her. She spared a thought for her sister, confident that they always had the other's back, but knowing that she'd hear more from Red about this situation later.

What had once been a sweet little clearing, with pink and white flower bushes that bloomed in the spring and a winter-frozen stream off to one side, was now a blackened and burned soil with the course of the stream forever altered.

The ship, named the *Ava Marie*, had landed hard, turning up earth and exposing great rocks to a sun that hadn't seen them in a very long time. A little man with a dark and scraggly beard was busy beating and screaming at whatever was inside the panel Snow had heard open earlier. He hadn't seen them yet, and it gave Snow a moment to look him over while determining what her next step was going to be.

A smuggler, and a rich one at that. He wore a tan leather coat that went nearly to his boots over a simply cut pair of trousers and a button up white shirt. His chosen wardrobe proclaimed him a man of means, but it was the pin on his lapel that announced him as a trader. The symbol, a wheel superimposed over a coin, was universal for someone who could get a client anything he or she wanted.

He was small, this angry man, and made even smaller by the large men who lingered around the ship. Wincing and cringing whenever his voice piped up to a screech or the wrench in his hand landed on some helpless part of the vessel, Snow and Red stepped forward into the clearing. When he finally noticed their presence, he went from startled interruption to impatient berating, skipping the introductions and not even bothering to ask for their help. In the end, it was the damage he was doing to his ship, and not the man's ire, frustration, or his barking command to "stop standing around like worthless ninnies and help me if you can," that brought Snow forward with her little patch kit.

Wanting to keep her sister in sight while Snow worked to patch the damaged craft and keep an eye open for other dangers, Red paced around the clearing. She could feel the captain's eyes on her as she walked.

"Who are you anyway?" she asked when he shooed her away from the open loading door at the back of the ship.

"Who am *I*? Who are you? Barging in here and taking over a man's job! You two are making more of a mess of it, anyway. Sticking your twitching little noses in someone else's business! I don't know why I'm even standing here letting you talk to me!"

"Us! We're the people patching up a hole in your piece of junk ship, that's who we are. Making a mess of it? It was already a mess as far as I can see."

"Not quite, Red; it's actually been very well taken care of. Despite the beating and the hard landing, she's a pretty piece of art that's been well-loved." From the looks on their faces, the crew took a lot more pride in the vessel than their Captain did. She looked toward the one beaming the most, assuming he was their onboard engineer. "It's an Emerald Dwarf, right? They were used on the mining colonies of Adom." Snow's voice took on a thoughtful quality, as if she was remembering an old friend or a story fondly told. She spoke aloud to no one in particular. "Lots of high quality gems can take up a lot of room, but in the end the Dwarf is light enough for fast travel. The G-Class vessels like this were the best of the best in their prime, but they've been outclassed for years now."

The little man, whose name they still didn't know, looked near to having a apoplexy when he looked at the patch job Snow had done on one of the large hoses in the engine compartment. It wasn't a pretty fix, but it would hold. Red had enough confidence in her sister's abilities to know that, but it couldn't have been any prettier unless the Dwarf had been brought to their garage. The trader's beady eyes popped from one sister to the other, and for a moment it was if the cherry red coloring of his rage had leaked into his eyes.

He tried to speak, his mouth opening and closing like a fish. When that didn't work, he even took to bouncing from one foot to another. *If the whole thing hadn't been strange and off putting,* Red thought, *it would have been hilarious.*

Still, he stared at them, perpetually bouncing. His intensely menacing gaze put both girls on edge. He stopped suddenly, coming to a conclusion as he took in their coloring: Snow's fair complexion and muted wardrobe and Red's bright eyes and red breeches.

"Those Rose girls, that's who you be. Should have known better than to get involved with the lot of you. Don't know why I'm in this damned forest anyway. Bunch of lousy…" his words trailed off into a mutter, and with a quick signal, the men climbed back aboard the vessel. Soon they lifted up out of the burned clearing and, with a burst, shot across the sky.

"Curious little man." Snow remarked.

"What an asshole," replied her sister. In response to Snow's lifted eyebrow, Red lifted her shoulders in a shrug. "It's true."

"True as it might be, I'm glad we helped him. That ship couldn't afford any more of his abuse, and the crew certainly weren't going to do anything more than they absolutely must." Snow thought about the crew. Big men surely, but slow. They seemed inclined to do as they were told and little else afterward. What kind of engineer would sit idly by while a man with a wrench beat his machine? There was something about the situation that Snow couldn't quite put her finger on, but it was suspicious.

"I wonder what he was carrying? Every time I looked too closely at the ship, he would huff and blow until I went back to scanning the tree line."

"Traveling salesmen are a nervous bunch. Never know what kind of cargo they're carrying," Snow replied.

By then they had arrived back to the bundle of kindling that Snow had stowed at the base of the tree. Scooping them up, Snow turned her attention back to the task their mother had set them to. Thoughts of Bastian, and the information their mother had coaxed out of him, occupied her mind while she and Red searched for firewood. She recalled the conversations they'd shared with a blush. Speaking with him had awoken some part of her that she hadn't known existed. Certainly his mechanics intrigued her, the way parts and pieces fit together, but she also found herself wanting to know more about him personally. What he thought about things, how he dealt internally with situations. What were the sum of all the parts that she saw, and most importantly, how had they shaped him into the man he was?

Red laughed and teased Snow when she noticed her sister's preoccupation. While growing up, Red was always the first one to jump into the fray. The flames never seemed to burn Red; instead, she soaked up life in all of its glory. Whether she was dealing with boys wanting a little kiss and cuddle, or traversing a conversation with the local washer woman, Red seemed born to it. Snow's shyness simply wasn't a trait her sister shared.

When they arrived home, it was with an armful of kindling to restart the fire and a rabbit Red snared. Jeanine was reading in her chair while nearby, Bastian turned a hunk of beef their mother had prepared over the fire.

Snow watched him for the entire night, keeping one eye on preparing dinner and another on Bastian. Jeanine wasn't very forthcoming about any information she'd gleaned from the young man and led the girls to believe that he hasn't spoken much at all to her in their absence.

"Bastian, why is it that you're so tight-lipped on where you come from? What happened to you for you to end up beaten and bloody on our porch? Who are you running from?" Red pressed him again after dinner.

Bastian paused with his fork halfway to his mouth. His eyes, both of them visible now that the swelling had gone down, were an odd combination of resigned and determined.

"I had hoped to..." his voice carried though he spoke quietly. "I don't want to involve you anymore than I already have."

"That's a load of bull."

"Red, stop!" Snow sat on the edge of her chair, manners warring with curiosity and some unknown feeling of dread that her sister would upset Bastian.

"Snow, it's all right." Bastian set his hand atop hers and looked at her for a long moment. He turned his attention back to Red. "I would prefer not to talk about it and not to answer any questions concerning the events that led me here. I wish only to recuperate and rest. If you want me to leave, I will. But I won't say anymore. Please, let it go."

Red looked ready to argue, but Jeanine sent her a sharp look that stalled any further argument from her daughter.

Jeanine turned her attention to Bastian. "I offered you a place to rest and heal in good conscience, without knowing what happened to you, as long as nothing happened to hurt those under my roof. Nothing has happened, and if it does, it will be me who presses the matter." Another pointed look at Red. "Now, let's finish dinner and speak no more of it."

———————◆———————

Some days later, Jeanine sent her daughters into the woods to see if there was any fish to be had. The sun shone brightly down on them, slowly melting the ice and snow as the twins set out to find a part of the river that was fit for fishing. They were walking along the snowy bank when a wild splashing from downstream caught their attention. Red quickened her pace at the sounds of distress; it was entirely too cold out for someone to be in the water.

Having spent more time in the forest than her sister, Red was quick to find her footing amongst the roots while Snow fell behind. Her sister was already hunkered down behind a bush when Snow finally caught up to her. It wasn't the first time, nor would it be the last, that Snow would consider taking a page from her sister's book and donning leather breeches instead of a skirt when they ventured into the woods. Settling next to Red on the ground, Snow followed her sister's gaze toward the river. She recognized the crew of the Dwarf immediately.

They both watched as one of the large men pulled another from a hole in the ice, each fretting until the two of them were safely back across the river where the Dwarf was settled, almost precariously, on the far bank. Once again, the ship had damaged the surrounding area, bending saplings under its weight and breaking apart a huge boulder. Snow wondered if the only thing holding the bank together were the roots of the enormous tree under which the wet crewman was now settled, wrapped in blankets and holding a cup of something steaming.

"What the hell are you doing?" The little man from before, more furious than ever, rounded the corner of the ship and barreled down at two more of his crew. "Get back out onto that ice and fish out my cargo! We don't have time for screwing around! You do what you're paid to do: follow orders!" Cowed, three of the men made to move back out onto the ice.

"You really are a damn idiot!" Red shouted, taking her sister by surprise. Snow stood up from where she'd been hiding only to watch her sister cross to the bank. Red stood on an outcropping of rocks that jutted into the river. She stood with her hand on her hips scowling at the smuggler.

"One of your crew has already fallen into the ice. The fact that he's tall enough to touch the bottom is probably the only thing that's saved his life, and you're sending out others?"

"You! What are you doing here?" His face became redder as Snow emerged from behind the bush. "Don't you come near my ship. She hasn't been flying right since you got your hands in the engine. It's your fault I've lost this cargo! Your fault I've got to send my men out onto the river! If you've got such a problem with the way I handle things, *you* get my cargo!"

"If my sister hadn't been there, your ship would still be sitting in that clearing, not flying at all, you ungrateful ass." Red turned her attention to the crew when they stepped out onto the ice again. "You, get back onto that bank before you fall into the water, as well. And get your friend into the ship, he's likely to catch his death sitting out in this chill."

Snow scampered after her sister, who by now was carefully picking her way across the ice toward the hole. "Red, what are we doing?"

"We're certainly not letting those men back out onto this ice. They'll fall through! We're going to fish their cargo out for them, or at least help as much as we can."

"You get off of that ice! I don't want your help, and I don't need it!" The smuggler was bouncing up and down again, his face still red and his eyes nearly bulging. "My men are going to take care of it before you screw anything else up!"

"Not gonna happen. Right now it looks to me like you're just going to keep losing men in the water, and your cargo along with them." Red stopped a few feet from him and crossed her arms over her chest. She held her head at a stubborn tilt that Snow had seen a number of times before. Red wasn't going anywhere, and she wasn't going to let anyone else back onto that ice.

"Fine, you can do it! Risk your own life, I don't care. But you had better get my cargo out, or I'll have your hide for it." He continued ranting to himself, his words trailing off.

"Snow, go on over and see if that thing has a winch."

"Of course, it's got a winch. It's a Dwarf!" Snow threw over her shoulder as she began her slow walk toward the bank.

The captain, who had been pacing back and forth across the bank stopped in front of Snow to stop her from approaching his ship. He stroked his bald head and his beard in one long pull, and set his beady eyes. "Hey, you better watch yourself. Don't you damage my ship!"

"She's not going to listen to you, little man. Do you want your cargo or not?" He only scowled at Red's words, keeping resentfully silent. She shrugged. "Then don't bother us and let us work."

With that, Red dismissed the man from her thoughts and focused instead on the task at hand. It took her a long moment to reach the hole in the ice, but when she did, the task didn't seem as difficult as she had originally thought. The large metal crate was sticking up out of the water, likely the work of the soaking crewman now resting comfortably in the bowels of the *Ava Marie*. A length of rope attached to a large hook sat at the edge of the water, and Red looked again at the box noticing this time that a series of rings were welded onto the sides of it for easy loading.

After a moment of thought, she called out to her sister. "Snow, how's the winch coming along?"

"All I've got over here is the rope that's leading out to you, though it's good quality and seems to be fairly new. Should do the trick!"

With a smile to her sister, Red went back to the rope and untied the hook, pulling it until a large coil sat at her feet. With a few deft movements and one good knot, Red found herself in possession of an arrow capable of being fired through the loop. The loop was small, and she'd have to find the perfect angle. She wanted the arrow to bounce and skid across the ice on the other side instead of flying off into the sky or down into the water. Still, Red was confident in her ability.

Snow, who had been watching her sister carefully, marveled at the skill that the shot would take. Accounting for the balance and drag of the rope, the direction and speed of the wind, and aiming just so, Red counted on the trueness of the arrow. She left more up to chance then Snow herself liked to deal with. Mechanics were so much simpler to operate and duplicate.

Red made the shot with surprising ease and walked carefully around to where the arrow rested on the ice. After that, it was just a matter of sending both of the loose ends of rope through the winch. Everything seemed to happen quickly after that.

Without a word of thanks or even a look in their direction, the captain rounded up his men and readied for flight.

"You're welcome!" Red called after him, but he hadn't heard her. In a matter of moments, the craft was lifting carefully off the ground to hover over the gaping hole in the river. The girls watched as the winch was engaged, and the cargo slowly lifted from the water. A few words stamped across the sides of the box piqued Snow's interest.

"What is *Johann Enterprises*?" Red asked, echoing a little of the excitement that Snow felt.

"*Johann Enterprises* makes mechanical parts. Their name is etched on nearly every part and piece back at the garage. Mother might know more."

The girls, lost in thought, continued upriver for a long while before they found a spot they considered safe enough to fish in. Soon they returned home with a string of fish and the traveling salesman and his cargo were far from their thoughts.

Red and Snow were in good cheer from their trip when they arrived home. Bastian and their mother were again seated in the living room. Most of his wounds had healed in the time that he had spent with them. Snow was glad for his recovery and surprised that she found herself dreading his leaving. They ate the fish that night, some of it going into the larder for dinner in a few days time. The company and conversation was enjoyable, and Snow found herself over and over again being drawn into conversation with Bastian. Red noted that her sister was quickly growing fond of the young cyborg and fretted for his leaving, as well.

Bastian looked around the table and spoke. "Thank you very much for tending to my injuries and allowing me to stay in your house. I can't express how much it has meant to me to have a safe place to rest and heal."

Snow flushed as his gaze lingered on her for a moment. Red became increasingly worried for her sister, though their mother silently approved. They all talked later into the night, only retiring at Jeanine's silent gesture.

Later, when everyone was supposed to have been long asleep, Snow tiptoed into the main room where Bastian slept on the couch near the fire.

Sleep had not come to her. Instead, she finished up alterations on one of her father's old shirts to fit Bastian's trim figure. She carried the bundle of clothing in her arms, pausing only to gaze at him for a moment while he slept before she settled it at his feet. Within one second and the next, he awoke.

He leaned up on his elbows and stared up at her, blue eyes watching her carefully. She stammered through an explanation about a new shirt and pair of pants to replace his ruined ones. "I know that you must be getting tired of the charity, but I've sewn these to be a better fit for your form. Our father was much broader and taller than you, and the clothing are dreadfully baggy, and I wouldn't really be surprised if they were awfully uncomfortable. I thought that you might—"

"Thank you," he interrupted.

There was genuine tenderness in his voice that left Snow once again wondering about his life before them, where he was from, and how he came to be on Tolstoy.

"Your name fits you, you know. Your sister, as well. Your mother told me the story. It's those trees there, under that window?"

"Yes." Snow looked over to the window, but all she could make out through the glass weas two lumps covered in snow, dark sticks protruding. "You should see them when they're in bloom. The bushes are older than we are; Mother planted them when she first moved into this cottage with our father. She knows things sometimes. Mother can tell you the way things will happen or the way they have. It's how she knew that she'd indeed have two daughters that would match her beloved rose bushes, and how she knew to let you in that night of the snow storm. She hasn't said anything, though. Nothing about what's to come."

She trailed off, not knowing what to say or how to say it. Snow felt that he was going to leave them, to leave her, and the knowledge upset her. Not enough to say anything now, though, before the actual leaving happened. Would she be able to even then? Bastian settled his feet on the floor; his chest was bare, and his hair was sleep disheveled, Snow blushed.

"I've made you a leather vest to go with the pants." She turned her attention to the pile and shifted through it until she pulled the vest free of the rest of the clothing. The leather was soft, supple, and embroidered in a slightly darker brown around the edges and button holes. She displayed it for him and when he reached out and touched the leather, their fingers brushed against one another. They held the contact for a moment before she pulled away.

"I'll leave you to sleep now," she told him as she turned to leave. He grabbed her hand in that last moment and smiled.

"Thank you." Snow smiled and went back to bed.

The next morning dawned and saw Snow's fears realized. She was the only one awake, as often she rose early to bake bread for the afternoon meal. His hand was just turning the knob when she stepped out into the living room, and he paused in the act to meet her eyes.

"You're leaving," Snow spoke quietly.

He nodded and stood quietly for a long moment. "I have things that I need to take care of, people that are looking for me, and others who would know that I am safe and well. Thank you, Snow White, for taking care of me. I would not have healed as well as I have if not for you and your family. I will return one day, and explain everything."

She nodded, silent. The sadness was there, but words were not. So she moved across the room, slipping her arms around him in a tight hug. He returned the gesture, and a moment later, the door was latching closed behind him.

Red came into the kitchen an hour later to find her sister sitting quietly on a stool in front of the stove, a loaf of bread rising on the counter behind her.

"Bastian left, didn't he?"

Snow nodded and Red, not enjoying the sight of her sister sad, crossed to her and wrapped her arms around her shoulders.

"He'll be back."

"I know."

Red was surprised at her sister's words and leaned away to look at her face. "Why?"

"Because he left this."

Red looked carefully at her sister's outstretched hand. In it lay a pendant dangling from an expensive golden chain. About the size of an acorn, it was adorned on one side with a family crest: an eagle soaring on a bed of alternating colors with a sheaf of wheat clutched in its claws. Red turned it over and saw a stylized letter 'J' on the back.

"Wow," she breathed.

"Yeah," Snow agreed. "This morning when he left, he promised me he would come back and explain everything. I found this shortly afterward on the mantle. It was in front of a picture of me Mother keeps there."

Red wasn't sure what to say. A bond had formed between Snow and Bastian during the time that he had stayed with them. Instead of offering platitudes or other hollow words, Red kissed Snow on the forehead and moved across the kitchen for coffee.

It took only seconds for the machine to issue a full pot, which Red promptly poured out into three cups, knowing that their mother would come from her bedroom soon. Jeanine, of course, already knew that Bastian had left in the early hours. The feeling of impending departure had been upon her for the last week; it hovered at the edge of her senses urging her to pay attention to those in her care. In preparation for this, she had planned an outing for the girls into the town. The mayor had recently paid up a neat little sum for the repairs she had made to a droid in his household, and shopping would give the girls a distraction from their thoughts.

So, she sent her children into town to purchase fabric and trimmings for new formal gowns for the both of them, using the excuse that they barely fit into the dresses they currently owned. A shiver went down her spine as she watched the two climb into the car and disappear down the lane.

Red and Snow rarely went into town anymore. Unless some kind of special event was happening, they kept to their trees and their cottage and minded their own business. Today the town was bustling and busier than it had ever been. Mummers of gossip about a rich man's missing son and heir tripped from every tongue they passed. In the clothing shop, ladies milled, and it was easier to pick up pieces of gossip.

"He's been gone for weeks," one of the tailors was telling her client as she entered measurements into a digital tablet. Her fingers scribbled with the stylus excitedly as she spoke. "Good looking boy, but there's a mystery about him. And the ransom!" She paused to show the woman an illustration on the tablet before nodding and continuing.

Snow turned them out while she walked down an aisle lined with an array of fabrics, trims, lace, and thread. Her mind was still filled with

Bastian, and she didn't have time for something happening another world away.

Red took considerably less time to choose her fabrics than Snow, picking a dark burgundy with grey lace trim and a silver underskirt. When they left sometime later, Snow had finally decided on a silver brocade with white and gold threads over a shimmering white underskirt. The projects would give her plenty to occupy her mind until his return. Everything was carefully packaged and tucked safely into the back of their vehicle.

Spring was finally settling into the township of Tolstoy, and on the drive back, Red decided to take a detour route across a meadow they generally avoided because of the time it added to the trip. An explosion to the left of the car caused Red to curse and turn the wheel sharply, and she nearly collided with a large hay bale on the side of the road. A ship touched down on the side of the road just next to the bale, a familiar figure emerging.

"It's our old friend!" Snow cried pointing at the smuggler as she threw open the door.

"Friend, my ass, he nearly killed us!" Snow paid little attention to her sister for she had already opened the door and was rushing to his side. Red retrieved the laser rifle from the back seat of the car and crawled across the passenger seat just as another ship, this one sleeker and much newer, also landed nearby.

Red meet up with her sister just in time to see Snow and the little man dodge a round of fire from the men disembarking from the newest ship.

"What the hell have you gotten us into?" Red whispered harshly to the smuggler. He wasn't apoplectic with rage and anger now; instead, he seemed very calm and very in control of himself. Jeanine, if she were there, would have said that he was a veteran of these kinds of altercations. But Snow and Red didn't know that, and they decided within short order to do as they had been doing over the end of the season. They would help the little man.

"These men are trying to steal my cargo. We can't let them have it! You any good with that thing?" He motioned to Red's rifle. She nodded in reply, and he turned to Snow. "What about you, got any experience with a weapon?"

"No, not that kind, but I'm quick with this." She flashed the dagger she kept on her person at all times and smiled at him. The excitement got the better of the girls, almost as if they were part of an adventure rather than a life-threatening situation. A voice from the others, familiar in tone, caught her attention before she could do much else.

"This doesn't have to go like this," the voice called. "It can be easy, all you have to do is hold up your end of the bargain!"

"Back into the ship!" the little man cried as he attempted to usher them up through the bay door.

"No, you landed this thing for a reason. It's likely not to have repaired itself," Snow said. "I'm sure that we can figure this out some way or another. How many of them are there?"

The man bit his lip, his teeth sharply white against his dark beard. "At least four. What do you have in mind?"

Snow thought for a moment, but it was Red who piped up.

"What is it that they want from you?" Red called as she peeked around to look at their opponents. The smuggler sputtered and spit. Red, realizing that they didn't have time for this, ignored him. "Whatever it is, just go and get it then head for the woods. Snow and I will come at them from opposite sides to draw them away from you. Get as far from us as you can and we'll find you afterward. Then Snow can do what she does to get the ship running."

The little man nodded and disappeared into the ship for a moment. Afterward, he took off toward the tree line, not once looking back to watch the girls. Red, steeled herself and handed her sister the bow— she'd at least fired that before and would remember how to handle it. They crept across the meadow keeping low to the ground and hidden by the subtle rise in the earth around them. They covered a small distance to each side.

After a long moment, and a flash from a small mirror that Snow had on her person, a volley of arrows and ammo sent the pursuers diving to the ground. The arrows rained down on the group of attackers for several seconds before Snow, then Red, ran out of ammo.

Looking for each other, they both raced backward across the field, dodging and weaving and they made their way to the forest.

Excitement tore through them, vibrating against their skin and through their veins. They had done it, for the little man was nowhere to be seen. The attackers didn't stand for a long moment, and by then, the girls were only a red and white silhouette on the distant tree line. They came together a few yards into the trees and, grasping hands, followed the trail the smuggler had made in the brush. It was easy to follow him; Red spent her time in the forest tracking deer and other animals that disturbed much less of the woods in their passage.

Everything felt surreal to Snow and Red, as memories of their time spent in forest feeling impervious to harm and foul deed flooded back to them.

They walked slowly and lightly where their quarry had been running and eventually came upon where he had taken to ground for a spot of rest. They found the man's satchel beneath an outcropping of rock, but he was gone. Curious as to what the thieves had been after, Snow reached for the bag, but Red stopped her.

"We don't know what's in there."

Snow shook off her sister's hand. "He's gone, and I'm curious. What was so important to him that he left all of the rest of his cargo behind for the thieves to take?"

Red, who truly was just as curious as her sister, waited with bated breath while Snow examined the bag. The first thing she removed was a small leather-bound ledger filled with scribbling and notes about various trades and illicit practices, that they had expected to find. The second was a tattered folder filled with loose papers and pictures. These drew a small gasp from Snow as she leafed through them. There were dozens of pictures of Bastian in the folder, each filled with notes on the edges. Pages and pages of notes filled with what she determined were kidnapping and ransom plans that spread out in front of her when she dropped the file folder.

She looked up in time to see Red reaching into the satchel and pulling out a large wad of money—real money, not credits—from the bag. It must have been then that the smuggler returned, because he grabbed Snow's wrist in a vice like grip and hauled her toward him. A knife appeared at her throat.

"Stop, it's us! We've made it! They're gone!" Red screamed as she dropped the money. Still the man's beady eyes stayed trained on her sister as his grip tightened around her wrist.

"Don't you be lying to me. You've got your eyes on my money, don't you? Well, you can just put the idea out of your head, because you can't have any of it!" he screamed.

"You've been playing me this whole time, haven't you? That's why you've been helping me, you want to get in on *my plans.* Well that's not going to happen, do you hear?" He pushed Snow away from him with a hard thrust and grabbed the satchel. He disregarded the folder, instead scooping up the small book from the ground and dropped it back into the bag. When he pulled his hand back out, he was holding a laser pistol.

"Now, what I am going to do with you? You know everything now, and I can't trust you not to come after me. Smart little girls you turned out to be." He swung the front of the gun from Snow to Red and back again, a wicked gleam in his eye. "Say goodbye to your sister, little girl."

Instead of the impact of the round through her chest, the shot fired up into the sky as Bastian burst from the forest and collided with the little man.

Bastien's face contorted in rage. He attacked the smuggler, slamming him into the rock outcropping. Fists flew as they came together, each of them landing blows. Unfortunately for his opponent, Bastian was part machine and had the power of his upgrades behind his blows. Bastian's fists landed over and over, breaking any attempts the man made to defend himself. The smuggler landed a number of blows himself, but they paled in comparison to the ones he received.

His eyes were wild, and his mouth was twisted as he beat at his opponent. The smaller man collapsed to the ground, sobbing and covering his head. Bastian raised his hand once more, to deliver another blow.

"Bastian!" Snow called. Her screams, which had been incoherent noises up until that moment, found his name with desperation and relief. He stopped his fist and turned to face her taking one single step in her direction. Then he stopped and waited.

Snow, on the other hand, did not stop until she pressed herself safely against him, her arms wrapped tightly around him, despite the rage and violence that she had seen in him just then. She breathed in deeply of the scent of the woods and sweat on his clothing. His arms tightened around her as he spoke.

"I thought… My brother said that two women dressed in red and white had run after him into the woods, and I thought you were gone."

Snow shuddered in his embrace. "I nearly was. But you came. How," she pulled back to look up into his face; "how did you find us?"

"Come and I will explain everything." As they left the clearing behind, Bastian weaved the tale of his abduction and ransom, his escape, and his arrival at their house in the middle of the woods.

"He meant to sell me back to my family, but the Johanns aren't a predictable bunch. Instead of sitting quietly and being ransomed off, I fought back and won my freedom, while my family sought out my captor. He will be brought to justice." Bastian finished his tale as they arrived back at the girls' car.

"Does this mean you'll be leaving now?"

Bastian replied by taking her face into his hands and leaning down to kiss her.

"I will be leaving, but don't worry. I'll return." He turned his attention to Red who was watching the scene. "I've a brother, Eric, who would be most interested to meet you, Red."

"Ha," Red replied. "If he was one of the men who hunkered down under a volley of arrows and took too long to stand, I'm not sure if I want to meet him."

Another man, looking much like Bastian with hair a shade darker and brown eyes instead of blue, walked up to the small gathering.

"Any man worth his salt would hide with a barrage like that coming toward him," the man said as he approached the group.

"You're Eric, I take it?" Red asked with a raised eyebrow.

"I am," Eric replied.

She sized him up briefly. "Well, no one's going anywhere until you all head back to our house for dinner. Mother would never forgive us if we let you all leave without meeting her." She reached out for her sister, who released Bastian with a sidelong glance and a warm smile. The girls, their arms intertwined, walked back to their car and settled in.

Eric eyed the car and then shot a look at his brother, wondering what Bastian had gotten them into. Bastian only grinned knowingly and headed towards the car, jerking his head for Eric to follow.

Before they could reach it, Red rolled down the window and stuck her head out to holler, "Well, are you getting in or not? We're not waiting forever!"

True Confessions of a Sea Witch

- C.L. McCollum -
Illustrated by Jessica Douglas

Once upon a time, there was a pretty, but air-headed little mermaid, and a brilliant, but misunderstood sea witch who was cursed to clean up her mess.

What? That wasn't the way you expected me to start? Too bad. You asked for *my* side of the story. You could hardly expect me to leave out any mention of myself. It's the principle of the thing.

Now where was I? Oh yes, you wanted to know what happened to the king's youngest daughter. Why I "cursed" her, or however her sisters are spinning the tale.

Well, the first thing you need to understand is that I had that girl's best interests at heart all along. No, truly. I swear I did. Do you think King Marianas would have left me here safe and sound in my little bungalow if he'd thought I intended harm to his precious youngest? Of course not! I'd be tossed right on my tail down into the darkest, deepest part of that trench he's so fond of, and you and I wouldn't be having this conversation.

No, the whole mess isn't nearly as sky and sea as the rest of the royal princesses keep telling the media it is. I'm hardly the "evil" sea witch they paint me to be. Witch, absolutely, but evil? Perish the thought. I'm about as evil as that sea sponge in the corner there.

The truth is, I've devoted my entire life to serving the king and his family. The midwife who attended all six princesses' births? Me. The healer who nursed the queen until the bitter end after she was poisoned by that bastard Lionfish? Again, me. The counselor who kept the king sane and focused on his kingdom and daughters in the wake of his wife's death? I'll give you a guess.

Uh huh, me.

I doubt there's a single subject in all the seas Marianas commands that is more loyal than I. I'd stake my life on it.

No, the trouble was never than I intended to harm the little guppy. The trouble was that I did everything in my power to keep her safe. But even all *my* power doesn't help much when some bratty little princess dares to command me to do a thing that might put her in danger. I'm loyal, remember? What's a subject supposed to do when one of the royals gives a command? Say no? That would go over swimmingly, let me tell you.

Bless her, she was just so *young.* You know, I've always thought fifteen was far too soon to let the younglings up to the surface. Sure, the land-bound call their girls near women at that age, but the humans only live to eighty or so if they're lucky. We mer live twice that! Fifteen's still barely a child. You can't expect a guppy to be mature enough to understand everything they might see up there. They're just not equipped to handle it. The depths forbid anyone listen to me when I bring that up, though. Oh no, that's arguing with tradition, that is, and I should be ashamed for thinking it. If old Mrs. Proudtail breached the surface at that age and was fine, then surely her children will be just fine, too. Silly of me to think otherwise.

Well, their precious princess, Sirena, certainly proved me right, now didn't she? Only her first surface visit and she not only interferes with the Sea taking Her tribute from a storm, she goes and fancies herself head over heels in love with the human she saves. Not a single word spoken between them, he's unconscious the entire stretch of their time together, and Sirena swears up and down "they've got a connection" and "he's the one."

She wouldn't know her "one" if he slapped her in the dorsal fin.

No, no, see, I'm not doubting that a mer can love a mortal. I'd be quite the hypocrite if I did, wouldn't I?

Oh you haven't heard that rumor? Ye gods, the gossips must be slipping. There was a time I couldn't show my face about the reef without someone whispering the tale behind my back. You see this scar here across my flank? That's what loving a man got me. He was a whaler captain, handsome as the sea is wide. Swore to the sun and back that he loved me as he'd never loved a human maid. Wooed me with stories from his travels and pretty bits of stone and crystal you can only find on dry land. Just swept me off my fins as if I were as weightless above the water as I am down here. I was going to go to him for good. I even found the spell to give me legs and lungs and all. That's the only reason I had it here when Sirena came asking. Just never had the chance to use the spell.

The monster I'd hoped to marry harpooned me.

There he was, showing off his catch and laughing with his crew about how no other fisherman had ever brought back a live mermaid before. He thought I'd make him a pretty penny, selling me to some royal court or collector out in the dry lands.

Of course, he didn't manage it. I was every bit a witch then as I am now. I conjured a whirlpool and swept the whole lot of them down to the bottom of the ocean. Took a while for the wound to heal, but I survived, didn't I? That's the part that mattered. Survived, and vowed I'd turn my love and devotion on a more deserving focus: the royal family.

I never expected my service to turn out this way: not *punished* per se, but definitely out of favor with most of the court. No more visits from the darling girls, no more gossiping with the dowager sea queen about her latest oyster tail accessorizing or listening to the whale choirs sing the hours.

You think I got off easy, but I've no one, now. That's what you don't see. I have have no one left. All because one idiot child couldn't keep her wits about her over a pretty human face. I almost wish I had cursed her like her sisters claim, that I'd damned her as I'm accused of. Then, at least, I'd deserve what's happened. Seems to me that would be more of a comfort than having my loyalty thrown in my face in such a way.

Oh, there's my darlings! I must have worried them, getting all maudlin. No need to fret; my babies wouldn't hurt a clownfish. Eels get a bad rap, don't they, Tide, my love? Just like their sea witch momma, huh? Now Swell, don't get your tail in a knot; I have two hands. No getting jealous of your sister. I swear, pets are so needy. But they're my darlings. Last bit of love I have to keep to myself. Makes me feel a little less alone.

Where was I? Oh right. The "curse." Honestly, I didn't know what to think when Sirena showed up. It's not like any of the girls ever came alone to visit—they always gadded about in a proper school, all six of them, except for the surface visits. She was a mess too, I tell you. Wringing her hands, fiddling with the oysters on her tail fin, tearing at her hair. That was not a mer thinking with all of her faculties.

She started raving about how she'd saved his life, and didn't that deserve his love, and I would give her a way to claim him, or so help her, she'd toss herself into the abyss. Really, it was a tantrum worthy of a tadpole, not a princess, but there was no calming her down. Sirena kept pressing me and shrieking at me. I tried to convince her not to go through with it, you see, and that just added spin to her whirlpool. She thought I wanted to keep them apart, to destroy her happiness or some nonsense. She even started throwing things about my workshop! Scared my poor darlings half to death, and nearly caused a typhoon right there in the room with some of the spell components she tossed so casually.

It was lucky I keep the walls covered and cushioned in sponges; it was meant as protection in case of accidents, but it certainly held up against intentional destruction, as well. Of course, some of my sponges will never be the same, poor things. They're resilient, though, and some of the colors they turned are just lovely, don't you think?

In any case, it became clear there was no talking sense into the maid's head, so I agreed to perform the spell. Not that I didn't send Swell streaking off to warn the king as fast as she could swim, mind. I'm no fool. I'd hoped he'd arrive to deal with his daughter before I could complete the working, but that was the day the kraken woke, remember? And well, dealing with that hungry beast was enough to distract even the most attentive father.

Still, I managed to at least set a time limit into the spell. It wasn't easy, let me tell you. The initial working I'd discovered for myself so long ago was intended to be permanent. Legs and land till death did us part, don't you know. But this one, I mixed to last only a moon's span. Twenty-eight days, and then she'd have to return to us. A mer can't survive long out of the water. She knew it. I knew it.

Sirena still seemed certain she'd convince her charming prince to marry her before the spell wore out. Not exactly the brightest of starfish, but it was… almost sweet to see how deeply she wanted to love him. Oh, to be young and naïve again.

But that's the gist of it. She asked for the spell; I cast it. She swam off to reach the shore before it took effect. As soon as I had the strength to move, I followed after to keep an eye on her from the shallows for the duration of the month. It really—

What about it? Oh for the love of—of course, her sisters said I cursed her. Why am I not surprised? I didn't cause any pain to punish her, nothing of the sort. Let me put it this way: have you ever swum too far in a day, twisted your tail, or pulled a fin? The pain feels a lot like knives, doesn't it? Now, imagine you've never, ever used your tail and suddenly decide to swim to the South Sea and back. In a day. How do you think you'd feel? Little sore, hmmm? Barely able to stand it until you got used to using the muscles? Now you're getting it.

Brand new legs, the maid had. With no other choice but to walk on them. Did you know it takes the humans a year or more to learn to walk as children? Nothing like our babes practically swimming out of the womb. Legs are terribly complicated, and require a great deal more physical coordination than we need. A fin is much more streamlined. With only a month to figure out her feet, she was never going to be pain free as she walked about. There was nothing I could do about that. I'd been prepared for it when I thought to sail with my captain forever. It was worth a little pain to be with him. Or so I thought.

Regardless, she thought it was worth it, as well. Even if she apparently thought it was only a product of my "terrible cruelty."

Idiot.

Her voice? Again, not my fault, believe me.

It wasn't her "cost for the spell." Please. I live on a very generous royal stipend. I hardly have to charge anyone for my work, much less one of the royal household. That's the whole point of the stipend. I keep myself and my spellwork ever available to their majesties, and they keep me in tuna and kelp. It was quite the favorable arrangement, prior to this little snafu. Left me free to pursue the mysteries of the deep, to perfect my craft. And the court had a witch on call for whatever little emergencies might crop up. Sure, I charged some of the other citizens. It was only fair with the amount of time and effort most of my spells take out of me. But I always traded work for goods, and before you start, I traded for something *useful*. A lovely bit of fabric to decorate my boudoir from some of the wreck divers; spell components from the reef farmers. That sort of thing. What use could I possibly have for someone's voice?

No, her voice was another byproduct of the spell itself, same as the pain in her legs. Humans don't have gills, do they? All speech is through the lungs and vocal cords. They can't even begin to make any of the sounds our kind do, and even if they could, *they don't speak our language*.

And we can't speak theirs. I had to use another spell to communicate with my whaler captain, and even then, there was plenty of room for misinterpretation on my end. And he certainly took advantage of it, didn't he?

Well, no, I couldn't have cast it on top of the other spell. Do you have any idea what kind of energy a spell of that magnitude takes out of a witch?

Of course you don't. What am I thinking? Frankly, I barely managed to drag myself out of my grotto to go after her when she headed to the beach. If not for these two pretties here, I'd probably not have made it at all and just ended up drifting away with the current until I could manage to find something to eat or a safe place to rest and recuperate.

Spell work is far more dangerous to the caster than it is to the one requesting such a spell. You should remember that.

All King Marianas' daughters should have remembered that.

It wasn't as if any of them were allowed to miss my lessons on how to protect and ward themselves against other magic workers. Seems Sirena only remembered the part of my tutelage that told her I could get her what she wanted. No matter the cost to me, or her, or even our kingdom itself.

Yes to the kingdom! Think, you fool: if Sirena had won her precious prince, what do you think would have happened then? She'd just disappear off into her new mortal realm without a word to her loved ones, never to mention our existence to her beloved husband? Do you really think he'd still love her, still *trust* her, once he discovered she wasn't truly human at all? That she'd concealed her very nature from him?

The spell would have ended in a month. There was no question of that. Had she won him in that time, she still would have returned to her natural form.

I told you: men see us as a *thing*, a creature to be caught, caged, and sold. Sirena would have risked us all to have her darling prince.

Just be grateful it didn't come to that. I know I am—grateful beyond words the prince broke her heart and turned to another before her deadline came due.

Oh there now, I'm fine, Tide, my sweet. Don't fret; Mommy's just a little emotional. You too, Swell. Calm yourselves, my darlings. We're fine. We're just fine.

So, that's the lot of it, then, as much of the tale as I was really involved in. Was there anything else you wanted to know? Or can I get back to my day now?

Is that why I *what?*

Of all the ridiculous—no, she's not dead! Why would you even think that? Ugh. Her sisters will be the death of me, I swear. I thought *Sirena* had a lack in judgment. Neptune help us, one of them will grow up to be the most idiotic queen in the history of the kingdom. All I'm going to say is, may Marianas live a long, long time. Preferably until his eldest pulls her head out of her tailfin.

No, Sirena is *fine*. Sea witch's honor and all. I will admit there might have been some mentions of suicidal thoughts towards the end there, all "I'll die if he doesn't love me" nonsense like young guppies sometimes do. Her princeling marrying his oh-so-human rescuer instead of Sirena really did a number on our little princess's self-esteem. Not that I expected her story to end any other way. But what do I know, hmm?

Granted, things were a little exciting for a moment there, what with her histrionic tantrum of tossing herself back into the sea without any warning to me that she'd need her gills and tail back earlier than scheduled. Getting her back to the surface to breathe until I could reverse the spell was stressful, to say the least. Sirena tried to fight me, shouting something about turning into sea foam since she couldn't be with her one true love. I tuned most of it out, to be honest.

Once she was back to normal, I turned her over to her father, and that was the end of it.

Honestly, I'm not sure where she is. Marianas said something about sending her away to learn her lesson. My guess is she's at some sort of sleep away camp for the troublesome children of royals who need a reality check. It's likely she's already declaring her undying affection for one of the other little ingrates. What can I say? Love's a fickle thing at that age.

Princesses. So dramatic.

The Dazzling Finister

- Ellen Million -
Illustrated by Rebecca Flaum

Once upon a time, west of the sun of Ergis and east of the moon of Zel'la, there was a settlement on a rich ice mining asteroid. Three computer units did the work of running and organizing the mine. The smallest and sharpest of these AIs was a MARya unit. While the other AIs maximized profits and efficiency, she developed a talent for preserving worker life, and thought of unique solutions to scheduling conflicts.

When the spaceworkers stripped off their helmets and drank, they propped their boots on the AI consoles to tease them as they played Ergis cards and gambled their profits to each other.

"What do you want for your share of the profits?" they would ask after a particularly good cycle.

The governing contract of the settlement required a percentage for the artificial sentients of the project, to allow them eventual independence. The oldest AI always requested memory, or motor units, or processing time with the super computer orbiting a nearby planet. The next oldest was saving towards a high-end android upgrade, and kept every credit for that eventual day.

"What about you, MARya?" they would ask her, and MARya set a subprogram to considering the question. "I'd like a feather from a finister," she finally answered, when the program had completed.

The finisters were sleek little quadrupeds the size of birds, and their brilliant, fire-colored, feather-like scales were tipped with phosphorus. The creatures were said to be smart and loyal pets, able to learn clever tricks and basic games. They were rare and getting rarer; the planet where they had been discovered had burnt in a freak solar flare. The only finisters that had escaped the devastation were those in captivity—a bare handful at best, and no one knew how they procreated, only that they didn't seem to. Every so often, a captive finister would simply vanish, with no explanation for their disappearance. MARya was intrigued by their mystery, as much as their beauty, and she downloaded every piece of data she could find on them.

The other AIs made mathematical ripples of amusement across their communication link at her odd request, and the spaceworkers laughed out loud. MARya joined them, giving a chime that she had selected for her own laugh, and expected nothing to come of it.

But the spaceworkers were fond of her, and over the years, she kept their safety and comfort first in her programming. Though she wasn't required to by contract, she always maintained their preference in air and water temperatures, provided their favored sustenance, and more than once clashed with her fellow computers in defense of their fragile health over efficiency and profit.

"They are fleshlings," she would remind her sisters-in-duty. "They need rest and oxygen."

When resources were scarce, she saw that rationing was sensible, and when energy had to be conserved, she always put aside her own pleasures first. During a partial collapse of a mineshaft, she sacrificed her own servos to rescue the trapped workers, and took the replacement cost from her personal credits.

A few months later, the foreman of the asteroid presented her with not only the feather she had requested, but a whole, living finister.

"How did you find one?" MARya asked through her speakers, toning her astonishment into the output. The finister preened itself in her main workroom. MARya had to adjust the focus of her cameras to appreciate the delicate details of its feathers and shapely little claws.

"Won it in a gambling match," the foreman said, exhibiting his embarrassment in the flush of the soft flesh in his face. "Knew you wanted one."

MARya, delighted, hired a fleshling crew to rearrange her processor banks for the accommodations for the creature, and special-ordered the rations it was said to be particular to. Using her servos and monitors, she trained the clever creature to play tricks and games, and was even able, to her surprise, to teach it Zel'la chess. Then, one day, she thought to use one of her controllers to put a modified virtual access port on her finister. It scratched at the port curiously, but did not seem bothered by the implantation. MARya activated it and stepped into the holo-grid with it.

It chose a male humanoid avatar, not the finister avatar she had carefully crafted for him.

"I didn't expect that," MARya mused to herself. She was used to talking only to herself; even in the holo-grid, most of the flesh spaceworkers still tended to treat her as another program, and they didn't find the holo-grid a comfortable headspace. The other AIs found her frivolous, and ignored her for the most part.

The finister inspected his virtual arms and hands, and touched the shock of orange hair that covered his head. He was nearly human in his features and build, with just enough subtle differences to be slightly alien.

"I thought a humanoid avatar would be more comfortable for you," he said with a slow, sweet smile.

MARya selected her own humanoid avatar, simply so she could express her surprise with a jaw drop.

"You're sentient!" she said. Although she had taught it chess, there were many programs not classified as sensate that had the capacity to follow simple rules; it had never occurred to her that there might be more to the finister.

The finister's smile grew dazzling. "You've always treated me as if I was."

MARya thought of all the times he had acted as no more than a simple-minded pet, begging for food and feigning foolishness before others. "Why haven't you let the other fleshlings know?"

Recognized sentience had been a hard struggle for the AIs to achieve. It sent her programming into a loop to think that the finister might deliberately set out to keep such a thing a secret.

"Being pets gives us a certain amount of freedom to observe and direct, without being obvious about it," the finister said, as if that explained everything.

MARya set a subprogram to consider that idea, and asked, "Do you have a name?"

The finister shook his head, and his hair had the same phosphorus flare that his feathers did. "Not the way the fleshlings do."

"I'm one of a thousand and three MARya units," she agreed with him.

"You can call me *your* Finister," he suggested.

"Only if you call me *your* MARya," she countered, and it seemed appropriate to give the chime she used as a laugh, though she wasn't entirely sure why.

"I like these," Finister said, touching the waist-length braids that MARya had selected, and she set them immediately as her program default.

"Fleshlings tell a story about a maiden in a tower with impossibly long hair." MARya nearly sent a databurst, before a subroutine reminded her that Finister was still a fleshling, and would not be able to handle the surge of information in such a fashion. Already, Finister felt more like herself than any spaceworker did, and certainly more than her sister AIs ever had.

"I know that story!" Finister said. "It ended with tears that could heal blindness."

"I've never understood tears," MARya confessed. "Such an inefficient use of fluids."

"And so confusing," Finister agreed. "Humanoids leak them for both joy and sadness."

"Sometimes, it seems like they aren't even sure which is which," MARya confided. "It's utterly baffling."

Finister laughed at that, but it was an understanding laugh, and MARya gave her chime agian.

The room in the holo-grid that she had chosen for them had been fitted with a setting of Zel'la chess, and Finister sat cross-legged before it and placed his pieces out. MARya settled opposite and did the same, marveling at the familiarity of the action.

"I have so many questions," she told him. "What was your planet like? Why are there so few of you?" She moved the crafter token into an early attack.

"It was bare and burning when I last saw it," Finister said sadly, defending his own crafter on the board with a sweeper figure. "But long, long ago, it was a green jewel, with mountains like glass and oceans of singing algae." He didn't answer the question about why there were so few of the finisters left, and MARya set a subroutine to consider the puzzle, but made a file reminder not to ask him again, because of the sadness in his eyes.

MARya told him about her first installation, and about managing subprograms at the mine. "The MARyas were among the first programs to be granted sentience," she told him, accessing the history files to show him. "We wouldn't have gotten there without the Predecessors, of course. The IOR units fought brilliantly for our independence, even though they were all memory-wiped before they could see the fruits of their struggle."

"Does it bother you, not to have a body?" Finister positioned his tokens into a flanking attack, and MARya broke through a weak point with a preacher piece. They had even control of the board, and though MARya had lost more pieces, she still held more of the stronger tokens.

MARya flexed her avatar's fingers, and stretched one arm before her. "I don't know what having an android body would do for me, that having an avatar here cannot do, and a machine is in every way superior to the frailties of flesh."

She rippled the avatar, turned into a bear, and then back into the humanoid girl she liked best, with thick braids to her waist. She picked up one of the pieces that her antics had knocked over.

"Don't you wish you could do that in real space?" Finister sounded thoughtful, a nuance of humanoid speech that had taken MARya a long while to learn. He toyed with a few of his tokens before moving a piece.

"I can have my sensors and servos reconfigured if I need to," MARya said, puzzled by his question. She wondered if he wasn't setting his own subroutine when he hesitated in reply and changed the subject.

They talked about the humanoids, about the confusing politics they dragged throughout known space with them. When MARya finally won the Zel'la game, they played a variety of other alien games, particularly enjoying the ones that involved simple boards and old fashioned counters. If MARya's programmed time alarm had not triggered, she was not sure how long they would have stayed there. "Your body!" she said in surprise. "You must need food again! I have duties to attend to!"

She deactivated the holo-grid and monitored Finister curiously with a few of her processors as she scrambled to do her mine tasks with the rest. The fleshling creature had not changed, exactly, but the subtle feather-twitches and flexing of tiny claws seemed to have new layers of meaning. The tilt of his head and the sidelong look was suddenly a message, the scamper of his feet had more substance than just play.

For three months, they met in secret. They watched the humanoid media together, agreeing that music was wonderful for different reasons; MARya loved the mathematics behind it, and Finister loved the emotion. They explored a gamut of games and fleshling entertainments, and MARya imported a variety of immersive holo-backgrounds for them to explore. She kept her privacy levels high, and if anyone joined them on the holo-grid, Finister used the default avatar MARya had first created for him, mimicking his simple pet behavior from real space into virtual space.

MARya found herself allotting more of her memory to thinking about him, and when she was working through her mine duties, looked eagerly forward to going back to the holo-grid to be with him.

Then, one rotation of the asteroid, MARya found herself spooling over a consuming mining scheduling puzzle, over and over and over and over, until her virus alarm went off, and she realized that the foreman was opening one of her private emergency panels.

"What are you doing?" she asked in puzzlement, most of her resources still consumed.

"MARya, you've been unresponsive for two days!" The foreman sat back on his heels and wiped his sweaty brow in relief as MARya automatically adjusted the climate controls for his comfort. "We had to call the programmers!"

MARya stopped the program in question mid-loop, and had to tamp down several related subroutines, putting aside the question of why aside as her sensors began reporting other details to her. She was missing two standard days worth of accountable time in her records, and worse than that... "Where is my Finister?"

The housing she had built for him was empty and cold. No hint of his warmth lingered in the carpeted floor, and not a single feather remained.

"I don't know," the foreman told her. "MARya, the mine…"

MARya gave a shriek that had the humanoids across the asteroid cupping their ears and staggering. Her programs all focused on the gap left by Finister, the loss as keen as if she had nerve endings and they were all on fire. All of the subprograms she had set to think over their conversations were spinning in an agony of abandonment.

Desperate to keep her from tearing the mine apart from the inside, the programmers and Intergalactic Enforcers who swiftly arrived delved into the asteriod's databanks and almost immediately found a bill of sale for the Finister. He had been shipped off the first day that MARya had been in her loop, sold to a fast merchant ship bound for places unknown. No fleshling had the capacity for over-riding MARya's protocols, and the programmers immediately found evidence pinning the virus and sale to the other settlement AIs.

"She had something we didn't," they reported in unison under the duress of the programmers and the threat of having their databanks utterly wiped.

MARya could feel their sullen jealousy, and wondered if they even recognized what they were jealous of.

She loved her Finister, completely and in every line of her code. Notes about him peppered every private database she maintained, and her programming had been rewritten from scratch in many places in her attempt to understand him.

"Put me in a ship," she told the programmers.

"It will be expensive," one of the programmers told her. "You'd have to buy out your tenure at the mine."

"A ship will cost your justice settlement," one of the enforcers told her. "You could spend those credits on a new pet…"

MARya made an earthquake that shattered one of the unused mine shafts and set every light on the settlement to humming at a tooth-gritting frequency.

"You'll be impossible to replace," the foreman said glumly, but he didn't try to stop her.

It took most of her savings and a promised percentage of future earnings, but she was fitted into a sleek little space-hopper, and set out to chase down the cold trail of her Finister.

For a full year MARya searched, taking passengers as she needed to backwater moons and obscure stations. She downloaded every databurst she could find that referenced finisters, chased every story, visited every exotic zoo, and ran her energy banks down to nothing.

She took risky trading routes and battled off pirates, fought off program viruses from unsafe data connections, and filled databank after databank with observations that she wanted to share with Finister. After a while, she stopped saving those thoughts and locked out those files, lost in a numb misery without him.

She was limping back to a planet with repair facilities when she found a passenger ship spinning wildly through space and sending out a weak distress signal. She nearly went right by it—she was herself nearly crippled, and she knew that no one would blame her for simply taking word of the distress to someone more capable. But she heaved a sigh through her ventilation ducts and pulled alongside, stopping the out-of-control spin at the sacrifice of one her own stabilizing struts.

Together, they scavenged necessary parts from MARya's crumpled ship, sealed up the damaged life-support systems, and got both of the fleshling crews to safe compartments within the larger ship.

"What are you doing out this far?" the other AI asked her, as they waited together for rescue crews. He politely did not mention the shameful state of her once-lovely plating.

"I'm searching for my Finister," she told him, and the databurst she added was concise and practiced. She had no expectations of understanding or information.

"I've heard of one of those," the AI surprised her by saying. "Twenty-seven jumprings from here, there is a humanoid woman, the Collectress, who has a zoo of amazing animals and creatures. Her acquisition of a rare finister made local newsbursts."

MARya examined the responses her programs cascaded at her, and decided that it must be what hope felt like; hope after a long, bleak period of despair. She had to vent plasma from her overtaxed energy banks, and for just a moment, it looked like the trail of one of Finister's phosphorous feathers.

Gratitude was not a common subroutine in ship's programming, though most AIs had a sense of honor to them. So MARya was further surprised when the AI offered more. "I have a program for a docking series that will speed efficiency, and the dock where the Collectress lives has terrible problems with these things. Perhaps that will get you closer to your Finister."

MARya gave the AI one of her processing units in gratitude, knowing that she wouldn't have space to keep it once she had been refitted anyway. She had to give up banks of her memory, as well, sacrificing years of mining data and copies of media that she had enjoyed. She could only afford a little cross-space probe jumper from the scrap of her ship, not even fitted for a crew.

After another year, even the probe-body failed her. The last jump was made on fumes and luck, and landed her smack in the middle of a little private space station that had lost its orbit and was falling into a moon. She used the last of her momentum and a slow burn of her final fuel cells to jolt them both into a stable orbit, where the station sent a call for help while they kept things together as best they could.

As they waited, in a slow rotation of the moon, the AI asked her, "What are you doing out this far?"

She told her, and the AI surprised her by having heard of the Collectress. "Ah yes, I've heard of her," she said sagely, fluttering some of the valves in life support to keep them from sticking. "You'll need something rare indeed to get the Finister back from her."

They drifted in companionable silence for some time, while MARya examined her databases for anything rare or valuable.

The station AI surprised her again. "I have a private holo-recording of a famous fleshing musician who stayed here a time. I have never shared it before, but it may catch the attention of the Collectress."

She transferred the file to one of MARya's databases before they parted ways, and MARya thanked her profusely. She was towed to the nearest repair station, where she was installed into a private short-distance shuttle. She had to give up a few more banks of memory to make the transfer, losing some details from her early installations, and some of the processing power that she had always enjoyed.

She missed the edges of her virtual mind, and the speed that her previous vehicles had taken for granted. It took a full year at shuttle speeds to reach her destination, and even then, the shuttle began to fail, spilling radiation from the leaking engine shields. Just as she was making a final approach to the planet the Collectress lived on, she heard a weak distress signal. One of the satellites had lost power and was in a slowly decaying orbit towards the planet's surface. The AI in the satellite was old and unsophisticated, but MARya couldn't let it perish, so she left her place in the docking line to boost it back into a stable orbit, resigning herself to another long wait to land.

The AI was grateful for her service, and asked her what had brought her so far from her asteroid mine to this planet.

MARya again explained her quest to find her Finister.

"The Collectress is a proud and vain woman," the satellite told her. "She loves beautiful things. There is a jewel in one of the matrices of my older processors. Take it in trade for your Finister."

MARya graciously extended a servo unit and accepted the jewel, thanking the AI.

"Shuttle MARya," the settlement hailed her at last. "You are cleared for landing. What is your purpose here?"

"I'm seeking work," MARya said. "I am an AI skilled in personnel and organization and may be of assistance in your docking processes."

Her references were good, and she easily passed their tests. "We've needed assistance for some time," the existing AI admitted to her. "But the Collectress doesn't like to spend money on anything outside of her collection."

MARya accepted a credit grade far below what she was used to, and traded her shuttle in scrap for a basic android model that was available, shedding the last excess memory modules she had. With the last of her debt allowance, she customized it to look passingly like the humanoid avatar she had chosen with Finister, with waist-length braids of copper wire perched on a dull metallic shell.

She fell into her work with the stored passion of three long years of travel, re-organizing the docking schedule and re-assigning the personnel. She used the program that the ship she rescued had given her, and in a matter of cycles had cleared the docking backlog. The staff cheered up and began working more efficiently as she found them tasks more suited to their skills, and MARya had the settlement humming with happiness again in short order.

Her work did not go unnoticed, and her program gave her a jolt of alarm and excitement when the Collectress herself came to give her commendation.

The Collectress was a humanoid, tall and stately, and dressed in rich velvets and rare silks. MARya knew her basic android body looked plain and clunky by comparison in its standard issue jumpsuit.

"You've done amazing things here," the Collectress said, giving MARya a haughty glance. "I believe I owe you a favor."

It was the moment that MARya had been working towards for so long, and her programs aligned to chatter nervous data at her before she could apply a logic pattern to dampen them.

"I understand you have a finister in your collection," MARya said, as casually as her mechanical voice could manage. The Collectress stiffened, and MARya observed a tight, jealous look on her fleshling features.

"I do," she replied coldly.

MARya understood from her research of the woman that she would never be able to trade the things that she had for Finister outright. Nothing she had was of that much monetary value, and the Collectress was possessive and controlling. "Let me spend a private night in your zoo," she suggested. "I would like to see a finister in flesh."

The Collectress considered, running fingers over the console that MARya used to interface with the settlement AI. MARya's android system gave a little shudder that she decided was disgust.

"Agreed," the Collectress finally said, and her dramatic exit left MARya's programs in a dizzy flurry of activity. Could her Finister be so close? Was her search finally coming to an end? If she could just talk to him, maybe they could devise an escape plan together. Perhaps she could persuade him that it was worth exposing his species' sentience in order to make the Collectress release him; regulations on slavery in the Given Galaxy were strict and swiftly enforced. She shut down the program that reminded her the Collectress might not have *her* Finister.

That evening, MARya came to the gates of the Collectress' compound, and was ushered in to the quiet zoo.

Free of the crowds of the day, the zoo was an oasis of exotic beauty. Tamed creatures were allowed free rein of the gardens; brilliant peacock grallians roamed the aisles, and little white sunbirds flitted between the branches of the arching trees. Every inch of space was groomed, with marble paths and perfectly arranged plants in every hue the setting yellow sun could show. Even the cages were beautiful, and each perfectly suited the creature it housed. A striped gazebeast roared from a perfect replica of its desert home and a thick-furred harmonygrazer paced the shielded edges of its cage, whining restlessly as it swished through the grass.

MARya paid none of them any mind, walking at once to the enclosure for the finister.

He was clinging to a tree, for all the world acting like a simple Terran monkey in rippling, glowing finery.

"Finister, my Finister," MARya called hopefully, voice pitched low.

He turned his pointed head to look at her, and MARya's programming stuttered over hope so keen that she had to halt that portion of her program before it overwhelmed the rest of her units. There was the virtual reality port she had installed, and the playful way he scampered over to greet her was familiar and delightful. Strangely, there was no recognition in his actions, only curiosity.

MARya's android hands were steady, plugging in the access cable and stepping into virtual reality with him.

Gone were the immersive backgrounds, a sacrifice of the downgrades MARya's memory had gone through. But she had saved her avatar, with the waist-length braids, and his, with the finister-orange hair tipped with phosphorus.

To her surprise, he did not choose his avatar, but slipped by default into the finister she had first created for him. "F—Finister?" MARya's processing units were too full of activity to maintain steady vocals. "My Finister?"

But the finister only frolicked with the ends of her braids, and did not speak.

"Finister, do you remember me? Do you remember our games of Zel'la chess?"

The finister groomed itself, settling all of its phosphorous feathers into place. When MARya pulled a Zel'la token from her databanks and manifested it between them, he only knocked it over and scampered after it when it rolled.

"Please, just give me a sign," MARya begged.

All night she talked with him, seeking some affirmation that he was more than the primitive pet he had been masquerading as.

"I wore out three ships trying to find you," she told him, seeking any flicker of intelligence in his round eyes or in the tilt of his head. He only sniffed at her braids and blinked at her, adorable and idiotic.

MARya's proximity alarms finally made her break the connection. Daylight was breaking over the zoo, and the Collectress was standing at the door to the finister's enclosure. "Did you find what you were looking for, AI?"

'My name is MARya. *His* MARya,' she wanted to reply, but her courtesy programming prevented her. So she only shook her head. "I had a lovely time," she answered instead, overriding her honesty program. "I would like to come again tomorrow night."

"One night was our agreement," the Collectress said, chilly scorn in every word.

"I have a file you may like in return," MARya offered. "It is a rare recording of a very famous humanoid musician." She gave details of the recording that the space station had given her, watching the Collectress' face brighten with desire.

"You may have your night," the Collectress agreed.

But the following night was no more rewarding than the first. MARya cajoled Finister, saying, "I've traveled so far to find you. Don't you remember me? You can trust me, Finister! Show me your true self, I beg you."

That morning, the Collectress came again to escort her away, and her gaze was pleased and full of self-satisfaction. "Still haven't found what you were hoping for, have you."

Something about the tone of her voice gave MARya's program the last piece of data she needed. The Collectress had done something to Finister, something that dampened his sentience. She identified the heat in her processor as rage, and made her servo fingers uncurl from fists.

"The finister is very entertaining," she said, as mildly as she could make her voice. "I have a jewel you may be interested in adding to your mineral collection if you give me another night with him." She extracted it from a shoulder blade storage compartment, and watched the Collectress' eyes light up with material lust.

"Very well," the Collectress said. "You may have one more night."

The third night, MARya didn't hook Finister up to the Grid, but sat with him in real space and stroked his shimmering scales carefully, looking for a mechanical device that might be inhibiting his mental capacity. She told him stories as she worked, telling the finister about the hard journey.

"I gave up half my memory in capacity downgrades," she told him. Nothing rewarded her careful inspection, and as the night spun to an end, her programs ran out of things to try. Pressure in MARya's facial servos led to a leak of solvents. "I've even learned to cry for you," she told him, and before she could stop him, the finister touched his tongue to her faceplate fluids.

He spasmed, flinching away from the caustic solution, and writhed on the ground while MARya leapt up in alarm. Then he vomited, three shuddering retches, and a little silver machine slipped out with the contents of his primary stomach. Shaking his head, he reeled back and sat up on his haunches, staring back at MARya's strange android form.

"F—Finister?" MARya queried, too much of her processing involved in keeping her flood of hope quelled to keep her voice recordings steady. "*My* Finister?" When her program found no more appropriate response, she gave the chime that she had selected as her laugh, a laugh that Finister had told her he enjoyed. "I have traveled so far to find you," she said with joy. "I wore out three iron ships for you, and gave up half my memory banks. It has been three years, but I never stopped searching."

"Stop!"

The Collectress was there at the door to the finister's cage, with a handful of uniformed men, two Intergalactic Enforcers, and a programmer fanned behind her. "Look, the android has damaged my creature! I told you, it is dangerous! I require you to remove it! It should be re-programmed!"

The Enforcers moved at once to detain MARya, a powered restraint held between them. "Wait," MARya said in despair. "Please! He is..." Her core program stopped her before she could explain. Finister had always concealed his sentience; it wasn't her place to reveal it now, even if it would save him from this captivity. "You must release him," she finished lamely.

The Enforcers were unmoved by her plea, and the power sapped obediently from her servos at the clamp of the restraint.

The Collectress smirked at her, before standing protectively over the finister, who growled at her, revealing two rows of sharp filament teeth. "You will dismantle the android," she said with authority. "It is too dangerous to be allowed autonomy."

"Are you pressing charges?" one Enforcer verified.

"I am," the Collectress confirmed. "Take her away."

MARya's shell obeyed the restraint program, walking woodenly away, until a voice stopped them all.

"You will stop."

The humanoid Enforcers turned, though MARya could not, and she could only see their expressions of surprise and amazement as they cowered back in sudden fear.

"I ask you what is the greater crime," said an achingly familiar voice behind her. "Someone who sacrificed everything to find me, or a woman who knowingly suppressed a sentient to add prestige to her collection?"

The Collectress flinched and stepped further away. MARya struggled against the restraint, but it was too effective for her programing to overcome. She cursed the poverty that had prevented her from installing full-range cameras.

"I loved you!" the Collectress protested.

"In the manner of love that only wanted to possess," Finister countered. "When you have searched for me three years, when you have worn out three iron ships, when you have given up parts of yourself, then you may know what love truly is."

Then, he walked around to where MARya's sensors could drink him in, and she was astonished at the sight of him. He was humanoid, like his avatar had been, with phosphorous orange hair.

"You are a shapeshifter," MARya said in amazement, double-checking that she was not somehow in virtual space without knowing it. "Not only a sentient, but a shapeshifter!"

He smiled at her. "We finisters have stayed out of the mainstream of the universe by shifting to fit in where we desired."

The Enforcers released her restraint with a stuttered apology, but MARya still felt strangely weak. "I had such an empty space left in my programming when you left. I—I think this is what love is."

"You know it better than fleshlings who were born with hearts," Finister said gently. He touched the solvent on her faceplate. "You even learned to cry for me."

MARya gave her chime of laughter. "I understand tears of joy at last!" She quickly dabbed them away before they might hurt someone or damage her jumpsuit. "What do we do now?"

"Do you wish to press charges?" The Galactic Enforcers had taken the Collectress by the arm. The fleshling woman was crying tears of anger and rage, and protesting her innocence even as one of the programmers lifted the silver intelligence damper from the slimy pile the Finister had regurgitated and identified it.

The Finister looked at her thoughtfully. "You tried to strip me of my very identity, to add prestige to your collection. You caged me against my will and kept me from the MARya that I loved."

The Collectress cringed and ceased her struggles. "I can pay..." she started to plead, but Finister stopped her with an upright hand.

"It is MARya that has suffered the worst," he said. "You wronged her most with your accusations. Offer her your compensation."

"A ship," the Collectress cajoled. "I shall install you on a golden ship, with all the memory banks you could desire."

MARya felt as if all of her programs had slipped into perfect harmony. "I will accept your compensation and drop any charges," she said peacefully. She had no programs with memory allotted for revenge. "I will have my Finister and our freedom. I need nothing more to be happy."

Her Finister took her stiff android arm and they walked away from the tearful Collectress and the agitated enforcers. A thought occurred to MARya.

"Do finisters live very long?" she asked him.

"Practically forever," her Finister replied.

MARya's android figure could not smile, but she made her happy chime of laughter. "Then it really will be a happily ever after."

- Audi Belardinelli -
Illustrated by María Andrée Paiz

Once upon a time, there was a princess running for her life. Her breath hitched in the back of her throat.

Briar Rose bit back bile as she stepped over the mangled bodies of friends, servants, and the many visitors who came from all over the kingdom for her birthday celebration. They lay silent now, the pain they'd experienced before death reflected on every part of their bodies. Briar Rose tried her best to avoid meeting their glassy stares in the darkness. The rush of blood pounded in her ears as she strained to hear anyone following her, fearing the worst of the one who was searching for her: the one that everyone had feared. The one who killed them all.

It was so quick, too quick for anyone to react when the darkness descended on the festivities like a thick cloud of poison. It slowly twisted the bodies of those she was now walking over until they were nothing but blackened masses of bones and flesh. The stench was overpowering to the point that her eyes teared, but she couldn't stop even to cover her nose; every moment she lingered was a moment closer to being caught.

When the darkness came, her parents had barely enough time to slip her into one of the many passages that lay in the castle's walls, known only to her family and the few close servants who assisted in her escape. The passages had once been filled with laughter, and happy celebration, as light reflected off the many hanging mirrors that hung in the hallways.

But now, they were gone. There was not a single remnant of the festivities that had once taken place. The decorations were replaced with death as Briar moved through them once again.

Fear had a tight grip on her heart, clawing at the shadowed walls until the dim light behind her was nothing more than a faded memory. Briar Rose's eyes barely adjusted to the darkness, leaving her half blind as she stumbled painfully through the tunnels. Hope seemed to fade the longer she moved towards it without any avail. Even now, Briar Rose could hear her crow calling out her name, seeking out the lone princess who escaped the fate of the rest of the kingdom. The screams which filled her ears for so long were now swallowed by the silence of the tomb all around her.

The edge of the wall grew cold to the touch, leaving her shivering in a gown that was torn into tatters of vibrant cloth in her haste to escape. It offered little protection, now she'd made it through the last of the tunnels. Soon, they would lead her out into the surrounding woods and from there, she'd have to find her own passage out into the outlying lands. It was a solid plan, one that would work if she could make it that far.

Briar moved as swiftly as her sore feet would allow until she reached the edge of the tunnel. There, her fingers found a wall in front of her. It was rough beneath her touch, drawing patterns along the edges of stones placed long before her birth for the sole purpose of helping those who needed safe passage.

It was her way out.

Briar Rose's heart pounded in her chest, louder now as the air stilled around her. She scoured the stones for the one that should move beneath her deft fingers and open to the world outside. Soon the disease would infect her, too; feeling the coldness from the stones seep through her fingertips, she struggled to seek the way out, knowing what that would mean if she didn't escape.

Death still lingered in the form of a witch who roamed the halls that she'd fled earlier.

Finally, her grip tightened on the edge of a stone which felt out of place. It caught on the tips of her fingers as she dug in and tugged until it fell with a heavy thud against the ground.

From there her breath caught as she took a small half step backwards. Briar heard the sounds of stones, grating and shifting as they moved against each other. Her eyes couldn't pick up what was happening; her fingers shook slightly when she heard the stones continue to move above her head. Soon a light slipped through the cracks. She blinked and squinted at the illumination which painted a fresh look on the passage she'd been running through. It grew from a mere flicker to encompass the hole where the wall once stood in front of her. Stones were gone, replaced with a large enough space that she could slip through.

The joy of freedom echoed through her as she slipped through the opening, her eyes adjusting to the sudden onslaught of light. She raised a hand to block some of the blinding brightness, until she realized it wasn't coming from above but in front of her.

A familiar voice called out from the light, one that Briar Rose would never be able to forget for as long as she lived. She pressed her back against the wall that had closed behind her already. It was too late to turn back now, and the light continued to overpower her to the point where she only saw white around the thin line of a figure moving closer.

"Hello, darling." The voice curled out to her like smoke, enveloping her until she couldn't breathe without feeling the awful presence that had taken the lives of so many others before her.

Briar Rose was frozen. Panic spiked in her blood as she fought to free herself and run in any direction, as long as it took her far from there. But nothing worked other than her eyes, blinking back the tears that started to form but didn't fall. Her only movement was the hand that had been covering her eyes falling slowly to her side. Briar was left completely defenseless as the light started to fade into black, and her body growing weaker as the figure became more solid with every passing moment. They grew closer, darkness swallowing up the light until Briar Rose could feel the warmth of the creature's breath on her cheek.

"You almost missed all the fun," her tormentor whispered.

"Noire."

The last word of a princess before she fell into a deep slumber and the world forgot about her.

———◆———

Once upon a time there was a hacker following a trail of code. Shredding through the last of the branches, Cobalt was nearly out of breath by the time he pitched forward into a small clearing. The forest swayed and moved, attempting to swallow what was left behind him, before he reached back to snag his bag at the last second.

A triumphant look flittered across his face as he clutched his prize, but it was short lived as he swung the pack onto his shoulders. No one else believed him when he'd told them of the trees; they only heard about it as children in the stories from their elders. They were just stories, so everyone told him. Each one had been made up to lead them to believe that the kingdom once housed something other than the smog that left the poor defenseless and the rich high above the pollution. The rich were untouched by the destruction they'd caused, leaving it to the rest to have to toil away with nothing but stories of a better time: a time of legend.

A time of a princess who could save them all.

Cobalt was one of the unfortunate many that had gone through life without so much as a credit to his name, much less the technology at his disposal for such a high living. Now, his heart raced in his chest and kept pace with his feet, carrying him further into the uncharted territory. The dark would only hide him for so long. Each step he took led him into the unknown and closer to the mystery that he knew was on the other side of the weak signal he was following. The security droids back in the city had made his escape difficult, proving to be more than pointless and barely operational when the time came to be tested. He'd made it through a weak spot in the fences. The burn on his neck had faded to a dull ache.

It only made him more determined to find her. The pain would subside, but the knowledge that his people were slowly choking to death would never leave.

The stories were enough to set him on his path as he ducked beneath another fallen tree. His eyes adjusted to the dimly lit path that he followed with every beep of the pad he clutched. It would lead him to her. He knew it. Even if no one else believed his mission, they hadn't stopped him. The other men and women forming the rebel coalition had only voiced their opinions, but hadn't stopped him from following after his own beliefs. If anything, they all needed a beacon of hope amidst the chaos that surrounded them.

The Glassers continued to build themselves new towers above the pollution and farther from the mess that was the city below, while poor people barely made it through the day without hacking and losing more of themselves to the sickness that descended on the city. Yet while they went up, he went out to find the key that would put an end to it all and save the people.

If he could find the lost princess, the one buried in legend, then he knew they would finally put an end to the Glassers' reign. No more need for gas masks or using any remaining credits on antibiotics to keep people alive. They would be free to live as they all should, without the stench of death lingering on every street corner.

The last quarter kilometer was uneventful, but the path he'd been following had been swallowed up by the briar patches. All it took was one look behind him to see that with every step he took, it was one step closer to being lost forever. The forest moved on its own. He'd close his eyes, and it would shift all around him until he had no idea where he was if not for the signal that called out to him: *her* signal.

Months of work had him scouring old and inactive commercial communication links. He scanned for any sign of life outside the city walls, and just when he was on the verge of giving up, he'd found this one. Cobalt grinned despite himself as he crawled through a tight aperture. He stumbled out the other side to a sight that took the breath from his lungs.

It was a castle. A castle buried within a forest that by all accounts shouldn't exist in the first place. The pollution that killed people within the city was toxic to all living organisms, and yet, he'd been travelling hours through these woods without a single sign of disease. It was peculiar, but not as much as finding what he'd been looking for.

The castle was grand in size, far taller than some of the first skyscrapers the Glassers had built in the past. Where the new structures reached for the sky, this one settled for the tops of the trees that protected it. Walls were in ruins, with stones and glass ground into the earth. His boots made a delicate crunching sound as he walked. The stone was then met in the middle with mirrored glass that shone despite the years of the forest growing within its many walls. They looked as if they'd been welded together, without a clear divide between where the stone ended and the glass began. The mirrors towered over where he stood, reflecting the moon high above and bathing him in a pale green glow.

His personal tech beeped as he gripped it tighter in his hands, careful not to damage the scrap parts he'd found and pieced together. Tech was scarce for those living on the streets as they were forced to live on little. Very few were allowed to mess with things that cost more than a Grounder's life. It beeped again, shrill and loud enough to wake him from a deep slumber as Cobalt's fingers moved swiftly along the glass surface to silence the handheld device. It pulled his attention from the castle before him to the present. He pulled it out to see the signal that he'd been chasing was far stronger here. It was inside. It meant that *she* was inside.

He picked up his feet and ran through the front gates, eyes only catching occasionally on the shadows that moved in the corners of his vision. Cobalt brushed them off as nothing more than tricks of the light against his tired eyes. A heavy wooden door stood in his way as he slipped the tech into his bag, shouldering it to the other side and putting himself up against the door. With a grunt, he shoved with all his might. It moved just enough for him to slip past, a sound of stone against wood echoing in the otherwise still building as he ducked through. A short, dark tunnel led further into a room which looked to be the main foyer when the castle had been at its grandest. It wound until he could no longer see the other end of the room without straining his eyes in the darkness. Yet that wasn't what caught his attention.

It was a box.

Taller than a fully grown man and just as wide, it took up space in the center of the room. It was pristine and shone so brightly that even the screen on his pad paled in comparison. Not a speck of dust covered the enormous container, as if time itself did not exist in this room. The castle walls, as well as the forest, did not stand a chance against the technology encased in this single room. As Cobalt moved forward, breath fogging the glass, his heart skipped.

There was a girl inside. Every story he'd heard, the ones that he'd forced the Elders to tell him time and time again, paled in comparison to the porcelain princess who lay within.

His hands were on the glass before he even had time to contemplate moving from her side but he needed them free to open her prison. The pad was still heavy in his bag. Cobalt reached in to grab the device without breaking eye contact, his fingers fumbling through the bag almost furiously until he swore under his breath and looked into the mess of items until he found what he was looking for. It shrilled loudly this time, as if he hadn't silenced it already, indicating that signal was indeed coming from her. He started tapping the screen with practiced ease until his concentration was fully focused on the tablet. There was a latch on the box, invisible to the unseen eye, but he had come prepared. The cell wasn't stuck in the past, but rather modernized enough that he could have sworn it resembled the tech they used to make the Glassers' towers.

Not that he had the time to stand around and gawk. He could only guess at the workmanship that must have gone into the air tight glass which kept her both locked away and safe all these years. Judging by the state of the ruined castle around them, Cobalt could see that the Elders' stories merely hinted at how long they'd been woven throughout the generations. His fingers continued to strike through patterns, selecting out numbers that repeated until he found the single combination that he'd been looking for. It was tucked away far enough that no one would have noticed it. No one except for a hacker with some time on his hands to decode and encode enough security programs that he'd helped many people slip through the cracks. This wasn't any different. He hit the last key with his index finger and held his breath.

He waited a few moments, hearing nothing but the sound of his breathing ringing in his ears amidst the stillness.

Nothing happened.

Cobalt checked over his calculations, scouring the code for any inconsistencies or mistakes that he might have made, but couldn't find any of them. He growled under his breath, losing confidence the longer it went without opening. It couldn't end like this, with him being so close and yet, unable to find a way to free her. He kicked the side of the cell.

That didn't help anything, either, as Cobalt began to pace around the box. His fingers swiped along the sides for any creases or latches that he might have missed with his initial inspection. There was nothing for him to find on the outside. Everything he needed was lying there inside, waiting to be woken up.

And he couldn't even open the damn box.

———————— ♦ ————————

Once upon a time there was a box that opened.

An unexpected hiss came from the lone object in the room as gas flooded the floor. Cobalt took a step back. It made the whirring noise of mechanics moving after many years of disuse, lifting the sides of the box until they shifted away and left an opening for him to reach through. It continued to retreat, folding into itself until the box revealed a platform at the base as the glass pane slid out of sight. He moved back in, hesitating slightly as he gripped the pad in his hands, keeping it between him and the box until it finished moving.

Her eyes fluttered open. A startling breath echoed through the empty chamber as she could barely move, finding her body was slow to respond to her thoughts.

Briar Rose blinked. The stiffness in her limbs made them feel heavy as she gripped the side of the platform she was lying on and sat up. The air felt thick and hard to breathe. Her gaze drifted around the room, her skin crawling with tension until she found what she was looking for.

Someone was in the room with her.

His features were foreign, unlike any one that she'd ever seen before. The clothing he wore struck her as odd, tight fitting, and out of place. His wild array of dark hair, sticking up in all directions, would never have been allowed in the palace.

She glanced down at herself for a moment to collect her thoughts. Briar saw that her own dress was the same that she'd been wearing when—"*Noire*."

Briar Rose's vision swam as she gripped the edges of the platform. Her breaths came and went in shallow gasps until she managed to counsel her fear. Noire wasn't in the room with her; someone else was. It was a figure that hadn't identified himself and was still staring at her with wide eyes. She swung her legs over the side and blinked back spots in her vision from the sudden movement.

This time her voice was harder. "Who are you?"

Her dialect was old. It was something he could barely understand at first until he leaned in and she repeated herself. It was the same language but softer, with a curl on the vowels that left him wondering where it came from.

"Name's Cobalt and I... uh," he stammered over the next part, having not thought this all through in the first place. What did someone say to a princess? "I'm here to rescue you?"

Probably not the best choice.

"What kind of name is Cobalt?" She stared at him, but curiosity won out over the fear and disbelief. Had someone else survived that night? Someone she'd never seen in her home before tonight? Was it possible that they'd escaped the clutches of Noire when Briar had run past so many others that had not been as fortunate? Her gaze dropped from him to the platform, and she slid downward until her bare feet touched the cool stone of the floor.

It was nothing like she remembered. None of the lights still shone from above, or the mirrors that reflected the engravings carved into every single wall from generations before. Nothing was lit except for the platform behind her as she took her first few steps and promptly fell into his arms. It was dark and cold but the embrace brought her back to herself. It reminded her of all she'd struggled for; to prevent this fate.

"You've been in there for some time now, princess. Any disorientation is to be expected," he spoke reassurances to someone who probably didn't even know what to do with them.

She merely picked herself up and began to move away towards one of the back walls without a word.

"Princess?" he called out after her.

"We must hurry."

Briar promptly turned around and grabbed his wrist, ignoring the confused look he shot her, as she began pulling him towards the far end of the grand room. Her free hand was out front; guiding them into the darkness. It swallowed them up as they left the glow of the room behind.

Cobalt dropped his tablet into his bag and followed after her. Her grip didn't slip from his arm as they moved from one room to the next, blackness falling all around them.

"We must hurry," she urged once more.

There it was again. Her ominous tone sent chills down his spine as he wet his lips. How did he begin to explain that she'd been asleep for a few hundred years, and there was nothing to fear anymore? Not out here, at least, although where he wanted to take her, her people were the problem that had been killing people for generations.

The Glassers needed to be dealt with, and she was the answer. Once the princess took her rightful place at the top of the towers they'd built into the sky, she would save them all.

"Princess, there's no one here but us. I need to explain," but couldn't as she cut him off with a shaking hand over his mouth.

Fear of the unknown made her cling to the shadows of the passages she'd once run down, before waking up back in her old home. Her footsteps were soft, barely leaving an echo for him to follow behind. Her grip didn't loosen while they walked.

Her voice was barely above a whisper when she met his gaze. "Cobalt, we must hurry before she finds us here. If she knows we're free, then there will be no stopping her until she has me again." If she hadn't been alone when Noire had grabbed her, others would have known what had happened and come to rescue her before this man. Her brow furrowed slightly, barely visible in the dimly lit tunnel. "How long was I asleep?"

He stumbled with an answer, grabbing his tablet and pulling it out for a more concise answer to her question. "If my research is correct, then you've been here at least two hundred years. But there's no way to know for sure." He gaped at her for a moment before sobering up and feeling her grip tighten on his wrist. "You were supposed to be a story. You weren't supposed to be real."

Briar Rose fought the urge to chew on her bottom lip. It was a nervous habit her mother had always warned her against.

Instead she slid her grip from his wrist to his hand, lacing her fingers with his and squeezing lightly. "Do I feel real?"

Her voice had softened significantly from moments before, afraid that this was nothing more than a trick played on her mind by Noire. It wasn't above her magic or the games that she liked to play.

"Y—Yes," he replied, dropping her gaze for a moment to look at her slim fingers tangled with his own. He squeezed back after a moment's hesitation. "Let's get out of here."

That much they could agree on. He felt her smile almost as much as he saw it, despite the darkness. She pulled them further down the hallway and out towards the opening where the gardens used to be.

Cobalt was so caught up in having found her and the both of them escaping into the night that he almost missed the sound of his pad beeping in his free hand. They'd made it through another few rooms, each one in as much disarray as the one before it, until the ground became so unstable that they couldn't find the path they'd been following. It was as if the floors had started to move on their own.

Another beep sounded off. This one was louder than before; he glanced at his hand. A second signal had appeared on his radar, replacing the one he'd been following earlier. It was far stronger than hers had been, and its range far exceeded any single living entity. It filled the entire castle. He turned the direction of the tablet and found that the signal was coming from every direction. No matter the angle he turned it, the signal only grew stronger.

"Uh, princess," he said while she continued to drag them both through the decrepit castle. "We have a problem."

"It's Briar Rose," she called out over her shoulder, only slowing her feet when she turned to glance at him. The look of hopelessness stopped her in her tracks. That expression did not bear good news. Briar grimaced before replacing it with a tight smile. "Please tell me that our problem comes with an exit strategy."

"Not exactly." He glanced up from the tablet again and met her eyes with a breathless sigh. "It seems we have company."

"Darling." The familiar voice iced her blood. "Do we need to continue to play these silly games?" Briar Rose held his eyes and her breath as a flap of wings cut through the stillness around them. "You hide, I seek, and I always find you. Do you not grow tiresome of the chase?"

"*You.*"

"Ah, Briar Rose, dear, it's been so long since I've last heard your voice. One could even say that it's been centuries."

Briar Rose didn't relinquish her grasp on his hand as she turned in the direction of the voice, finding nothing except a pair of glowing red eyes.

Those couldn't belong to the crow. Not after all this time; not if she believed what Cobalt told her, that she'd been asleep for over two hundred years. It wasn't possible. And yet, there it was, perched high above them. She strained her neck to see it, sitting there on the edge of a wall which had caved in under the weight of centuries.

"Why don't you show your face, witch? Or are you afraid to after all these years? You didn't scare me as a child, and you do not scare me now with your tricks." Her voice was steady, though the tremble in her fingers was only masked by the warmth of Cobalt's hand.

A laugh rang out as she eyed the bird that moved almost mechanically in the way it watched them. It opened its beak as if to speak and sent forth a light that shone down on the floor before them, presenting an image of Noire, or what was left of her.

She was no longer the dangerously beautiful woman she'd been the last time they'd met, but instead, she shone brightly where gleaming metal replaced her body. Her left eye glowed a similar green to the bird's while the rest of her face remained unchanged and lineless. Both arms were hidden in the length of a cloak, but she couldn't hide the silver hue of her fingers curling around a staff that Briar Rose knew well.

"You're a cyborg," came a breathless gasp from Cobalt, reminding her that she no longer stood alone against the woman who killed her entire family. At least she had him watching her back. There wasn't much trust yet, but it was better than being alone.

"You're what the Glassers are trying to become." Cobalt recognized this as the new technology they were researching. It prolonged their lives by incorporating what they had created into bodies that would eventually fail while the technology would not. It would make them stronger and more resilient to the poisons they fed into the world through the building of ever newer tech. He'd yet to ever see one in person. By the time someone was replacing parts of themselves, they were so high up that they never reached the ground again, let alone allowed themselves be seen by a Grounder, even through hologram form. They were the elite. The most rich and powerful could afford such upgrades to their lives, while the rest of their people lived in squalor, barely managing to feed themselves each day.

The woman blinked in and out of sight with a thin smile on her lips. It left his blood running cold as she looked through both of them for a moment, before resting her gaze on Briar Rose once more.

"You really should think twice before running again, Princess. It didn't work out so well for you the last time, now did it?"

Briar Rose's fingers tightened on Cobalt's. She was already looking past the image before them, dancing high above. It was just an image. Noire wasn't there, and even if she was, she wasn't the same witch who destroyed her life so long ago.

"I'm still alive, aren't I?" It wasn't much to go by, but it was enough right then. All they needed to do was escape the castle, and they'd be free.

"And why do you think that is? Was it out of the goodness of my heart? Perhaps I have other plans for you." The image flickered as her expression hardened and loomed in closer to the two of them. Behind Briar Rose, Cobalt had pulled out his tablet, entering a few lines of code to disrupt the signal from the crow. It was just another signal. If it wasn't one thing, it was another; Cobalt shook his head as his eyes darted from the hologram to the screen in his free hand.

"You will not win," Briar Rose challenged.

Noire laughed. "Look around you, my dear. I've already won. It's only a matter of time before—" Her image flickered in and out, cutting out mid-sentence until the hologram died and left them bathed in darkness once again. Even the crow looked to be short circuited as Briar Rose blinked.

"What was that? How was she—" Briar shook her head, her jaw still slack at seeing the one person that should have been long dead, just like her, but wasn't. "What just happened?" She turned her head back towards Cobalt. All she saw was a meek look on his face as he slid something into the satchel across his chest.

"Just a little bit of what I do. Now, shall we?" He gestured for her to take the lead once again.

Briar shot him a curious look that darkened, a sign that her questions had not come to an end. Luckily, she didn't bother pressing him for further information, knowing that speed was of the essence.

The room had changed, significantly, and Cobalt knew it stemmed from the growing signal radiating all around them. It wasn't anything that he wanted to stick around to discover for himself.

They moved on, passing beneath the deactivated crow's gaze. There was no telling how long the jammed signal would take to reset. There were far more powerful hackers at the Glassers' disposal, but it was enough to buy them the time they sorely needed.

Briar Rose led them further into the castle, ducking through broken doorways and over misshapen floors until she came to a place she recognized.

She knew every nook and cranny of the castle that had been her home for all her life, or did she? Some walls looked to be out of place and stuck in the middle of rooms, forcing Briar Rose to slow her movements while leading them through the darkened passages. Her fingers reached out to brush along the cold stone and feel the roughness beneath her touch.

"This shouldn't be here," she whispered, glancing over her shoulder at Cobalt and slipping her hand from his to press up against the wall. It felt real enough. She strained against it, to see if it would topple over. "This passage should be open and lead us out the back into the gardens, not... be in the way."

She moved around it with cautious footsteps until she neared the end. It stood freestanding from any other wall in the room. Her eyes darted to the high vaulted ceiling and found it completely intact.

"Strange," she mused for another moment before gesturing for him to keep behind her as they walked around the wall and back on the path they needed to follow.

They only took another ten steps out of the room before she heard the first sign of trouble: a loud scraping noise. Immediately, a low beep came from Cobalt's satchel. Briar glanced back. She couldn't see anything in the direction from which they'd come. Cobalt's gaze quickly followed hers to the passage reaching into his bag. He pulled out his tablet to find that the signal was concentrated nearby. Wherever the signal was coming from, it had moved. He cleared his throat before meeting her wide eyes with a nod.

"That bad news from before? It's moving with us."

All the questions she had earlier about the thing in his hands and how he knew what it was jumped to the forefront of Briar's tongue. She glanced at the pad in his hands. Yet before she could say a word, a loud noise assaulted their eardrums.

They both jumped back towards the outer wall of the room. It came from behind them, but there was nothing in the darkness. Nothing but the sound of something far larger than either one of them could make as it came closer and louder than before. It sounded like rock tumbling down—like the walls themselves were ripping apart.

It wasn't until a breath or two later that either one of them saw the source of such a clamor. It thundered and shook the floor. Briar Rose stumbled, grasping the wall behind her while Cobalt held his ground and continued to stare. The floor behind them shook and broke apart, leaving gaps where they'd been walking moments earlier as the walls leaned in, beginning to collapse.

The entire room was coming down on top of them.

Briar Rose gaped as she watched her childhood home move as if alive. It wasn't falling down around them but tearing itself apart until the passage crumbled behind them, threatening to trap them forever. Briar felt the warm touch of his fingers against her hand, and looked at him.

"We should run. Fast." Cobalt's words cut through the low rumble surrounding them.

She nodded and let him lead this time as the sounds of crashing and creaking rose up even louder than before.

She had to cover her ears to keep the screaming walls out of her head while they raced down the empty passages. Briar matched his pace as the pathway grew terribly crooked and managed to dead end a few times. She had them backtrack and turn down another path opening up. Every time they turned their heads to look at the walls, everything had changed again, forcing them to move elsewhere rather than straight out.

Stones flew and landed at their feet. Briar screamed, then shoved her fist against her mouth to keep moving forward. She didn't stumble or collapse, but rather ran harder than before as Cobalt kept in stride behind her, ready to pick up the slack if need be. Soon the pounding in his chest was only matched by that of the walls that collided into each other from above, and he covered her head with his arms when rubble fell down on top of them. Another groan of rock warned him, and Cobalt shoved the two of them against the far wall, barely avoiding the collapse of the ceiling above. His grip on her tightened as he surveyed the damage they'd barely escaped before turning back to see the color drain from her face.

"We have to keep going before this place comes down on our heads." Cobalt moved to catch her unfocused eyes. "Princess?"

His eyes pleaded with her, begging her to snap back into herself. After a moment, she met his gaze and nodded once. If she was back with him, maybe they'd be able to survive this.

"It's just up ahead. One last hallway and we should be there." Her voice trembling, Briar Rose moved forward with shaky legs as the floor shivered and pitched forward.

Cobalt's hands slipped off her once again, letting her take the lead as she hurried off down what he hoped was the last passage. The walls moved in closer as they ran. His arms scratched along the rough stone until they could no longer run side by side but he had to hang back and let her lead them out. The noises grew louder until he couldn't pick which direction they came from. The entire room began to shake and shiver beneath their weight. It felt like it would collapse if they stood still long enough.

And then came the dead end.

Cobalt's stomach dropped as he heard the sounds that had been chasing them grow louder while they were trapped. He turned to look for another path they could take, but found none. This was it. There was no going back when the hallway they'd been running down wasn't there anymore. It was gone, along with the rest of the castle, once grand and spacious but now nothing more than another box, this time of stone.

"Briar? Not to sound defeated or anything, but do you have any ideas on how to get out of here? Because from where I'm standing, it's not looking too good." Cobalt could barely hear himself over his heart thumping in his chest. He waited for a response that didn't come.

"Princess?"

Cobalt turned to see that he was alone. The walls encased him, moving fast until he could barely put his hands out before his fingers brushed along the rough edges.

"Princess!"

His voice echoed off the walls with no response. Panic started to choke him along with the walls that continued to move closer. Cobalt threw out the palms of his hands against the jagged wall and shoved with all his strength, to no avail. It continued to close in without a pause. The surface was rough and scratched at his clothes as he put his shoulder to the stone and fought back, his weight thrown against it to stop it from squeezing him flat. It didn't slow and there was no princess around. Somehow she'd disappeared, swallowed up by the castle.

That was when he felt not stone, but air against his back as he stumbled, right into Briar. Her hands were on his back, holding him up until he spun around and wrapped his arms completely around her, crushing her tight against his heaving chest.

"I thought you were gone."

Silence. Then he felt her arms move around him as he took a long-awaited breath. No walls were closing in on him anymore. Instead he heard the sounds of the outside world. Everything that he'd been running through and away from on his way to her was now a welcome distraction to the blood pumping in his system. His adrenaline would start to slow soon enough, but not before Cobalt made sure they were safe. He heard the wind above rather than the creaking and groaning of the castle collapsing around them. Moonlight streaked down and lit them up. Reluctantly, he pulled back. For the first time he saw all her features clearly.

Cobalt wanted to say something. It was on the tip of his tongue, something he felt earlier when he'd been alone in that place with no escape, but when he caught her staring up at him, he lost the nerve. Instead there was a laugh that rang out from above; a haunting noise that sent a chill through the both of them. He fought to keep his eyes on the princess when a bright light started to envelop the both of them. Her hands grabbed his arms, tightening as it became increasingly harder to see. A figure moved out of the corner of his eye. It gleamed in the moonlight, reflecting off mechanical parts which long since replaced the body of the Glasser witch.

She wasn't a hologram this time. Cobalt blinked, the bright light skewing his vision of Briar as he clutched her close, neither one letting go. They went stiff, unable to move anymore.

"Silly girl, did I not tell you that these games of yours would only ever work out in my favor?"

———————◆———————

Once upon a time, there was a girl and a boy in a box locked shut. They are there still; waiting until the day that box is discovered again. Then, only then, may their story start anew.

APPENDIX

Bobbie Berendson W.
www.metallicvisions.com

August Clearwing
www.augustromance.com

Jessica Douglas
www.jessicamdouglas.com

Rebecca Flaum
www.rebeccaflaum.com

Tawny Fritz
www.tawnyfritz.com

Rebecca D. George
www.rgeorgeart.com

Katherine Guevara-Birmelin
www.coroflot.com/katguevarart

Karin Van de Kuilen
www.spider-design.nl | www.facebook.com/karinvandekuilen.arts

Mitchell Lehnert
www.coolkidmitch.tumblr.com

Kristi Luchi
www.facebook.com/kristiluchiwrites

[cont.]

Wendy Martin
www.wendymartinillustration.com

Ellen Million
www.ellenmillion.com

C.L. McCollum
www.facebook.com/clmccollumauthor

Emma Michaels
www.emmamichaels.com

María Andrée Paiz
www.mariapaiz.com | www.facebook.com/theartofmariapaiz

Michelle Papadopoulos
www.michellepapadopoulos.com

Iole Marie E. Rabor
www.iolemarierabor.com | www.iolemarierabor.tumblr.com

Kym Schow
www.touchfeel.deviantart.com

Elaine Titus
www.facebook.com/elaine.titus.author

Visit www.herdcatspress.com for more information on upcoming projects

Made in the USA
San Bernardino, CA
06 July 2015